Final Reckoning

Final Reckoning

Barry A. Nazarian

SEAVIEW/PUTNAM
New York

Library of Congress Cataloging in Publication Data

Nazarian, Barry.
    Final reckoning.

    I. Title.
PS3564.A97F5   1983   813'.54   82-19234
ISBN 0-399-31011-8

Printed in the United States of America

To those who were sure,
to those who are still uncertain,
to all the men of my generation who served in Vietnam—
from one who did not.

Part One:
Sam

Chapter One

Samuel Clement had sensed that he was in for it since breakfast.

That final meal had been taken aboard the crowded transport during the small hours of the morning when it was still dark. Now, a lightened sky flattened the horizon against the blue of the South Pacific, growing darker above the island from the incessant bombardment of the battleships. It seemed to Clement that no one, not even the invisible Japanese, could survive the eruption of those twelve-inch shells, so constant and unrelenting that they obscured the beach his boat would soon be approaching. The entire landing area was smoke and flames, and still the first wave of amphibious vehicles, crammed with marines and their equipment, continued to circle while the big guns carried out their destruction.

But Eddie, appearing like a man returned from the dead at breakfast, had told him that they would catch hell anyway, and Clement believed him.

The unexplained appearance of Eddie aboard ship had confirmed Clement's initial sense of dread. It was not the joyful reunion between old friends that it might have been, even though Clement was happy enough to see Eddie miraculously alive. It was a grim business, this beachhead, and Eddie had talked mostly about business when he approached him. Clement was standing apart from the other marines, marked by a red hospital tag tied to his wrist that indicated he was not to have breakfast.

"You get shit food for weeks," Eddie said, coming up to him as though their meeting were another chance encounter back in the old neighborhood. "Then, hours before you go in, they give you steak and eggs. At three o'clock in the morning."

Clement bent his gray head without speaking, feeling that the uninitiated had not yet earned the right to complain. The younger men surrounding him did not seem to be doing too much with their food anyway, pushing at it with preoccupied stares. Like Clement, there was room for little else in their minds except the beach. Last night, they had cheered the bombers from the ship when the low flying planes had lit up the blackness with a thorough pounding of the island. But in the morning, the landing was too imminent and real to allow anyone to escape his own thoughts, or share them.

During the final climb down the cargo nets and into the bobbing L.C.V.'s, the bodies clinging to the heavy netting parted momentarily, and Clement had glimpsed Eddie standing at the railing above him. His eyes were vacuous, and there was nothing about his expression that conveyed any sense of accusation, but somehow Clement knew that Eddie's unexpected survival was to be compensated for by the loss of his own life, and he dropped into the landing craft with the premonition that he was as good as dead.

As the bottom of his own barge began to lift and fall beneath him, Clement was torn between gratitude over landing safely and the stark realization that he would soon be out of the boat and exposed to a withering fire marked by flashes along the distant tree line. Abruptly, the enemy jolted him from the realm of thought into a frenzy of instinctive action by exploding the water on all sides of the vehicle with a barrage of light artillery even before they had come to a complete halt.

When the landing ramp fell away, the water that the first row of marines waded into was already being whipped into a foamy crisscross, and three of the five men in front of him were cut down immediately. Clement did not see what happened to the others, because his body was taking him over the side of the craft, away from the exposure of the opened front.

He was wearing an assault jacket whose large pockets were filled with only light equipment, and when he plunged below the surface of the water, he had to fight the action of his life preserver in order to keep from floating upward toward the danger of the daylight. Something heavier than air was filling his lungs, and he thought he had begun to drown until he noticed that his chest was making the motions of breathing again. It was then that he felt the mask being pressed firmly against his nose and mouth, held in place by a hand that was not his.

He twisted in an attempt to thwart the life-giving process, but the pressure against his face increased, and one of the men restraining him protested that he was a doctor in a faraway voice that Clement sensed rather than heard. Clement jackknifed his legs in protest, pushing against the sandy bottom in an attempt to reverse himself and take what was coming to him on the beach.

For a moment, the people with the mask almost pulled him back into the realm of reality, but he broke the bond with an effort that caused the blood to roar in his ears. He could hear the sea rushing past as he straightened out and made his way up toward the light above him.

The surgeon bent over the operating table to peer down at the patient again before he stepped away. "This *is* Samuel Clement, isn't it?"

The scrub nurse nodded, and the lines around her eyes indicated that she was smiling behind her mask. "He was raving like that when they brought him down from his room."

"Well, he may have been premedicated, but I'm not starting while he's still thrashing around." The surgeon glanced over at the anesthesiologist. "See what you can do to calm him down when he stops fighting the mask."

Clement reentered the nightmare of the beachhead with a gasp, and he was forced to bob in the water a full minute until he gained enough breath to move on toward the beach. The few hundred yards of ocean that separated him from the shoreline were dotted with the floating bodies of men who had been killed before reaching land. There were no breakers on this beach, since the coral barricade of the atoll prevented the waves from moving inland, so the dead and the dying floated close to where they had been hit, held upright by the indignity of their life preservers.

Twenty yards inland there was a segment of metal tread half buried in the sand, and Clement made for it in a frenzied run as soon as he had cleared the water. His mind's eye slowed the motion of his break for cover, and he saw himself in the sepia tint of old newsreels, wondering if his form would be one of those that flopped down abruptly and became motionless, another anonymous death that would be indifferently recorded by the camera for ignorant people in another time and place.

But nothing in that humming air touched him, and he reached his objective in a diving roll. His fear had begun to edge toward anger by then, and he let loose on the rectangle of a pillbox, clearly visible through the vegetation that began less than one hundred yards in front of him. There was a soft, sliding sound behind him, and he knew that another marine had dropped into the same shell hole, either seeking protection or falling senseless to the sand as a result of the murderous fire from the jungle. For the moment, Clement was indifferent, concentrating all of his attention on firing into the narrow slots of the Japanese bunker, which were marked by flashes of machine-gun fire. If the man behind him had been killed, he was beyond help. If he were still alive, he would be moving up to join him.

But Clement never learned what had actually happened, because the ground suddenly shifted beneath him and he was assaulted by a wall of noise so loud it was as much a tangible part of the explosion as the fragments of the incoming shell. The body of the marine behind him slammed into his back, rendered lifeless by the impact of the flying metal, or perhaps already a corpse, and given the semblance of life a second time. In either case, dead or alive before the explosion, Clement's unseen companion had saved his life by shielding him. There was no clothing and very little skin on the back of the man Clement rolled out from under, although once lying face up, there was almost no evidence he had been hit at all.

Two more men had come up immediately after the shell had landed, and when Clement looked up from the body, one of them tapped his chest and pointed ahead at the bunker. Clement nodded and turned away from the dead man, indicating with a thrust of his rifle in the direction of the pillbox that he understood he was to cover. The men were in motion before he had completed this acknowledgment, and Clement noticed that the marine bringing up the rear was equipped with a flamethrower. More than a few troops in his vicinity were directing small-arms fire toward the narrow slots of the bunker, and both men survived a rush on the pillbox that brought them into position on either side of it. The unencumbered marine rolled a grenade toward the center of the bunker without exposing himself, but only after it had gone off in front of the thick wall did Clement see the point of the gesture.

The fire from the machine gun altered its pattern, shifting radically to cover the area on the flank from where the grenade had been thrown, and with perfect timing, the other marine stepped up to the bunker from the opposite side and trained his flamethrower on the opening directly in front of him. The screaming inside was loud enough to reach Clement in spite of the din from other parts of the beach, and the first marine immediately got off another grenade, this time venturing right up to the opening and pushing it through the slot. There was an explosion delayed by only seconds, and Clement found himself coming to his feet and cheering with the others who had been pinned down by the same fire.

His elation was short-lived. A half dozen Japanese soldiers emerged from behind the bunker, impossibly alive, some with their uniforms still smoldering. Clement dropped to one knee, expecting that they would be cut down before he had time to raise his rifle. But the marines around him remained motionless. They were staring at him, he realized, and he took his eyes off the charging Japanese long enough to see what was responsible for the look of condemnation that had suddenly come over every face within sight of him.

It was the dead soldier at his feet in the shell hole. At first, Clement thought that the body had somehow rolled over onto its stomach again, but it was not the ravaged back that lay red and exposed on the sand. It was not even any longer a body. There was meat beside him, hock bone and white fat, devoid of organs or the human form, as though Clement had performed a methodical butchering moments before on the beach, complete even to the blue circles that indicated the stamp of the grading inspector. It was the tangible evidence of his guilt, confronting him from a part of his memory he had suppressed for decades.

Clement found his voice then, screaming at the gaping men on all sides of him that during the worst of it, he had taken no life. But the Japanese were on him like vengeance itself, and not one American made a move in his defense when they hurled him to the ground. One of the last conscious sensations he had was the breath of his attackers on his face, as cold as the air of the slaughterhouse. And then there was only the burning intrusion of the knife, entering his abdomen like a surgeon's scalpel just below the navel.

Before the operation, the woman had visited his room unchallenged, and she managed it again immediately afterwards. But she made frequent trips to the door, darting her head out into the hallway in order to check on the movements of the floor nurses. There was a scalpel tucked behind the bib of her uniform that she felt fully capable of using, though in all likelihood, she would be given adequate enough warning to conceal herself in the bathroom. Everything had gone as smoothly as she planned it, from her entrance on the floor to the location of his room. But they had removed him for surgery just when the drug was beginning to take effect, and most of its power seemed to have worn off during the course of the operation.

For the past five minutes, Clement had rewarded her efforts to draw him out with nothing more than a useless delirium, and she knew she had very little time left before someone would be entering the room to check on his recovery from surgery. She decided it would be safer to leave and come back later, so she gathered her things and stationed herself just inside the door. When the hallway was clear, she stepped out of the room and marched toward the stairwell with her head down. She could kill ten minutes in the lounge upstairs. Anyone there would merely assume that she was a nurse from another floor.

It was the throbbing in his wound that woke Clement when she returned. His right arm was secured to some part of the bed, and there was a tube taped to it near the seam of the elbow, but he managed to find the dressing over his stomach with his left hand by working it cautiously under the crisp contour of the sheet. He might have been patched, he concluded, but there was no denying the fact that he was alive. Clement moved the fingers of his free hand in front of his face after he had brought it out from under the covers, noticing that the red tag had been removed from his wrist.

He felt clumsily along the surface of the night table next to the bed for his glasses, but they were not where he remembered putting them. Their absence confused him, and he wondered again if he really knew where he was. The room he found himself in was dim, and he could only take in its blurred outlines as he moved his eyes in a brief survey without the benefit of his glasses. He identified two chairs and a clock on the opposite wall, but there was nothing he could recognize that would date the room. Because he had been so thoroughly drugged, his mind was as hazy as his vision, and he had difficulty in raising his head even inches from the pillow. He lay back and shut his eyes, ordering his thoughts with an effort that was strenuous enough to seem physical.

Gradually, he allowed himself to succumb to his disappointment. Not only had he not died on the beach: there would be no going back to it. He was in Florida, four decades away from the war with the Axis. He could not see his surroundings in any detail, but it took only the briefest second glance to assure himself that his was the only bed in the room. Military hospitals, he knew, did not accommodate patients in private rooms.

It was then that he became aware of the footsteps on the opposite side of the room. He called out in the direction of the movement, but there was no reply, and he was not even sure if he heard the sound of his own voice. He finally opened his eyes, although it made him dizzy to do so. The white form of a nurse wavered near the foot of his bed. There was a pear-shaped blur of yellow where her face belonged, and he realized that her back was to him.

Only when he shut his eyes again did he become aware of her scent. His recognition of it was a delayed reaction, directly attributable to the fact that he had been so recently and vividly drawn back to the war years. It was a part of that time, that musky smell which brought back a whole host of associations. He was seeing sights and experiencing sensations that had been so deeply buried, they evoked an identity that might have belonged to another person rather than to a distant part of his own life.

Something brushed the edge of his pillow and he opened one eye. The nurse was stretching up toward the metal stand that held his intravenous container, and her waist was inches away, almost level with his face. Clement's vision was unimpaired at that distance, and he opened his other eye, mesmerized by what he was seeing. The white material of the nurse's uniform was translucent, and the light entering from the window outlined the body beneath it. The profile of a well-proportioned pelvis was betrayed by the dark shadow of underwear, which ended in the V-shaped suggestion of panties. It was any shapely female form, ageless and anonymous in a well-defined silhouette.

But Clement knew it. There was no particular detail that evoked the recognition. Rather, the totality of the form and the distinct scent of perfume worked together on his senses, communicating a familiarity by the same indefinable process that distinguishes close friends or family in the most distant or blurred photographs. If his right arm had not been stationary, Clement would have reached out and attempted to touch the body brushing against the side of his bed, so sure was he that the person in the room was a part of his earlier delirium. As it was, he called out again, twisting his head sharply to take in the face hovering above the circle of his vision. The suggestion of the features, framed by the yellow of the hair, confirmed his suspicion.

"Vera!" he said out loud, but the woman ignored him, and he could see the shape of her arm intercepting the tube that led down to his bed. "What are you doing?" he protested, sensing that the movement somehow threatened him.

Again, there was no answer. Only a silent response that seemed to flow instantly down the length of the tube and enter his arm, rendering him unconscious in a matter of seconds.

"What have you done, Sam?" Her voice came to him from another time and place, although the whisper was distinct enough for him to know that she was very close.

"It was war, Vera," Clement answered, barely moving his lips. Spots of white light exploded against a field of red. Clement followed the whirling forms with an inner vision, unwilling or unable to open his eyes.

"It's still war for some of us, Sam," the voice told him. "There are debts to be paid."

Clement nodded blindly. "I know. I was there, Vera. On the beach. Fighting."

"Damn you and your beach!" The response was a savage hissing in his ear. "Remember what you *were* during the war, not what you wanted to be! What have you done with it, Sam?"

"My God." The question touched a nerve that had been numbed by memory. "I never touched it. It wasn't mine."

"It was *ours,* you fool! I've come for it, and I'm going to get it back."

"Are you here, Vera?" Clement called out. "Can we really go back? I saw Eddie. Maybe we can still change things."

"You would be stupid enough to wish that." The voice dropped in pitch, and he could feel the movement of her breath against his ear. "Now listen, Sam. You took everything you wanted, and you can sob about it for the rest of your life. But I'm out here, and I'm still hungry. Thirty-five years of hunger, Sam. What have you done with it?"

Clement's body had gone stiff, and there was the grip of something cold inside his intestines. "You're just like Eddie and the beachhead!" he protested. "You're not real. Kill me if you are!"

"You can't die, Sam. Not yet. I gave you something before your operation to make you remember what you'd done with our investment, but all you've done is moan about some beachhead. That wasn't *our* war, Sam, no matter how much you dream about it. We got what we wanted, remember?" Clement became aware of her hand working lightly across his stomach. "You'll forget all this later when the drug wears off, and I won't leave any marks. But I've finally found you, and I'll be back!" The hand cupped his testicles, where, like the touch of a lover gone bad, the fingers closed cruelly in a grip that made him cry out in pain.

She was hovering near the bladder of his intravenous again, and he could catch the stabbing motion of her hand. He called out to her, but it was literally a matter of seconds until the color in front of his eyes grew deeper, floated inward, and became darkness.

Clement came awake abruptly the second time. He caught the

nurse reaching for his wrist, but before she could control his free hand, he shot it out from under the covers and captured her arm.

"Please, Mr. Clement, you're a very strong man." The voice was firm, but clinical and without alarm. "I'm glad you're finally awake. You took a little longer than we expected."

Clement squinted up at her and relinquished his grip. "Where's the other nurse?" he said sullenly.

"I'm all you get, I'm afraid." She crossed his pulse with a light touch of her middle finger, and Clement fell silent while he took the opportunity to clear his mind.

"Do you have a blond working here?" he finally asked. "Fine figure?"

"This is a hospital, Mr. Clement. You take the luck of the draw." She pressed his glasses into his hand before she released his wrist.

Clement slipped them on immediately, and the room came sharply into focus. He found the nurse at his dressing table, a thick-waisted woman in her early forties with salt and pepper hair. "I'm sorry," he said. "I thought there was someone in my room before. Someone I knew, who was a nurse. That's why I grabbed your hand. She hurt me."

"Vera?"

"Yes, that's right." Clement attempted to sit up, but the pain in his lower abdomen brought his head abruptly back down onto the pillow.

"You've been repeating the name, Mr. Clement. I've been the only one here, and nobody's hurt you. Intentionally, that is. You're going to have a little pain with a suprapubic prostatectomy. As for the blond, I think the halathane was responsible. You were fighting the mask in the operating room, and they made sure that they really put you under."

"Oh. I thought I was drowning. In the ocean."

The nurse crossed the room and placed a plastic pitcher next to the water glass on the night table. "You were in the middle of the war most of the time. I could hear it from my station at the end of the hall. Take this ice water slowly, you might find that you feel nauseous." She smiled while he sipped tentatively at a styrofoam cup. "Were you in the service, Mr. Clement?"

"Is that a professional question?"

"No need to take offense. I'll be in to check on you in another hour, Mr. Clement. You can call me sooner on the intercom if you need me before then." She turned and strode toward the door.

"I'm having nightmares," Clement protested, putting his hand to his forehead. "I'm not really as bad as I seem."

But she had already gone.

They woke him for lunch, which he disturbed but left uneaten on his plate. The meal reminded him of the breakfast on ship that he had dreamt about, but when he fell back asleep, neither the beach nor Vera's unnerving visitation disturbed his rest. He woke late in the afternoon, when the room was filled with sunlight. His wife was there, a benevolent presence and the final evidence that all the shadows of the previous night had finally receded.

"You were watching me while I was sleeping," he said to let her know that he was awake.

She drew her chair closer and leaned in to kiss him. "You looked so peaceful. How are you, my dear?"

Clement raised a shoulder slightly. "As well as a man can be with a tube up his thing. Todd?"

He looked toward the door, but she shook her head. "Hospitals. It would not be easy for him to come."

Clement pressed his lips together. "I suppose. Kara? I dreamt about the war last night. I was fighting. I wanted to fight."

"You have always wanted to fight, silly man." Her way of speaking made the last words both a term of endearment and a mild rebuke. Even after thirty years in the country, she spoke with a slight accent.

"But this was an actual test. I thought I was there. Everything had a quality about it that made it real, something I've never experienced."

"You should not wish for such dreams. When I had them about the camp, you comforted me and told me they would go away in time. And they did."

"But you lived through it, as a victim," Clement protested. "I've never seen the South Pacific, even as a tourist. I did last night, though, and everything was just the way Eddie described it. I was glad it was real enough to believe, because I believed it, and I . . ." Clement faltered, self-consciously.

". . . you fought well. As you would have, dream or not." Kara had brought her needlework, and she continued to follow the motion of her fingers when she finished his sentence for him, aware of the emotion behind what he was saying.

"Yes, that's what I thought. Until I was awake long enough to realize where I was. And why I was here." His frown reflected disappointment. "I guess they would call that a subconscious urge to escape, actually. Rather than wake up and find out that I was going to waste away."

It was the first mention either of them had made of the operation, and Kara looked up from her sewing. "They found nothing, Sam. Nothing they could see during the surgery. The doctor said two days for the test in the lab."

"Which is the only real test."

"If they should find something, we will face it then. There will be no wasting away. Mrs. Evan's husband had a cancer they found ten years ago, and he is healthy now. Running, even, she tells me. You are the one with the doubts, Sam. I have always known I married a fighter."

Clement shut his eyes without a reply.

"Todd was on the phone with a girl last night," she said brightly. "He did not say so, of course, but I could tell from his voice. It's a good sign, I think." When he continued to hold his silence, he heard the scrape of her chair on the floor, and there was the cool touch of her hand on his forehead. "Are you all right?" she asked.

"I'm not worried about the verdict from the lab, if that's what you mean."

She responded as she so often did, brushing his hair lightly with her hand as she stood by the side of the bed. He took her in through half-closed lids. Kara was fifty-one, seven years younger than he was, but she could easily have passed for a woman in her late thirties. She was Austrian, with the graceful, elongated body type that seemed to defy age, and tight, healthy skin that was creased by wrinkles so fine, they disappeared in all but the brightest light. Clement's hair was full, but it had turned completely gray, while Kara's remained dark and shiny with very little attention on her part. She was wearing a white blouse and a wide beige skirt that fell well below her knees, but her slim body coupled with a bearing that Clement thought of as European gave the simple outfit an accent of style.

He looked away from her, letting his eyes shut completely. "There was more about the war," he offered, feeling a comfortable drowsiness coming over him under her touch. "I mean, while I was coming out of the operation. I saw Vera. Right out of those same times. The bad times."

"Yes?" The hand continued its gentle sweep through his hair.

"She was real. Absolutely real."

"So. It is a good thing, all these tubes, after all. I would not want you alone with the other woman, particularly when she was younger."

He drifted further toward sleep. Her voice was a sounding, telling him all was well. "It wasn't like that. It was frightening. She came for me," he added so softly that she had to lean toward his pillow in order to hear it. "She said she'd finally found me."

"No one is coming for you," she soothed.

But when there was no response other than his even breathing, she bit down on her lip and squeezed her eyes shut under the weight of her feelings. She was the only member of her family who had survived the Nazi occupation, and her own son had been permanently disabled in a war that had shut a large part of him away from her. It took all of her strength to face the possibility of losing her husband, but she was determined to control her emotions regardless of what the surgeon told her. It was the waiting she found so unbearable.

Clement was awake and vulnerable when the doctor made his fateful visit. He had refused medication for the past twenty-four hours, partially because he feared the return of his nightmares, but mainly because he wanted to confront the ultimatum of his diagnosis head on, without the numbing benefit of any drug. The surgeon's face was neutral, and Clement wondered if it was considered professional for him not to betray anything he was going to say by his demeanor. He did come immediately to the point.

"You had a benign prostatic hypertrophy just as we suspected, Sam. But we removed the gland anyway."

"I'm pissing blood."

"Perfectly normal." The doctor took in Sam's full gray hair and the heft of his shoulders. "You're in excellent shape for your age, and we perform this operation routinely on men who are a lot older." For the first time since he had seen Clement in the hospital, he broke into a broad grin. "I thought you might want to tell your wife." He made a motion in the direction of the phone, but Clement stopped him with a raise of his hand.

"No. She'll be in later."

"Of course." The doctor turned away from the phone and strode over to the door, but he paused before stepping out into the hall. "I've got a lot of people to see, but I'll get back to you before you go home. That should be tomorrow, barring any complications."

"Good. Doctor?" Clement hesitated momentarily. "I'm going to live?"

"Only another twenty to thirty years, judging from your present condition."

Clement dropped his eyes to his lap. "Thank you," he said. The doctor parted with a few bright words that were lost on him, and he was left alone with the realization that his life was not going to be cut short despite his suspicions. His expression remained sober.

So, he was not going to face his furies after all. Or if he did, they would come still later, in a different form.

The syringe had contained sodium amytol, a chemical that could cause a patient to reach into his mind and unlock some of the thoughts trapped in the subconscious layers of his memory. The only evidence that it had been used on Clement would have been the syringe itself, since the drug entered his bloodstream through the intravenous tube rather than by direct injection into his body.

But the syringe was not detected until it had come through one of the hospital sterilizers along with other miscellaneous instruments that had been left on a metal tray outside an operating room. By then, any trace of the chemical it held had been thoroughly purged, although the duty nurse did notice the syringe itself for obvious reasons.

"Real glass," she remarked to a supervisor who was occupied sorting through clamps in another part of the room. "And a metal nozzle to hold the needle in place. Doesn't Dr. Howard believe in disposables?"

The supervisor was an older woman, and she set her lips in a line of impatience before she crossed the room and took the instrument from the girl.

But her expression became thoughtful once she had examined it, and she nodded slightly when she recognized the dated logo stamped on the glass of the plunger. "We didn't get this from Howard, or any of the O.R.'s for that matter." She placed the syringe back down on the table and returned to her work. "Put it in one of the storage lockers when you get a chance. They must have run short of regulars on the night shift, although I don't know where they dug that up. I haven't seen one of those since the war."

Chapter Two

As it turned out, it was an appropriate day to see *Yank in the R.A.F.*, and the picture itself contributed to his sense of destiny.

Sam and Maura lingered in the dim interior of the theater, making their way reluctantly down the stairs leading from the balcony after everyone else had gone. Sam had loved the escape of the movie houses since he was a small child, and in recent months, he had added the excitement of Maura to the special associations of the weekly drama. Twice during the film, she had allowed his hand to brush the side of her breast when he had made a point of shifting his weight with his arm around her.

His shoulder was still aching from the cramped restriction of the position when they made their way out of the building and stood huddled against the early evening cold at the bus stop.

"I like Tyrone Power," Maura announced. "I think it's his eyes."

Sam dug into the pocket of his trousers at the sight of the bus approaching them. "It's his uniform. You put one on and you've got the look. No more job, no neighborhood. Nothing ordinary left."

"What's wrong with ordinary, Sam Clement?" she argued,

25

and they continued talking as they boarded the bus, oblivious to the animated conversations taking place on all sides of them.

It was not until the bus was two full stops toward Pennsylvania Station that the news caught up with them. The driver had pulled up to a corner near one of Newark's better residential areas, and a man in a gray suit and matching fedora followed by two uniformed police officers mounted the steps to the aisle as soon as the doors folded open. The trio stationed themselves at the front of the bus, but even from his position near the back, Sam could see that they were making a thorough survey of the fifteen or so passengers that had fallen silent at their appearance.

They seemed to focus simultaneously on a small figure as he made his way to the exit. Without explanation, the two policemen flanked the passenger while the gray suit stood directly in his path, forcing him to a halt. There was a brief discussion in subdued tones, and then the four men climbed off the bus together. Clement and the others saw them walking across a broad lawn toward the distant lights of a house as the bus shut its doors and swept back out into the traffic of Orange Street. A man with a ruddy complexion seated across the aisle intercepted the bewildered look that passed between Sam and Maura.

"They're not wasting any time," he volunteered. "Figure he worked in one of those houses there, and they were waiting for his bus to bring him."

Maura turned away from the window and looked over at him. "Why?"

The hum of conversation had renewed itself as soon as the police had left the bus, and the man across the aisle had to raise his voice slightly in order to be heard. "Japanese. Probably one of those houseboys or something." When Sam and Maura continued to stare at him, he smiled, allowing himself to glance knowingly at several people sitting around them who were obviously listening. "Where you kids been all afternoon? South of the border?"

"We were at the movies," Sam said, feeling a need to point

defensively toward the distant marquee of the Tivoli as he took in the expressions turned in their direction.

"Yeah, well what we got today was the real thing," the stranger announced while several heads bobbed a confirmation. "The Japs just bombed Hawaii."

As soon as Sam and Maura were aware of what had happened, further evidence of the emergency confronted them every step of the way home. Pennsylvania Station was only a few short blocks from the Ironbound District of Newark where they lived, so they took time to cross through the crowded terminal rather than walking around it. There were men in uniform everywhere, crowding the high-ceilinged plaza of the waiting room until the trains that would take them back to their units arrived. Clement caught the tenor of their excitement, and he pulled Maura by a hand up the broad stairway that led out onto the platforms. The packed windows of the incoming trains were mottled by the olive drab of soldiers who had boarded at previous stations, and Sam envied the special kinship that became apparent as the new arrivals pushed their way into the crowded cars.

"Mostly the Fourth, the First, and the Ninth," he told Maura knowingly as they made their way back down to the main floor and pushed through a revolving door out into the cold of the December night. "I didn't see any marines, though."

They turned to watch a police car sweep up to the curb and discharge several more men in uniform before they left the lights of the station and moved down Raymond Boulevard toward the industrial section of town. The Ironbound District took its name from the rough oval of railroad tracks that bounded several square miles of row houses, and the heavily screened windows of the local plants remained bright with the activity of the night shifts.

Three blocks from Clay Street, they passed a group of civilians carrying rifles and wearing a variety of metal helmets. The men maintained a dignified silence as they drew abreast of the couple, and when they had passed, Sam turned to see that the one bringing up the rear had a large hunting knife tucked in a diagonal under the band of his belt.

"Damn. They're guarding the plants."

"Of course," Maura agreed. "This is a very critical area for industrial purposes." The observation had the singsong accent of a newsreel narration. "Even at the phone company, they've been telling us to be alert for sabotage. Now that we've been attacked, I guess anything could happen—even right here in Jersey."

"They'll never get away with what they did twice," Sam said thickly, and they drew into each other suddenly, overcome by the drama of an event that seemed to have imbued them and everyone they had encountered with a sense of mission.

Sam brushed her cheek with his lips and they took the last few blocks home at a quickened pace. Clay Street was typical of the lower-middle-class neighborhoods that manned the factories of East Newark, and people were gathered on stoops along the length of the block in spite of the cold, talking with a ready familiarity that seemed natural and appropriate under the stimulation of the crisis. Sam and Maura came to a halt where several cars and a collection of bicycles jammed the curb in front of one of the row houses. "Everyone's at Branagan's," Sam observed, and they hurried down worn slate steps to a basement door as the sounds of a large gathering came to them through cellar windows that had already frosted over.

Joe Branagan's house had been a gathering place for Sam and his friends since they were in elementary school for the simple reason that it was located near the center of the block. The Branagans were slightly better off than most of their neighbors. Joe's father ran a liquor store on nearby Market Street, and he owned the duplex his family shared with a tenant. The Branagans also had their own telephone, and Joe had been allowed to finish off the small basement in return for the privilege of sharing it with his friends when his parents weren't entertaining.

A brief photographic history of Sam's crowd overlooked the

young people packed between the cellar door and the stairs by the rear wall. A picture of Joe Branagan's sixth-grade class hung from the near wall, with Sam Clement frowning out from the last row, the flaps of a leather aviator's cap hanging below his shoulders like elephant ears. The ledges of the basement windows were lined with trophies from the local softball team which was sponsored by Joe's father, and in a high school prom picture centered over the coal furnace, five tired couples in gowns and rented tuxedos squinted out at the photographer against the incongruous background of a beach.

Sam made a quick survey of the room as soon as they had ducked under the low lintel of the entrance way. The timing of the Japanese attack seemed ideal. Everyone was available on Sunday, and there was no one he could think of who was not adding to the din of overly loud conversations in the tightly packed room. He was making his way toward Eddie Syms when a hand gripped his shoulder, pulling him abruptly around.

"You see the plant tonight? Purcell has a few of the night-shift people guarding it. Hell, I'd like to walk around with a rifle tomorrow while somebody else does the work!" It was Tom O'Hearn, not a member of Sam's immediate circle, but a worker at the same liquid gas company that employed Sam and Eddie Syms.

Sam pulled Maura close to him with an arm around her shoulders. "You think there'll be work tomorrow?"

O'Hearn took a long pull on a metal flask he was holding, tucking it into his back pocket when Clement shook off an invitation to share it. "Of course there's going to be work," he said. "They're going to want everything we can produce now. For the war." His eyes narrowed slightly. "You're the damn shop steward. I guess you'd better be there."

"For a while," Clement said, aware of Maura's head turning abruptly in his direction.

"What's that supposed to mean?" O'Hearn's expression was skeptical.

"It means enlisting. If it's war, I'm going."

"You're crazy," O'Hearn said. "They'll call you soon enough as it is." His eyes darted to the side long enough to take in Maura's rapt expression. "Of course, I couldn't go now or any time, even if I wanted to. I got bad arches, same as my Pop. That's what sent him home early from the last war."

Sam felt Maura putting pressure on his arm. "Well, we'll see what happens tomorrow," he said conclusively, and they drifted away from O'Hearn toward the rear of the room where they could see Eddie nodding quietly in the face of Joe Branagan's animated gestures.

"Are you really going?" Maura asked, pulling him to a halt as soon as they were out of O'Hearn's hearing.

Her blue eyes were clear and receptive, but somehow Sam felt it was appropriate to look away. "Of course. I'm eighteen, so no one can stop me."

"What about us?" she offered.

He faced her then. They had only been going out for the past two months, but it suddenly seemed as if there were the closeness of years between them. "I'll probably get leave before I really go anywhere. And we'll have plenty of time. After it's over."

They embraced, joining several other couples locked tightly against each other while the gathering roared on around them, reflecting an atmosphere of permissiveness that seemed to have begun with the shock of the news earlier that afternoon. Sam felt the actual press of Maura's hips against his own before he looked up from over her shoulder and found Branagan winking at him from across the room. He broke the embrace, but Maura leaned into him, lacing an arm around his waist as they approached the group gathered at the back of the room.

"Have you heard it's Hitler, too?" Branagan called out to them, putting a hand to the side of his face as if in disgust. "I met someone on Raymond who said there were German planes involved in the bombing."

Several members of the group reacted with meaningful glances, and Sam tightened his expression, taking a pull from a bottle of Vat 69 that was moving around the circle. He was surprised to see Maura follow his example before she passed the liquor to the next couple. "I believe it," he said, and the eyes of the others made him the center of attention as he assumed a natural leadership. "This business of the Japanese peace envoys in Washington is more like a carbon copy of Hitler's style. The last *March of Time* that Maura and I saw showed how Hitler talks peace until he's ready to make his move, so he can put countries off their guard. Just like the Japs at Pearl Harbor."

"Shit." Branagan ventured the word in mixed company without drawing even the raise of an eyebrow. "The Secretary of the Navy just said we can win a war on both oceans at the same time." He nodded in agreement with himself. "Right in last month's *American,* before anybody had any idea of the attack."

"That may be tougher with what's left of our Navy," Eddie Syms observed quietly.

Branagan waved the suggestion away. "Hell, they didn't do any real damage in Hawaii."

"That's not what they said down at the Fed."

The circle shifted its attention to Eddie Syms. He was close to Sam's height, but without the same obvious power in his frame, and when he spoke, the others leaned in slightly in order to hear him. "I was downtown a couple of hours ago, and the stuff coming over the radio made it sound as if things were pretty fouled up out there. I didn't hear anything about the Germans helping, either."

Branagan faltered momentarily. "What were you doing downtown?" he finally asked.

Eddie had deep brown eyes and dark hair, a combination of features that lent a brooding expression to whatever he said. "I tried to enlist, but the Federal Building was closed. They were turning people away all day, I guess. A truckload of about fifteen guys came all the way over from the Oranges, and they told them to come back on Monday. The Marines are opening early in case there's a big rush to join up."

"Good," Clement said, and he felt a responsive squeeze where Maura was holding his arm.

Branagan turned in his direction. "You enlisting?"

Sam nodded, and he locked eyes briefly with Eddie. "If it's war."

"Hell, if it's war, we're all going," Branagan said in a voice that was overly loud, and the whole circle seemed to nod at once.

Joe had told Sam it would be all right to use his father's Packard, and for a half hour after they had left the noisy basement, he and Maura moved against each other with an urgency that betrayed their unspoken thoughts. The car had been cold, but they had warmed it with their breath, and their bodies were actually flushed with a light perspiration underneath their heavy clothing. Maura broke away for a moment, putting her hands on either side of Sam's face and gazing at him with a special intensity.

"You're really going tomorrow?"

"If it's war. And it will be."

"That could ruin things at the plant for you," she reminded him. Sam had raised the worker support necessary to make his small factory a union operation, and the grudging respect he had earned from the management meant only that they would take full advantage of any opportunity to be rid of him permanently.

Sam put a hand to her lips. "They have no say about anyone enlisting."

"But when you come back—"

"I'll get a job with someone else if they won't take me. I got a pretty good record. I'll leave tomorrow if the President gives the word, and Eddie will come with me. If the others want to follow, let them. I'm their union leader, not their conscience."

Maura's grip tightened and she drew his mouth toward hers with hands that were shaking. "Oh, Sam, it's all happening so fast. One afternoon goes by and suddenly there's no time left!"

They came together again, and his hands worked up under her open coat, sliding unopposed over the swelling in her dress that marked her breasts, finally working under the dress itself, until he could feel the soft warmth of her skin just below the

band of her girdle. He pushed further down when she continued
to press her mouth against his, drawing in his breath sharply
when his hand grazed the roughness of the hair there. She lost
her own breath then, twisting in a way that allowed him to drive
his arm against the elastic restraint of her underthings until his
fingers were moving freely between her legs, probing what had
been forbidden to both of them only hours earlier.

He did not take them further, although there was an agreement implicit in the way they were touching that even the final
barrier would be broken once he had actually committed them to
the gamble that was sweeping an entire nation. The thought
interrupted his passion, or perhaps it merged with it, because he
was suddenly overcome by the imminence of so much that was
unknown to him. He wanted the sky to lighten the day so it could
all begin. He had found in a matter of hours that he loved
Maura, that he loved life itself enough to respond to the ultimate
threat without considering the consequences. There was only the
passion of his commitment and the night, stretching out in darkness beyond the clouded windows of the car like the future itself.

Clement's mother had been asleep on the couch when he had
come home during the small hours of the morning, and she was
still there when he rose early to have his coffee and make a
sandwich for his lunch box. He paused to take in her frail form
before leaving for work. She was arched like a doll over the
flowered pillows of the living-room couch, her arms straight
against her sides and her gray hair pushed up near the top of her
scalp as though she had fallen asleep where she lay. The observation caused Clement to frown, and when he stooped down to
kiss her, he caught the glint of a bottle between the pillows of the
couch.

She had never been much of a drinker, even after his father
had died, but years later, when Sam had graduated from high
school, she began to indulge herself several times a month. The
habit never grew, and it was confined to evenings, but if Sam
found himself in a position to discover her, she became angry

and defensive, seizing on some reason she had stored in the back of her mind earlier in order to justify herself. Sam could never tell her that he was not overly concerned, because to do so would have been to admit that he saw her in the backwater of old age, someone to be loved and defended while she continued to recede into a well-deserved sense of her own reality.

He pressed his face against her cheek after he had kissed her. She had her friends, all of them in the neighborhood, and many of them widows. Her small needs would be met by his father's pension without the added benefit of his salary. He had also put aside some savings in the year and a half that he had been working at the plant. She would have that and whatever he could send home. He rose to make his way down the fire escape that served as a back stairs to their second-floor apartment, but she had come awake under his touch, and she called out to him before he opened the door.

"You never came home last night."

Sam opened the door, but he turned to face her. "I did. I was just a little late. Maura and I had a lot to discuss because of the news and all."

She was beginning to wake up, pulling herself into a sitting position while she worked at her eyes with the back of her hand, and Sam glanced uneasily into the kitchen at the clock over the stove, determined to avoid an argument.

"You had news so important that you couldn't call the Skorskis downstairs to let me know you were safe? I knew this would happen if you got way ahead of yourself and ended up with a steady."

"It's not Maura."

Her leg came in contact with the bottle, and she shook her head with a grimace of disgust. "So what's this news? This news so big it's worth doing this to me?"

Sam rushed his explanation while he stepped out into the hall, keeping his head craned through the doorway. "Yesterday the Japanese bombed Hawaii. The country's waiting for Roosevelt to declare war, and when he does, I'm joining the Marines. I love you, and I'll come home as soon as I'm inducted if they let me. Otherwise, I know I'll get leave before they send me overseas."

Before she could respond, he was taking the metal steps of the fire escape two at a time.

News of the attack filtered into the Newark area all morning. The large open room where Sam worked with six other men contained rows of pipes and nozzles to fill hundreds of heavy metal cylinders with oxygen and nitrogen. It was a noisy operation, and the loaded cylinders were rolled across the broad concrete floor and onto a loading dock, adding a hollow ringing sound to the drone of the pumps. But Sam had placed a radio on the low table in the corner of the building where they took their lunch, and during the morning, one of them managed to be close enough to it to keep the others posted on what was happening. If the floor manager noticed, he overlooked the radio. The neighboring ball bearing plant had piped the hourly bulletins of *The New York Times* right into their shop, and the entire city was tuned to their radios with World Series intensity.

By coffee time, Sam had learned that besides Pearl Harbor, Hickam Field, Ford Island and Honolulu had all been heavily bombed. The entire plant was also aware that the President was going to address the nation at 12:30, and all three buildings in the yard were going to share a common lunch break in order to hear it.

O'Hearn was not concerned. "There's more danger right here than anywhere else," he said, tapping the table hard enough to spill coffee over the brim of the cardboard cup beside him. "You guys mark my words. I'll stay behind on account of feet I was born with, and then get blown up along with the whole goddamned plant!"

"You mean sabotage?" Eddie asked.

"Bet your ass! They got the Pulaski Skyway guarded, they got the utilities guarded, they even got private security for places like this. There's gonna be some explosions sooner or later."

A balding man in his late fifties waved his hand in O'Hearn's direction. "That's all bullshit. We got unique isolation in this country. They ain't gettin' over here except in planes."

"They're here already," O'Hearn said knowingly. "There's cops pulling in Slopes all over Ironbound. They hide down here 'cause you can't tell 'em apart from the Filipinos."

"Slopes ain't Japs," someone corrected. "Slopes are Chinese."

"Same race," O'Hearn defended.

"Japan's already been at war with China a lot longer than with us," Clement said, and the others around the table looked over at him. "The Chinese are glad we're in on their side. Down on Mulberry Street, they're the ones saying the war won't last six months."

"I hope we get over there before it ends," Eddie put in.

The bald-headed man wiped his mouth with the back of his hand and nodded in Sam's direction. "I hear you kids are joining up."

"If it's war," Sam said.

The man glanced at the clock over the table and stood up, drawing the rest of them reluctantly to their feet. "Well, some of the guys in building two were thinking of enlisting, but I guess they plan on waiting a while."

"That's their business," Clement said, exchanging glances with Eddie before he turned and walked with a relaxed stride in the direction of the waiting cylinders.

As well as falling silent, the entire shop stopped eating when Franklin Delano Roosevelt addressed eighty million Americans over the radio, telling them that their nation had been at war ever since Japan had begun her unprovoked attack. The radio commentator began to outline the Congressional procedures for formalizing the declaration of war, but his voice was drowned out immediately in a wave of cheering that started at the back of building three and brought the thirty workers assembled there to their feet.

The men were packed around the lunch table, with most of

them spilling out onto the floor in order to hear the radio. The front door of the building was close to where they were gathered, separated from the table only by the glass-faced rectangle of the floor manager's window. As soon as the last wave of cheering had died down, Sam walked resolutely in the direction of the exit. Eddie fell silently in behind him.

None of the workers dispersed, and Sam knew from the growing murmuring that he and Eddie were being watched, but he kept his eyes straight ahead, coming to a halt with a neutral expression when Clay Purcell, the floor manager, intercepted him by stepping out of his office just before he reached the heavy steel door.

"Lunch break's over," Purcell said, tapping his watch with a tight expression. "You people even got extra today."

"We're joining up," Clement said firmly, but without any trace of anger. "You don't even have to pay me for this morning." He heard steps behind him, and he resisted the temptation to turn around. He was sure the entire shift had moved in to follow the argument.

Purcell crossed his arms over his chest and remained blocking the way. "You're too smart for this, Clement," he said just loudly enough for Sam to hear. "There's nothing in your contract about walking out for no reason."

"I'm not acting for the union," Sam announced. "I'm doing this on my own."

Purcell was about to protest when he checked himself. Something else was intruding on them, and they both turned to frown through Purcell's heavy glass window, as if it looked out on the other side of the building instead of the rear wall of the office.

As it turned out, there was no need to see. In a growing crescendo, the voices of the men gathered in the neighboring yard of the ball bearing plant were yelling out a semblance of "The Star-Spangled Banner" in an impulsive reaction to their President's speech. It might have been maudlin, except that the entire nation had just gone to war, and it authenticated itself further by the raspy, masculine delivery of the workers. A tuneless bass took up the chorus behind the gathering at the front door, and in seconds the entire building was filled with the sound of the national anthem.

"Let's go!" Sam yelled, raising an arm over his head in case his voice had not carried over the singing. In a move as gentle as it was powerful, he simply lifted Clay Purcell by the elbows and deposited him to one side of the door. Then he was out and into the light without looking back. The workers who had carried the singing in the yard next door applauded and banged against the mesh of the fence with their lunch boxes, and Sam was surprised that they had guessed where he was going. It was not until Eddie squeezed his shoulder near the front gate that he turned and looked back at the yard behind him.

Seven men had followed him through the door of the building, including O'Hearn, who lagged near the rear with a shuffling gait that bordered on a limp. The others poured out onto the blacktop to cheer them, joining the workers who were lining the fence. Sam looked over at Eddie and grinned. Then he squared his shoulders and headed down Raymond Boulevard, leading his contingent out of the Ironbound and toward Pennsylvania Station where a bus was waiting that would take them to the enlistment center.

The Federal Building was less than a fifteen-minute ride from Pennsylvania Station, but by the time Sam and the others reached it, it had been mobbed by men of enlistment age for hours. Waiting on line that cold December afternoon, Sam and Eddie learned that over two hundred men had already assembled outside when the recruiting offices had opened their doors that morning. They learned also that Congress had given President Roosevelt his official declaration of war within an hour of his address to the nation by a vote of 470 to 1, and that the sole dissenting vote was that of Congresswoman Rankin of Wyoming.

"Women," one of the men from the shop muttered with resignation, but minutes later, he regretted the generalization. Just as the cold was beginning to wear through some of their initial excitement, volunteers appeared along the line ranging down Broad Street, giving out sandwiches and coffee. Some of them looked as though they were members of auxiliary organizations such as the Red Cross, but the woman who served Sam and Eddie was wearing a winter coat over the hem of a flowered housedress, and she was with a small child who dug eagerly into her shopping bag, distributing sandwiches she had obviously made herself.

On more than one occasion, the line came to a complete halt while the processing officers shut their doors in order to work with one group of applicants without being interrupted by the next. As the afternoon wore on, Sam began to fear that they might not be taken at all that day. The front of the line had already passed back word that the Navy had disconnected its phones in order to concentrate on the men who had already appeared at their doors.

"I know they sent out a mobile recruiting unit," Eddie said, frowning as he took in the number of men who stood between their position and the front door. "I'm not sure if they'll tell us where it is, but it's worth a try."

Sam bounced lightly up and down on the balls of his feet, wrapping his arms around his upper body in order to keep warm. "I'll hold our place if you'll give it a try. I sure as hell don't want to go home tonight and tell Maura that we never even made it into the building."

"Okay, stay here while I see what I can scrounge up," Eddie said, and he broke into a run, skirting the crowded curb and finally disappearing into a knot of applicants near the front of the line.

In less than ten minutes, he appeared outside the front door again, stepping several yards out into the street when Sam failed to catch his waving signal. "I guess he wants us to go up there," Sam said, squinting toward the head of the line, and the eight of them raced toward Eddie's distant figure, with Sam arriving breathless in the lead.

"Talk to this guy," Eddie said, pulling Sam through the front doors and silencing the question he was about to ask with a meaningful expression.

Sam looked up to see a middle-aged man with a camera beckoning in his direction from the other side of the lobby. "You Sam?" He smiled as Clement and his group fell into step beside him.

"Yes, sir," Sam told him, attempting to glance over at Eddie to find out why he was being questioned.

"Well, any objection to being processed ahead of the others? And being in the paper?"

The corridors outside the recruitment offices were lined with candidates seated on the floor, and Sam glanced at the waiting men surrounding them and nodded emphatically. "Are you with the Marines?" he asked.

The man with the camera shook his head and laughed. "No, but I think that gentleman is, and he just might take you as a group if I ask him." Sam followed the direction of his nod and caught the uniform of a first sergeant through the doorway they were approaching. "That's Sergeant Parker," the photographer explained, catching Parker's attention by tapping on the edge of the open door. "I'm just a reporter from *The News*, but the sergeant's been very cooperative in helping us capture this incredible response on the part of you young people."

There were other men in uniform aiding Sergeant Parker, but they waited several minutes before he could make the time to join them. "Sergeant," the reporter began as soon as Parker approached them, "this is Samuel Clement. He just led eight of his fellow workers out of the plant where they were working and brought them down here to enlist. Right after the President's announcement."

Parker's harried expression broke long enough for him to smile. "You look like a man we could use," he said, taking in Sam's build. He glanced over at the reporter. "Blond-haired and blue-eyed, too."

The man from *The Newark Evening News* winked before he

turned back to Sam. "We just did an item like this," he explained to the others as well as to Sam. "We had five members of the Seton Hall track team come down together to join the Air Corps. If we can follow you people through your physicals, we'll have something on the workers as well as the students. What about it?"

There was an enthusiastic chorus of affirmative comments as soon as the words were out of his mouth, but Sam colored slightly and shook his head. "I want to get processed as soon as possible," he said, "but I didn't do anything special. Eddie here came down yesterday before I even heard the news."

"He's all wet," someone said behind him. "We followed him when we went union, too."

Everyone laughed but Sam, and when even Eddie shook his head indulgently, he shrugged at the reporter and allowed Sergeant Parker to lead them across the room. There, they were seated at a long table, and after the reporter snapped a preliminary picture of them poised with pens over their applications, they began the frantic processing that would lead to their enlistment.

For most of his physical, Sam walked from one station to another in his undershorts and heavy work boots, which he was told not to remove. All of the men stepped through the lines in their footwear, but the boots became a badge of identity for the plant workers. They had already drawn attention to themselves because of the reporter's constant picture taking, and Sam led them through each exam like an officer with a particular pride in his unit. The priority of the newspaper coverage allowed them to cut a four-hour process down to half that time, and before five o'clock, they had been X-rayed, fingerprinted, punctured for blood, and given innumerable other tests whose purpose was neither evident nor explained. A final picture of Sam was taken as he stood with his arms straight out and his eyes shut, demonstrating his coordination to an Army psychiatrist. Then they were permitted to get dressed in order to be sworn in.

Sam knew there was something wrong as soon as the sergeant

motioned him away from the others as they were filing into a small room off the hall to take the oath of allegiance. Parker seemed reluctant to meet his eyes, and he had the same sort of uneasy expression on his face that Sam's uncle had displayed when he had taken Sam out of the fourth grade in order to tell him his father had died.

"We're pretty busy here," Parker said, lowering his voice and leaning in toward Sam. "But I just wanted to tell you that we appreciate your response, regardless of the outcome."

Sam's eyes darted behind the sergeant to the little room where Eddie and the others were already forming a rough line in front of the flag. "The outcome?" Sam repeated.

Parker put a hand to his mouth and cleared his throat. "Well, I'm afraid we're not going to be able to take you. You're in great shape," he added quickly. "It's just the eye requirement. You didn't have any idea?"

Sam shook his head dumbly before he found his voice. "I can see all right if I narrow my eyes," he said hoarsely. "Even in football."

Parker put a hand on his shoulder, and Sam noticed some of the men still seated in the hall were looking over at them. "I don't doubt that, son, but this is different. We don't have anything to do with how they come up with the requirements. It's just up to us to enforce them." Sam remained staring at the floor, too numbed by the news to offer a response. "It's fine with us if you finish up with your group," Parker said, allowing his voice to brighten. "The man from the paper thought that might be a good idea."

Clement could not trust himself to respond. He shook his head slightly and turned away, feeling the sergeant's hand slide awkwardly from his shoulder. Without speaking, he moved toward the door, stepping over the legs of the other recruits who were seated along the length of the corridor. There was nothing that Parker could think to call after him, and the last sound Sam heard before he reached the exit was the oath of allegiance recited in a ragged unison by those who had so suddenly and irrevocably left him behind.

Chapter Three

The Japanese attack on New Jersey was announced the day after Sam's rejection, when he was still sleeping off the effects of an all-night drinking bout. At noon that Tuesday, military intelligence detected hostile aircraft off the coast of Virginia, heading north. Minutes later, Washington reported that the planes were a mere two hundred miles from New York, and that the strike force consisted of one hundred bombers. Families were evacuated from Mitchell Field on nearby Long Island, 280 planes were put into the air, and 2,500 men were deployed.

By one o'clock, Boston had ordered over twelve thousand air raid wardens to report immediately, and 250 New Jersey air raid stations were put on alert. A half hour later, sirens all over the New York metropolitan area sounded the first warning, and shortly after that, Warden Frank Skorski banged up the stairs from his apartment directly below the Clements, dispatching Mrs. Clement to the safety of the basement and rousing Sam from the stupor of his sleep with a frantic shaking of his shoulders.

"Wake up, kid! We need every able-bodied man we can find!"

For a moment, Sam thought the voice was part of the lingering nightmare produced by his rejection, and he rolled away from it, throwing an arm across his face. "I can't fight," he muttered under his breath. "They won't let me."

Skorski brought his eyes open with another shake of his shoulders. "You can and you will," he said dramatically.

Sam blinked and worked himself into a sitting position, still uncertain as to what he had heard. But Skorski refused to disappear, nodding a confirmation in the face of Sam's questioning glance: a short, heavy-set Wizard of Oz in a broad-brimmed steel helmet. "We're under attack, son. I got your Mom downstairs with my Marian, but we've got a whole city full of people to warn, and I could use your help."

"Jesus." Sam had passed out fully dressed after a solitary night in the local bars, so he had only to throw his legs over the side of the bed. He gripped his head with both hands, but his growing excitement allowed him to reach his feet and stumble after Skorski, who was already heading toward the hall. "Where are they?" he called out as they clattered down the stairs.

Skorski pushed a finger toward the ceiling without turning to answer. "They're coming in from the air. Bombers, just like Pearl. The filthy bastards." He paused in front of his door and pointed to a large metal tripod resting on the floor of the hallway. Next to it lay an elongated cylinder with the distinctive grips and muzzle of a machine gun. "I've had that baby on standby since Sunday," Skorski announced. "It's as old as the last war, but it's oiled and ready. Now Skyhawk Five has a real sting."

Sam rubbed at his eyes. "Skyhawk Five?"

"That's the name I picked for my station. Our station. Everyone in civilian defense gets to choose a code name." Skorski was squeezed into a pea jacket that parted where a button had come undone near his ample waist, and he reached into one of the pockets, producing an armband marked with the triangular insignia of an air raid warden. "Wear this," he offered, "on account of I have the helmet." As he worked it around Sam's sleeve, he continued to glance anxiously toward the light at the end of the hall that filtered in from the street. "There's a whole invisible network out there that only a few people know about, Sam. Skyhawk Five is only one station in the Second Defense Region. We got thousands all over New York, New Jersey and Delaware. There's plenty of fighting to be done in a bombing blitz if a man has the stomach for it." Skorski patted Sam's arm and stooped down to pick up a large portable radio standing outside his door. "You can tell from what's going on in England that the city of Newark is going to face some real hell out there, and the Office of Civilian Defense is the only hope they have. You can be a part of that hope, son."

He shot a hand out to deliver a slap of encouragement, but Sam had already stooped down toward the floor of the hallway, and when he rose, his shoulders were bent under the weight of the heavy machine gun and the awkward burden of the tripod.

Skorski bobbed his head in a curt approval. Then he squinted toward the light at the end of the hall. "Let's go get us some planes," he said.

One of the frequent bulletins coming over Skorski's radio warned citizens to stay clear of the streets, and although sirens were sounding in different locations of the city, many of the people Sam and Skorski passed seemed to be going about their business as usual.

"We'll get our area battened down first," Skorski panted, squeezing out the words with difficulty because of the hurried pace. "Then I'd better chase some of these people off the streets before those bastards hit us." He glanced up at the sky. "You can stay behind to man my station."

Sam's drinking and the overbearing weight of the gun had robbed him of his customary strength, and it was all he could do to nod his agreement, silently hoping they would reach their position before he became ill.

But there was already a man pacing the corner of Jackson Street and Raymond Boulevard when Skorski planted his radio on the sidewalk to indicate they had arrived.

"Otis, what the hell are you doing here?" Skorski demanded as soon as he had caught his breath.

Otis was also wearing the armband of the Civilian Defense, and he mirrored Skorski's indignant expression. "I'm alerting vehicular traffic. I suggest you get to your station and do likewise."

"This *is* my station," Skorski said, gaining volume along with his breath.

Otis put his hands on his hips. "The hell you say." He pointed toward the roof of the building behind them. "That there was where they put me when they flew those test flights over last October—"

"—those weren't the final assignments!"

"—and this here," Otis went on, ignoring Skorski's interruption and dropping his hand to indicate the cellarway of a local restaurant, "is my designated place of refuge for pedestrians!"

"Since when?"

Otis opened his mouth to bark a reply, but just then, the music coming over Skorski's radio was interrupted for another bulletin. Skorski dropped to one knee and made a show of turning up the volume, as though the boxy Philco gave him the endorsement of special equipment. The three of them listened in silence as a local commentator announced that Brooklyn and Staten Island Navy personnel were being cleared from their areas.

And then, before the music had resumed, Otis seized the initiative by stepping out into the street and waving a passing bus over to the curb. Unlike Skorski, Otis wore no metal helmet, and the driver responded to his frantic gesturing by pulling up and opening his doors with a bored expression, ignorant of the emergency that had raised the status of his bus stop to an air raid station.

He looked up in complete surprise when Otis rapped sharply on the metal entrance steps with his flashlight instead of boarding the bus. "All right," Otis said with authority. "I think it would be a good idea if you emptied your bus right here. We'd like everybody in that restaurant." He pointed to the basement entrance behind him.

The driver frowned down at him, opening his mouth slightly and gazing in the direction of Otis' outstretched hand. Having been out-maneuvered, Skorski could only second the command. He waved the driver toward the restaurant with a smile of encouragement while gesturing emphatically toward the radio on the sidewalk, unaware that it was emitting the soothing bars of "Night and Day" as played by the Harry James orchestra. Sam had put the gun aside and was gazing expectantly toward the sky, swallowing rapidly in an attempt to stave off his growing nausea.

The driver hesitated long enough to take in the trio before he slammed his doors on them, sweeping Otis' flashlight from his hand and pulling out into the street with enough acceleration to pass several of the cars in front of him.

"We're under attack!" Otis yelled after him, but he was forced back to the refuge of the curb by the traffic that continued to stream down Raymond Boulevard.

Skorski picked up his radio and waved Sam away from the corner without looking back. "Let him have his way," he offered with satisfaction. "There's a whole city left to save out there."

Alerted school authorities had released many students from class, and Skorski detained a flock of them hurrying home in order to urge them to hurry home. But it was not until they approached the Renold Insurance Building on Raymond that he found an appropriate object for his sense of mission.

"Sweet Jesus, they got a whole company full of people in there still goin' about their business! Like lambs to slaughter," he muttered, and he hurried up the steps of the three-story building, waving Sam after him without looking back.

The first floor was divided by rows of desks, and by the time Sam had crashed through the swinging doors of the entrance with the machine gun, Skorski was shouting over the receptionist toward the approaching manager. "Tell everyone here to do just what we say! Your lives depend on it!"

Fifteen people froze where they were, and only a faint female scream from the back of the room broke the silence. Several of the clerks immediately behind the manager fastened their eyes on Sam with drained expressions, and one of the men slowly raised his hands toward the ceiling. Skorski barked his announcement with the force of frustration. "This is an air raid, don't you see? An air raid!"

The manager was wearing a bow tie, and he pulled at it nervously when he confronted Skorski. "Is that why we heard sirens? We thought there was a fire at one of the plants."

Skorski's glance took in some of the women standing behind him. "Mister, there's enough enemy steel on its way through the air to put this whole city ablaze." He held up his hand to silence the immediate reaction. "There's no reason to fly off the handle! We're just one part of an invisible safety net that Civilian Defense is throwing over the whole coast!" Dropping his voice, he turned back to the manager. "I want everybody flat on the floor under their desks, but first let's get those shades down. And pull the curtains over them."

"You heard him," the manager ordered, and in seconds the circle of office workers had scattered toward the walls. "It's daylight," he suggested tentatively while Skorski nodded his approval.

"It is *now,*" Skorski shot back without explanation. He turned away briefly to motion Sam forward. "You got a way we can get up on the roof?"

"The elevator's the fastest." The manager pointed toward the metal doors of the shaft.

"Good enough." Skorski cupped his hands around his mouth. "All right, we're going upstairs to deal with the Japs! Everybody find a place under a desk!"

While they were scrambling to comply with his order, the elevator arrived in response to his ringing. Sam sighed with relief as the doors slid back. He was ready and willing to face the fire of the enemy, but if he had to shoulder the weight of the gun on the stairs, he had serious doubts about reaching the roof without getting sick.

A black elevator boy slid back the metal gate, and his mouth opened slowly as he took in the prone figures scattered around the dimly lit floor. His glance settled on the gun draped across Sam's shoulders. "Is they dead?" he asked.

"There'll be no dying here," Skorski said, patting his head lightly as he stepped into the elevator. "Just get us to the third floor as fast as possible."

"Ain't no one up there," the boy said, shutting the gate and putting the elevator in motion. "Only fifteen folks for filing on the first. The otha' floors is fo' the files themselves. I don't even put on the lights, 'cept when they send me up there."

"Hold at the second!" Skorski screamed, and they stopped suddenly enough to be thrown into each other. Skorski bent down on one knee and put both hands on the shoulders of the elevator boy. "Listen, son, I just remembered something important. We have to cut the power off, and by the time we assemble the gun, the enemy could be right on top of us. Could you take the stairs and get to the electric?"

"Sho' could. Those are the switches in the cella'."

Skorski nodded with approval. "Good. And when you've got the power off, get up those stairs as quick as you can and duck under a desk. The top floors may be the ones that get blown out, but it's the basement where the gas settles. Understand?"

The boy nodded, already pressing his hand to his face as though he detected the scent of something alien in the air. Skorski pulled back the gate and sent him bounding across the floor in the direction of the staircase. In the time it took to reach the basement, Sam had managed to fit the cylinder of the machine gun to the tripod, and Skorski had manned the controls of the elevator.

As if on cue, the music coming over the radio cut away once more, and they paused long enough to hear that all civilian flights from Newark Airport had been canceled. In addition, the planes of the 119th Observation Squad had been scattered around the airfield, making them less accessible targets.

"No picnic for the bastards this time!" Skorski said through his teeth, and he pulled up on the control lever, moving them in the direction of the roof with an uncertain, halting motion. It was difficult to tell how far they rose, because almost immediately, the light on the ceiling dimmed, and Skorski sent them jerking upward into the growing darkness with a series of tentative pulls at the controls. Within seconds, everything around them had faded from sight and they were at a standstill.

"Sweet Jesus, what the hell is going on?"

Skorski's disembodied voice came to Sam from less than six feet away, but Sam's reply was lost in a series of thundering salvos that filled the entire elevator shaft. In cutting the power, the elevator boy had not only brought the rising car to a halt. He had also plunged the cellar into a total blackness that prevented him from finding the stairs. In desperation, he remained where he was, pounding for the elevator on the metal doors of the shaft and breathing only through his uniform cap, which he had pressed against his mouth.

Only Sam realized the same switch that cut off the lights had robbed the elevator of its motion. "It's the power," he repeated over the explosion bouncing against the walls of the shaft. "You told him to cut the power, so we stopped!"

"Damn the luck! And just when they're hitting us with everything they have!" The pounding in the basement grew more desperate as the elevator boy felt increasingly certain that he smelled gas, and the sound was overwhelming by the time it reached the level of the stranded car. In a frenzy of motion, Skorski swept back the metal lattice of the gate and threw himself against the barrier of the elevator doors. A nightstick dangled below the hem of his pea jacket, and he managed to pry them apart using it as a lever. When there was an opening big enough to squeeze through, he called out to Sam. "I'm going down there!"

But the words were lost in the booming from below, which had grown deafening when the doors were forced apart, and Sam climbed over the barrier of the gun to hear what Skorski was telling him.

"If we don't return their fire, there's not going to be any city left!" Skorski shouted, and he let his lower body slide out into the void of the shaft. Sam bent down to support him, but the momentum of Skorski's movement took his heavy body down past the saddle of the doorway, until he was clinging to the edge of the car by the faltering grip of his fingers. "Jesus, I'm going!" he screamed.

Sam flattened himself against the floor of the elevator and covered Skorski's hands with his own, but they began slipping against his grip almost as soon as he had captured them.

"Get the gun up there!" Skorski shouted as he felt the final ripple in the metal saddle of the doorway slip beneath his fingers. "It's all over for me! Get the bastards!" He might have said something else, or even screamed, but Sam could hear nothing over a final wave of sound erupting in the shaft. He knew only that Skorski's hands were no longer beneath his.

He rolled to the center of the car, pounding the floor in frustration with the ball of his fist. Then, as though he had jolted a loose connection somewhere in the mechanism of the elevator, the light over his head began to come to life with a dull glow. Sam scrambled to his feet screaming Skorski's name, and the echo of his own voice made him suddenly aware that the thundering had subsided. The outline of the open doorway came slowly into view as the bulb in the ceiling brightened, and like a ghost gaining form, Skorski's head appeared outside in the shaft, just below the level of the elevator floor.

A husky voice came at him in subdued tones from beneath the shadow of the helmet. "Lower the elevator," it said.

Sam found his feet and inched the operator's lever downward. The car responded in a slow descent, and the rest of Skorski's body came into view. When the bottom of the elevator cleared his feet, Sam could see that he was standing on the linoleum of the second-floor landing. They had only risen half the length of the second floor doorway before the power went out, and Skorski had plunged downward for a distance of two feet.

The older man reddened slightly in the face of Sam's startled expression, but he straightened his helmet and boarded the elevator with a dignified limp. "I banged my ankle when I hit the deck," he said. "But I guess there's others out there a lot worse off now that it's all over. Take her down. At least we can help with the wounded."

Sam stretched out a blackened hand, and they moved toward the first floor. In the renewed light, he noticed that all of his clothing was smudged by dark patches he had picked up when he pressed himself against the elevator floor. Skorski had lost most of the buttons on his pea jacket, and he hopped on one foot, favoring his injured ankle when Sam brought the car to an awkward halt.

But nothing they had been through jolted them as openly as the scene they confronted when Sam drew back the elevator doors. The entire office was gathered in a large semicircle outside the landing. Not only were they whole and uninjured, but through the windows that had been uncovered on the wall behind them, the city of Newark went about its business undamaged and heedless of the danger it had managed to escape.

The members of both parties confronted each other while a muted trumpet wailed melodically through the lead to "Sentimental Journey" from the speaker of Skorski's radio.

"False alarm," someone near the back of the crowd muttered awkwardly after they had stared wordlessly at each other for several moments.

"So." Skorski narrowed his eyes and made a show of nodding with a knowing expression.

But the absurdity of the situation and the realization that there would be no fighting combined to overcome Sam. He had barely turned away before he surrendered, becoming ill on the floor of the elevator in front of all of them.

That night, in the solitude of his room, he heard Col. George H. Baird announce that in New York, New Jersey and Delaware alone, 2,684 young men had been accepted for Army enlistment in the first two days since the attack on Pearl Harbor.

It came close to being the worst winter of his life. In a sense, he brought much of the pain on himself, since others were rejected for a variety of reasons, and many never even volunteered. But Clement had always been a leader in the most natural sense of the word, and as the neighborhood gradually emptied of men his age, he found it impossible to deal with what he considered a personal failure.

He could not bring himself to report for work after his dramatic attempt to enlist, even though he later learned that O'Hearn and one of the others who had also failed his physical returned to the plant the following morning. Eddie visited him briefly on Wednesday, telling him that the entire group had refused permission for the publication of their pictures once they had learned of Clement's rejection. That same afternoon, Sam saw that the members of the Seton Hall track team had been featured in the paper's war coverage, without any mention of the men from his plant.

Eddie sensed his pain. They had shared the early death of their fathers and developed the sort of friendship that almost compensated for not having any brothers or sisters of their own. But without speaking of it, they both knew that there would be a barrier between them for as long as the war lasted. When Eddie left for basic training in early January, they embraced stiffly in the hallway of Sam's apartment, both of them shaking with an emotion that reflected Sam's rejection rather than Eddie's departure for a war that might mean his death.

Sam never did return to the plant. He had accepted the death of his father, and years later, he had gone willingly to work even though he was capable of college if he could have afforded it. But there was no way he could compensate now for his failure to serve, and it continued to eat away at him. He remained at home during the day, and drank his small savings in the evenings, avoiding the local bars in order to be free of conversation.

He saw Maura only once. He informed her that she was no longer interested in him, she denied it, and they quarreled. He was too caught up in himself to care about the truth, and his mother was happy enough to tell her that he wasn't in when she attempted to see him. In time, he cultivated a certain fondness for his punishment, warring with himself during the torpor that came over him each evening. His mother was grateful that he had not been taken, and she indulged him without complaining. He had always been a good son, and in time, he would find work again.

He did make the effort, but only after the money had run out; and in a sense, it led to a job. But all of that began with Vera.

It was late January, and he had been out to the Breeze Corporation, a manufacturing company that made aircraft equipment and was located a comfortable distance from the Ironbound area of Newark. He had thought of applying for a job on the night shift, but before he even approached the gates of the plant, he decided that he could not do it. If he wasn't able to fight, he could not bring himself to contribute to the war effort merely by helping to produce weapons, regardless of the attractive wages and the growing sentiment that such a job was just as critical as carrying a rifle. He had less than eighty dollars left in his savings, but it was still enough to buy a little more time, and he turned from the lights of the factory, deciding to postpone the end of his self-imposed isolation for a few weeks longer.

He was heading down South Street with the intention of finding a local bar when a high-pitched sound came to him through the cold night air. At first he thought it had been produced by the plant, but it wavered slightly, dropping in tone, and he knew it was human. By the time he had identified it as moaning, he had traced it to the outskirts of a vacant lot less than a hundred yards away. Even from the sidewalk, he could see a small figure flanked by two larger ones. There was a fourth man with his back to Clement, and he seemed to be working at the body of the shorter man while the two others held him stationary.

Clement glanced over his shoulder. The street appeared to be deserted, so he approached the group to investigate on his own. The man administering the beating delivered another muffled blow to the stomach of his victim before one of the others nodded a warning, causing him to turn abruptly in Clement's direction.

"Who goes there?" he asked with a sharp formality that worked to disguise his voice, and Clement did not recognize him until he had turned completely around. It was Tom O'Hearn, and although he was in his winter coat, the white of an armband circled his sleeve, and there was a cartridge belt and holster strapped around his ample waist. "Jesus, it's Sam Clement," he said.

The short man was no longer moaning, but looking at Sam with widened eyes, as though he were waiting to see if another member was to be added to the group. There was a thin stream of blood running from one corner of his mouth, and several reddening marks on his bare midriff, which had been exposed by the unrelenting grip of the two larger men on the sleeves of his coat. Sam looked down to see that his feet were not resting fully on the ground. "What the hell are you doing?" he asked.

O'Hearn's smile disappeared at the sound of Sam's tone. "Butt off, Sam!" he said indignantly. "I happen to be doing my job."

Sam stretched out an arm that shook under his growing anger. "Your job's over on Raymond," he said, pointing in the direction of the Ironbound.

"During the day, maybe." O'Hearn tightened his expression with an anger of his own. "At night I work for Breeze. I'm part of security."

The whimpering had started again, and Sam nodded in the direction of the prisoner. "What does that have to do with this man?"

"He ain't a man. He's a fucken' Jap. They let some of 'em come back from Ellis Island and the first thing they do is sneak around this plant lookin' for trouble."

The victim must have understood English, because the sudden grunting he produced was obviously in response to what O'Hearn had just said. Both men turned from their confrontation long enough to follow the indication of his head, which he jerked in the direction of the street with increasingly desperate sounds. There, under the arc of a lamppost, Sam saw the slight figure of a woman with a small child pressed tightly against her side. Even from the distance that separated them, he could see that she was anxiously reflecting the nodding of O'Hearn's prisoner, darting a pointed finger in the direction of the apartments on the other side of the street.

"Jesus Christ!" Sam exploded, turning back to O'Hearn. "That's his goddamned house! He lives here, you jerk, and you're beating the shit out of him in front of his family!"

O'Hearn tapped his chest hard enough to make a thumping sound. "Listen, don't you tell me what to do! I got responsibilities to the defense establishment and I ain't ducking 'em." He turned back toward the prisoner. "Like some people I know!" he added with a meaningful inflection.

Sam took one last glance at the figures huddled near the edge of the sidewalk, but the look on their faces was hardly necessary to peak his anger. For months, he had directed his growing frustration inward, drinking to exhaust himself as well as to escape the fact that he was not permitted to fight. He could fight, and so well that it was impossible to resign himself to what had been done to him as easily as the others who had been left behind. He took a deep breath to gain control over his voice and the bulk of his coat tightened briefly under the visible expansion of his chest. "He's an American like anyone else," he said tightly.

O'Hearn turned back toward him to argue, but even before he could open his mouth to reply, Sam unloaded on him. It was the shoulder-backed punch of a natural athlete, and it was delivered with the momentum of a man whose energy had been bound up for months. Sam knew that there was no way he could handle all three of them, but something perverse inside of him actually welcomed the opportunity. His fist collided with O'Hearn's jaw so hard that Sam grunted with pain as the impact of the blow traveled down the extension of his arm. O'Hearn simply dropped soundlessly to the ground.

Fortunately, O'Hearn had been the only one of them armed, although both of the men with him were almost as large as Sam. Without hesitation, they released their prisoner and advanced on him.

Clement let his mouth fall open and threw his hands upward, stretching his arms over his head. "All right," he said. "No need to get rough."

One of the men had gotten behind him, but the one in front accepted his surrender, dropping his arms with an expression of disgust.

Almost immediately, Clement lashed out at him with his leg, catching him directly in the crotch with the heel of his heavy work boot. The man doubled up and Sam brought him the rest of the way to the ground with a driving tackle. He had grabbed a rock and delivered one satisfying blow to the back of his opponent's head when something caught him from behind, knocking him senseless.

"Hello, beautiful."

Sam squeezed his eyes open and shut several times in order to adjust to the light before he found the source of the greeting. He was lying on a trolley bed in the corner of a noisy room, and there was a nurse peering down at him with an amused expression. He felt a throbbing in the top of his head, but as he tightened his muscles cautiously, he concluded that his body was still intact. "Is this a hospital?" he asked.

The nurse had shining blond hair, and it bobbed with her head when she nodded. "It's actually an emergency room. You're at City Hospital, but we didn't want to take you upstairs until we got a little information. We couldn't find a wallet. Were you robbed?"

Clement felt a wave of nausea sweep over him when he arched his back and slid his hand into his pants pocket, but he swallowed rapidly, and gradually it passed. "I did have a wallet. I guess whoever hit me took it," he said without further explanation. He propped an arm on the edge of the bed and she helped him into an upright position with a surprisingly strong grip on his arm. "I can't stay here," he said. "I've got money to pay for what you've already done."

The nurse shrugged. "You're taking a chance. You've probably got at least a slight concussion, but you can suit yourself." With an increasing sense of orientation, Clement realized how attractive she was. She had slate-blue eyes, and one of the clearest complexions he had ever seen. She looked close to his age, but there was a coolness in her expression, and the way she carried herself made her seem older than Maura. "Want to file a complaint with the police?" she asked.

"Did they bring me here?"

The nurse was already writing rapidly on a form she had attached to the top of her clipboard. "No. A couple of Orientals did, but they ran like the wind once they got you to the front steps. Technically, my shift is over, but I'll stick around long enough to get you released if you don't want to bother with the law. I'll need your name and address to begin with."

There was a large lump on the back of his head, and one side of his face was badly swollen, as though he had been kicked while he was down. But by the time he was released, neither of those injuries bothered him as much as his eyes. He was less than half a block from the hospital when he was forced to lean against a building, holding his head between his hands in an attempt to check the whirling effect of his vision. He was still trying to regain his sense of balance when she found him on her way home from work.

"You aren't still nauseous, are you?" she asked, taking his hand from his face and peering up at him without announcing herself. When he blinked several times and met her gaze, she took him by the arm and led him cautiously back out onto the sidewalk. "I'm Vera, your nurse," she said. "If you still feel sick to your stomach, you'd better let me help you back to the hospital. Nausea can be a real danger sign with concussion."

"Thanks, but I feel better now," he told her. "I only have to get as far as Clay Street."

"That's a few blocks from my apartment. If you keep a tight grip on my arm, you might make it."

Sam felt his strength beginning to renew itself, but he was still worried about the return of his dizziness. "Do you really live near Clay Street?" he asked, letting her guide him in the direction of the Ironbound.

"Only until I can move again," she said dryly. "Come on, but you'll have to wait at my place while I change. I'm not staying in this waitress outfit any longer than I have to."

They spent twenty minutes in her apartment, which was less than a five-minute walk from his neighborhood. She passed briefly from her bedroom to the bathroom in her slip, arching an eyebrow and telling him not to get any ideas when he looked up from the living room couch where he was lying down. He did not want to tell her that it was actually a novelty for him to be alone with a woman in her apartment. He had never gone beyond the petting he had experienced with Maura in Branagan's car, and he sensed an air of sophistication about this girl that intimidated him. Copies of *Glamour* and *Bazaar* lay in a neat fan on the coffee table beside him, and there were cigarette stubs ringed with lipstick on a stand-up ashtray at one end of the couch.

She walked him home with both arms locked around his waist, and Sam found himself telling her about his confrontation with O'Hearn. He had missed the company of a woman more than he realized, and he felt a sudden disappointment when she broke away the moment she had led him to his doorway. As he turned to thank her, she grimaced openly at the swollen side of his face, laughing with him when he attempted to hold his head at a more flattering angle.

"I don't know how to thank you," he said awkwardly.

She was already backing away, but she looked at him with that half serious expression he found so appealing. "I saw on your admission form that you're out of work. You could always take me out to dinner when you get a job," she said.

He decided not to wait that long, and late the following night, he was outside her apartment when she returned home from work. This time, she told him to remain in the lobby of her building, but she was downstairs in less than ten minutes, and they had several drinks together at a local pub, coming home arm in arm during the early hours of the morning.

They began to see each other frequently after that. Sam was already accustomed to sleeping most of the day, and he would meet her each night at eleven-thirty when her shift ended. Her full name was Vera Campbell, and she was not a nurse, but a nurse's aide.

"I've done my eighty hours of classroom and ward work," she told him one night at the Essex Pub, a small tavern that they had made a habit of frequenting together. "Now I'm supposed to put in one hundred and fifty hours at a hospital each year."

"But you're working every day," Sam said.

"Of course. I have a private job looking after an old lady on weekends, and once I've had a little more experience, I'll leave the hospital for good. This war has already created a shortage of nurses, and it's just begun. People who need private care aren't going to be too picky about degrees. Or pay. I saw this coming a year ago when I got up enough money to leave home." She pulled deeply on her cigarette and narrowed her expression. "I told you, if I'm making a living anywhere in the medical profession, it frees someone else for war duty. You better face that, Sam. Men are going to be scarce around here, and the good ones can write their own ticket."

Sam looked down at the table and shrugged. "It doesn't matter how I feel about it anymore. If I don't get a job next week, I'll be flat."

Vera beckoned with her hand toward the back of the room

before she mocked him with a frown. "And that means the end of us, since you're too proud to let me pay for anything."

She smiled over his shoulder at someone approaching their table, and he twisted around to see that it was a man in his early fifties he knew only as Max. Max was one of a small circle that they shared their company with, and Vera originally introduced him as one of the regulars the first time she had taken Sam to the Essex Pub. He had a salt-and-pepper mustache to match his graying hair, and his face was lined in a pattern of wrinkles that reflected an expression constantly on the edge of humor. Sam had liked him from the start, and Max usually managed to stop by their table long enough to enliven the conversation without intruding on their privacy. Sam found that he was more comfortable with everyone he had come to know through Vera, since he was meeting people who could not possibly judge him from the perspective of his past.

Max put Vera's hand to his lips and saluted Sam with the suggestion of a bow before he sat down between them and thrust his hands into the pockets of his dirty brown overcoat. As always, his battered gray hat remained on his head. "Heil Hitler," he said, raising his glass. "What are the young people up to this evening?"

Vera gave him an affectionate squeeze before she withdrew her hand from his grip and pointed at Sam. "Flash Gordon here still hasn't come up with a job. Should I leave him, Max?"

"Only for me," Max said, pulling at his beer. Then he turned to Sam. "Can you drive with those eyes?"

Sam reddened slightly. "I could fly planes if they gave me the chance."

Max winked at Vera. "I already heard you can fight, kid. If you have a license, I got a proposition you might want to consider."

"I've got a license," Sam said, frowning in the face of Vera's amused expression.

Max pushed away from the table. "Good. My proposition is

right out back. You can take your drink, but leave the lady. People who look like that are probably good for business."

Sam followed Max across the noisy room and through the swinging doors of the kitchen with a growing curiosity over what the older man could have to offer. He had tried to buy Max a drink on several occasions, and although he always refused, Sam had the idea that only his pride kept him from accepting. Nobody seemed to notice their intrusion in the busy kitchen, and Max seemed to know just where he was going. They crossed a narrow hall, and he pushed open a heavy metal door, leading them out onto the apron of a loading dock. He gestured toward a car that gleamed under a single light bulb suspended over the bay where it was parked.

"Think you could handle that?" he asked.

"Jesus." Sam jumped down into the bay and walked slowly around the vehicle, whistling his appreciation. It was a '41 De-Soto, painted jet black with red upholstery. Even the tires were the newest Sam had seen in months. "What would I have to do to deserve this?" he asked.

Max opened his hands. "Make deliveries. I may get a truck later, but the business is still growing. That's why it's part-time for now. Still, the pay should be enough to keep Vera in Luckies."

Sam slammed the door of the DeSoto shut with a solid refrigerator sound. "I didn't even know you had a business, Max. How come they let you keep your car here?"

"I guess because I own the place," Max said, raising his shoulders in a shrug without bothering to take his hands out of his coat pockets.

In February of 1942, the nation changed to War Time in order to save precious daylight, the last civilian car rolled off the assembly lines, Singapore fell to the Japanese, and Sam Clement made close to thirty dollars a day. In the beginning, he drove one or two nights a week, delivering linen to the industrial laundry that serviced the Essex Pub, or carrying enough cases of liquor back from New York to fill both the trunk and the back seat of the DeSoto. In time, he made periodic trips to Boston, where he found Max owned another club that was larger and had the status of a complete restaurant. Max warned him against speeding, and once Sam found him taking the car's mileage from the odometer, but as Sam continued to prove dependable, he assigned him further deliveries with greater frequency.

He saw Vera less, but their relationship grew more intimate, and late one night when they had both finished work, she lay against him on her living room couch, allowing him to loosen her bra so that he could trace the contours of her bare breasts under her sweater. She met his mother briefly, and everyone they had known since they met considered them a couple.

Sam enjoyed being active again, especially at night. He felt as though he were moving in a different world after nine o'clock, and working helped to heal the wound of his rejection from the service. He also made money. It was good to begin with, and it became increasingly better as the weeks went by. Ultimately, it was the money that made him hesitate long enough to question his new life.

"Something's up," he told Vera one evening at her apartment. They were going out, and he sat on the edge of her bed while she moved around the room in her slip, finishing her dressing. "I did the Boston run yesterday, which is why I'm off tonight. Do you know what he gave me?"

His tone caused her to look up, and she crossed over to where he was sitting, pulling at the backs of her stockings.

"You're not going to tell me he stiffed you," she said.

Sam shook his head. "He gave me too much. Fifty dollars for one night's work." When she continued to frown at him, he took her hand, locking her eyes with his own. "Vera, something's not straight. Sometimes I deliver boxes that aren't even marked, and I always drive at night. That's probably why Max doesn't want me speeding. He's afraid of the law. Why else would he pay me this way?"

She pulled her hand from his and glared down at him. "Because he likes you, you jerk, and you're good at your job! Clubs have never been busier, and Max has two of them. What did you see in New York when we finally got through the door of one of those places? People doing everything from the rumba to the boompsa-daisy in order to forget the war!" She turned her back on him and bent over her stockings. "Can't you get it through your head that there's more opportunity in this war than the chance to get yourself killed?"

He put a hand on the small of her back. "That's not all, Vera. I'm not the only one who drives that car. A few times a week I have to adjust the seat. And the mileage is different."

"So?"

"So, I saw blood on the back seat yesterday. Two stains that couldn't have been anything else."

"There's plenty of harmless reasons for that," Vera said without looking up from her stockings.

"Along with night runs and big money? Maybe, but I'll be interested in what Max has to say about it when I ask him."

She turned on him at that. "The hell you will!" she warned. Then she paused, as though she had just become aware of herself, and her expression softened. "I'll speak to Max. He's still your boss for all his joking, and it's not your place to question him. We don't want him angry with you."

"He's not angry. He wants me to work full time for him. He says it's going to mean more money, if you can imagine that." He bent down, helping her to straighten her stockings so that the seams were centered in the backs of her legs.

"Get the upper parts," she said. Her back was to him, and he raised the hem of her slip so that he could see underneath it. She moved her hips slightly under his touch, swaying in an even tempo to the music of Tommy Dorsey's band, while Bunny Berigan's gravely voice pushed against the speaker of the radio, singing "I can't get started with you." When she spoke again, her voice had lost its anger. "Is it so wrong to get ahead, Sam? To become someone better?"

"You know I want to," he said. There were dark bands

around the upper part of her stockings where the clips from her garter belt were fastened, and when he moved the slip high enough to expose the white silk of her panties, she turned slowly, keeping it bunched above her waist so that he could look at her.

"Is there anything bad about taking what you want if you know you're right?" she asked.

He could only shake his head, swallowing at the stretch of her body as she pulled the slip up over her head and let it fall to the floor behind her. He reached up tentatively, and when she leaned into him, he put his arms around her back, unhooking her brassiere. When it came away, he saw that there were marks on the sides of her breasts from the tight restraint, and he touched them, sliding his hands around and watching in open fascination as her nipples hardened under the brush of his fingers.

She pulled him in then, pushing on his shoulder until he slipped down her body to his knees. He loosened her garter belt and drew it into a tight circle along with her panties, slipping them both down around her ankles. The triangle of her pubic hair was dark gold against the even whiteness of her skin, and when he ran a hand behind her and into the fold of her buttocks, she arched into him until he worked with his mouth at the fold between her legs.

She fell back onto the bed then, pushing her legs free of her underthings, but when he lay down beside her, she restrained him with a hand, keeping him prone while she worked at his clothes. When she had removed everything except his undershorts, she straddled his chest, facing away from him, so that when she bent down over his middle, the entire area between her legs was exposed to him. She lifted the band of his shorts, taking a firm grip on the shaft of his penis, and causing him to moan openly as she slipped down over it with the tightness of her mouth.

She seemed to know when she had brought him to the edge of his control, because she stopped the working of her mouth and rolled off of him, reversing her position, and pulling him on top of her by locking her arms tightly around his neck. As soon as he was moving inside of her, she reached behind him and held his scrotum, fondling it without hurting him as he pushed awkwardly against her. He came at once, and she shuddered under him, extending his exhilaration until he finally collapsed, hot and spent beside her.

For a full minute, there was no sound in the room other than his heavy breathing. Then he rolled over onto his side, pushing gently at the damp strands of hair that framed her face. "I don't know how that happened," he told her in a voice that was less than a whisper. "I guess with two people who love each other—"

She put a hand to his lips, silencing the explanation. "It's all right, Sam. Every girl has to have a first time, and I'm glad mine came with you." Then she rose from the bed with her panties in her hand, clamping them into a pad between her legs as soon as she was out in the hall and approaching the bathroom.

He slept with her when they got back that night, and the memory of her body lingered with him the next day when he went to see Max. He had decided he wanted the job: easy money, blood, and the threat of the law notwithstanding.

Part Two:
Todd

Chapter Four

V era's visitation lingered with Sam even after he was home from the hospital. If Kara sensed that he was not completely at peace, she gave no indication of it, leaving him to his thoughts that first night and withdrawing quietly to their bedroom. They had met only after each of them had survived troubled times, and they had the mutual respect of veterans for things better left unsaid. Kara kept her silence, knowing he would come to her if he needed her. She was not to lose him after all; she was content to let him cope with his own survival.

Clement wondered himself if his own unrest was due simply to gaining a new lease on life. He had been convinced that he was going to die. Couldn't Vera merely have been part of that entire drowning man mentality, a part of his past flashing before his eyes? He sipped at the drink he had made for himself and stared into the shadows of the dimly lit living room, allowing himself to conjure up her face as he had remembered it. It had been a deliberate mental exercise, shutting out an unwanted past. When he reversed the process, he found the characters and events still lifelike and vivid, preserved in a special cellar of the memory where they had not been allowed to fade in the light of each new day's experience.

Vera was there before him in all of her forms, squinting at him in the sunlight of brighter, younger afternoons, or newly naked in the dimness of rooms whose dated furniture evoked moods and feelings he had long suppressed. Clement put a hand to his eyes and brought back the woman he thought he had seen in the hospital. The images mixed and distilled in the darkness of the quiet room, leaving the unmistakable aura of the same person. He sighed and worked his way painfully to his feet, allowing himself to finish the remainder of his drink before he headed down the hall in the direction of his son's room. In retrospect, he was suddenly surer than ever that the nurse he had seen was real because of one telling detail that was unlikely to have been the product of his imagination.

Vera might have drugged him, but in spite of the vagueness of the image, he was certain that the woman who leaned over his bed had aged with him over the years. It was the set of her posture, the network of veins in the hand that had slipped under the sheet with a lover's familiarity—even the register of her voice, recognizable, but lowered by the years. All of these belonged to Vera, but a Vera that had grown older. It was possible that Clement might have conjured her up as she was thirty-five years earlier, but it was too much for him to accept the fact that a delusion of his own creation would have aged in such perfect lockstep with him.

Ironically, he felt his own son might be able to provide him with a final confirmation.

Todd was a problem. Until he had left for the Marines, he had been slightly indulged, but that had been Sam's doing, and a fault shared by many parents of his generation. The boy was basically good, and his own sense of pride prevented him from accepting everything his father was willing to give him. He had volunteered for Vietnam, Sam frequently reminded himself, and his own officers said he had acted heroically in combat. He had also been wounded.

Sam's feelings about the leg his son dragged slightly to one side were ambivalent. There were times when he felt that Todd's wound was part of the retribution for his own failure to serve, but the infirmity was slight enough so that Sam found himself envying the obvious sign of Todd's courage. In the most general terms, before he drew into himself, Todd had embodied almost everything that Sam would have wanted to achieve in his own life.

He was at home with the young people who had grown up in the better suburbs of Fort Lauderdale, an area as far removed from Sam's old neighborhood by its standard of living as it was by distance. The income from Branagan's liquor store had allowed Joe's family a phone and a finished basement, but Clement's success had blessed his son with a life-style that seemed the embodiment of every advertisement his father had ever seen. And Todd himself looked the part. He had inherited Sam's blond hair and blue eyes, but he was built leaner, along the lines of his mother, and he seemed at home in the tasteful clothing that Clement still wore with a slight sense of affectation. Unlike his father, Todd had served with honor. He could walk well enough, Sam reasoned, and his future was secure from any real physical labor as the future owner of Clement Realty. Since the war, it had become apparent that Todd did not see his situation that way.

The leg seemed to be at the center of his resentment. He would not talk about how he had been wounded, refusing even to discuss the war; yet, more than once, Sam had heard him refer to himself as a cripple. Sam had attempted to draw him out on the subject, but Todd ignored these efforts with an attitude that bordered on hostility. Shortly after his release from the last of the veterans' hospitals, he had walked pointedly out of the room when Sam mentioned his outstanding service in front of a small group gathered to celebrate his homecoming. Clement understood that Vietnam had been a war involving some confusion, but Todd had returned safely and with honor. There was no apparent reason for his resentment.

For their part, Kara and Sam made it clear that Todd was free to finish school, seek another job, or leave the area entirely. Todd chose to complete college, but during that time, and in the years that followed, he remained inside himself. He had never been a taker, even before the war, and Sam felt that Todd's acceptance of a job in the firm was not a sign of dependence, but a compromise that allowed his son a minimum of exposure to the outside world. He was polite to his clients, and civil to his parents, insisting on paying a fair rent for his room, but living apart from them in the manner of a slightly resentful guest. On occasion, he would see a woman, but only for sex, Sam suspected, as he never brought any of them home, or seemed any less indifferent to the world around him the following morning.

He had acquaintances, but none of the close friends Sam had seen in evidence during the years before the war. Sam thought of the boy he had once known as he heard the faint strains of familiar music coming from Todd's end of the long hallway. They were the same records his son had played before he left home. Clement grimaced as he approached the light under the door. In a sense, Todd's development seemed to have been frozen at a point in time almost a decade earlier. He was now nearing twenty-seven.

"Mind if I bother you a few minutes?" Sam asked, knocking softly on the door.

"Dad. Come in."

Clement pushed back the door to find Todd looking at him from the opposite side of the room, the same familiar, neutral expression on his face. He was in his pajama bottoms, seated cross-legged on the floor. There were several magazines on the rug beside him, but none of them had been opened. He had been smoking a joint, which he tamped lightly in the ashtray beside him, making no effort to conceal it.

Sam limped over to the bed and lowered himself into a sitting position, facing Todd with one hand on the soreness in his lower abdomen. "I wanted to talk to you about drugs," he said.

Without insolence, Todd raised the joint in his direction. "Peace. I'll stop if you like."

Clement shook off the confession. "Not that. I've known about that longer than you think. I mean that I might have been drugged in the hospital. Beyond medication."

"Drugged?"

"Given something to put me off my guard. Make me talk. You know something about that kind of thing, don't you?"

Todd responded with a slight lift of his eyebrows. "You think I do?"

Sam sighed and leaned over the edge of the bed, stretching his hand toward the joint, which Todd surrendered without comment. "I told you, I wasn't thinking of grass," Sam said, peering at the glow between his fingers. "I mean the things you might have seen in the service. When you were in the hospitals. There might have been stronger stuff available. Things they would shoot, maybe." The terms slipped from Clement's mouth as naturally as they had decades earlier. The stretch from the bed had set his incision on fire again, and just as unthinkingly, he touched the joint to his mouth and pulled in the comfort of the smoke with the unconscious motion of an old habit.

Todd's eyes rolled with surprise in his direction before Clement realized what he had done. For a moment, they were silent. In almost a decade, they had discussed nothing more personal than sports, even when Sam had left for the hospital with the thought that he might be dying. Clement knew that if it hadn't been for the threat of Vera, he would never have dared to approach Todd on such a subject, but with his past springing back on him, there was suddenly nothing he didn't want to tell his son. Perhaps to articulate the confession he could never make, perhaps because of his mood and the effects of the marijuana, Sam touched the joint to his lips a second time, turning the tip a bright red and passing it wordlessly to Todd.

Todd shared it without expression, but the ceremony seemed a tacit acknowledgment, as though both men had breached a barrier that hinted at an intimate part of themselves without risking any open revelations. "I really never did any drugs *except* at the hospitals," Todd began suddenly, gazing without focus at some point across the room. "Not including grass, which we didn't count over there. But the hospitals were a different scene. I was in New York for the first workup on my leg. Queens, actually. That was about a month before I came home, and I had plenty of money from my tour." The voice was distant, but for the first time Clement caught a tone in it—a quality of relaxation—that made him feel his son was confiding rather than supplying the necessary responses to another guarded dialogue. Todd's eyes looked beyond his father, and he smiled in recollection. "One day, they sent someone from the V. A. out to see us. This is still at St. Alban's Naval Hospital, which isn't even open anymore. Anyway, this guy was conducting some rap session that was supposed to heal the war for a bunch of us they gathered in the lounge, and he asks us if there are any drug problems in the wards." Todd shook his head. "This big black guy, Alphie, tells him absolutely seriously, 'Not really, sir. You can pretty much get what you want if you have the money.'" He raised his eyes and grinned over at Clement. "Right in front of the press." For a moment, Sam shared his amusement. Then Todd seemed to catch himself, looking away to finish in a more neutral tone. "Anyway, we did a lot of different stuff, some of it hospital issue, some of it brought in from the outside. They knew it, too. What are they going to say to the spinal cases? It's bad for their health?"

Clement nodded sympathetically, but Todd was already coloring slightly, as though he realized that he had strayed from what he was going to say. "So what were your symptoms?" he asked quietly.

"It was after my operation, and I was feeling fairly groggy. I don't know if it actually happened, but I remember suddenly seeming much more alert. Not just high, or free from pain. I could travel in my mind. I went back to the war, before I met your mother. I think I was open to all kinds of suggestions. And things weren't just dreamlike: I had full-blown illusions."

"And when you came down?"

Clement sighed. "Real depression. That was fairly abrupt,

too. I don't know what I would have done if the operation hadn't tired me enough to shut it all out with sleep."

"You'd have looked to get high again, like the guys I left behind in the hospital."

There was too much feeling in the remark for Clement to ignore it. "You haven't really left it all behind, have you? You can talk about it, you know."

Todd's expression darkened. "Nothing to talk about. I'm not a philosopher. And I'm not one of the violent ones, either, so there's no danger I'll explode." He remained silent a moment to close the subject. "Anyway, for whatever it's worth, I think you were wired. They don't use stuff like that for post op., so it wasn't part of your medication, I'd guarantee it." Despite the implications, Todd refrained from asking the last, obvious question.

It was Clement's turn to stay inside himself. He rose from the bed without any mention of Vera or his suspicions. Like Todd, he could say very little without having to say everything, and he knew he was not capable of that. But he made a point of locking his son's eyes with his own when he paused at the door to the hall. "You've been a real help. I'm glad that we talked."

"Any time."

"Good night, then." Clement stepped out into the hall, shutting the door softly behind him.

After he had gone, Todd remained seated on the floor for several minutes before he crossed the room and slipped into his bed, snapping off the small reading lamp on the night table beside him. But even in the darkness, he remained awake and alert, as he had expected. The encounter affected him more than he would have liked. It had also touched off certain responses deep inside him.

In time, he lapsed into a fitful sleep, struggling with the incongruous image of his father smoking a joint with practiced ease, and wondering again if the fifty-eight-year-old owner of Clement Realty had actually been drugged by someone. There was nothing in the safe and predictable personality he had long ago consigned to his father that would allow for what had just passed between them.

And then, for the first time since the nights at the hospital, Mai appeared before him. She seemed diffident and vulnerable as she had when he first met her at Camron Bay, but he could find something behind her smile that betrayed the hell to come, and he knew he was about to relive it yet another time. He was unsettled, but not surprised. He had been disoriented by the conversation with his father, and the confusion remained with him as he lay in the darkness, somewhere between consciousness and dreaming. That had always been her territory.

Clement stared south at the sky over Miami. His was one of the rare Florida homes with a second story, and there was a small terrace off his master bedroom. Kara slept soundly inside while he looked out at the night and attempted to evaluate what he had learned. Until a few hours ago, he could believe that Vera had materialized only if she had managed to overcome odds that made it virtually impossible for her to trace him. Now he realized that Todd had left his name—the name he had never changed—in a number of hospitals as far north as New York. As recently as two months ago, he had been to Lyons in New Jersey for special therapy.

It had been a different world in the Forties before the explosion in commercial aviation. Then, Florida had provided the anonymity of distance. Now, if Vera had really found him, there could be no effective escape: only a postponing of the inevitable. Clement took in the familiar borders of his grounds and the lights of the houses beyond them, aware of Kara's even breathing coming through the open door of the bedroom. He would stay, he decided, regardless of the temptation to escape and begin again as he had done so many years ago.

And she would come down on him like fury.

The letter was waiting for him when he made his initial appearance at the office the following week. It was typed on pastel stationery of the 5 and 10 variety and signed with her name, although the letters had a square, masculine shape that she had no doubt used to disguise her writing. The letter itself was characteristic of her caution, designed to arrange their meeting without the betrayal of anything the slightest bit inappropriate to his normal business:

Dear Sam,

Forgive this short notice, but I will be leaving the area as soon as we have reached our settlement. If I don't hear from you, I'll assume that you can meet me at the airport by four this afternoon. I'll be waiting outside the Everglade Lounge. I think we can agree on market value, so please bring the appropriate papers.

Sam studied the note in the privacy of his office, noting how clear she had made her terms in the limited language she had permitted herself. The first statement was both a threat and a promise. She would be willing to leave him the life he had made for himself, provided she was satisfied with what he would give her. She would never believe that he had walked away from the entire agreement years ago, had hidden the bale and made his fortune in spite of it rather than because of it. The appropriate papers she referred to would be a sum of money he could only guess at. Negotiable, but approximately the maximum amount she judged he would part with before he considered it worth resisting.

Clement slipped the note under the blotter of his desk and padded down the carpeted hallway outside his office as quickly as the remaining soreness in his abdomen would allow him. He had eight salespeople working out of three suites that shared a common lobby, so that anyone entering his office would have to pass the large, circular receptionist's desk directly in front of the doors to the building. The girl on duty looked up from her typing to smile at him.

"Going to lunch, Mr. Clement?"

Clement shook his head. "I've got to wait for an appointment, Tanya. She hasn't been in already, has she? A woman about my age, with blond hair?"

"You haven't missed her. I've been here since nine."

Clement worked at keeping his voice free of concern. "Well, I'm not too sure of that description. I've only met her once."

"If you're sure she's a woman, she hasn't come in yet. Except for the staff, Mrs. Conway's the only woman who's been by the whole morning."

"I see. Then hold my calls for the next half hour, would you? I'm going to need a little time to myself."

Clement sat back in his chair, his fingers to his mouth. The fact that Vera had managed to negotiate the lobby undetected didn't surprise him. The use of the note rather than the convenience of a simple phone call was a tactic in itself, informing him that she could reach him where and when she wanted.

He would give her nothing, he had decided, and not simply because there was no amount of money that would ultimately satisfy her. He had been faced with death in the hospital, and he had realized then that his deepest regret was that he was leaving life without any chance for atonement. Facing Vera would supply that opportunity, as well as removing the very real threat of her vengeance from his family. An end to it, he thought with a smile that reflected an emotion very close to relief. A final reckoning that would justify the good years.

Clement had never kept a gun, even at the office. He had moved through the second half of his life without a thought to defending himself against misfortune in any form, partially, he supposed, because he had always been expecting some form of retribution. It was going to take a conscious effort to revert. He hadn't lived outside the law in many years, and sitting in the quiet of his office, he realized how dependent he had become on the society surrounding him. If he were hurt, he sought medical attention; if he were treated unfairly in business, he had the redress of the courts; if he were threatened, he could rely on the police. Now he would have to defeat Vera in an arena he had not entered in over thirty-five years, and judging by what he had seen so far, her skills had not suffered from lack of use.

He had only one advantage he could think of, but it was considerable. As long as he could eliminate her, he was willing to forfeit his own life. For her part, the coming struggle would mean nothing unless she survived. That could be a weakness if he found the proper opportunity to exploit it.

Clement shook himself from his reverie. He might still be able to rid himself of her without making the ultimate sacrifice. The first step, as Max would have advised him, was to hear what the lady had to offer.

He leaned forward and stabbed at the console of the intercom. "Tanya, I've had to set up a meeting for this afternoon. Could you see what you can do about canceling the rest of my schedule?"

Something malevolent was with Kara in the garden. Nothing palpable justified her apprehension, but she had survived too much in her lifetime to ignore an intuitive sense of danger. Her neighbor stood on the other side of the split rail fence that divided their properties, and Kara focused on her conversation, wondering if Rowena Bloom was responsible for her premonition.

"So I actually ran into Janet and her boyfriend downtown," Rowena was saying, "and they were carrying *groceries.*" Rowena's eyebrows were painted, and she raised them knowingly when she gestured toward the house directly across the street. "Of course, Bess pretends that she's still over there with the rest of the family, but I'm sure she drives here once or twice a week just for the sake of appearances. Janet Fowler's living with that boy. You can count on it."

Kara pulled off her gloves and rose from the last of her weeding. "How should I count on it?" she asked with a slight frown, taking advantage of her imperfect English to avoid passing judgment on Bess Fowler's daughter.

Rowena laughed. "Just an expression, dear. It means you can be sure I'm right." She shrugged. "Not that it makes any difference. The young people are all doing it nowadays. Living together, I mean. I'm surprised that you've kept that beautiful son of yours at home so long." She put a hand to her breast. "Lord, if I were twenty years younger, I could have been the girl next door!" She wrinkled her nose and waved a good-bye with her fingers before walking back in the direction of her house.

Would you like living next door if you knew the truth about my husband? Kara wondered. Rowena Bloom was the president of the local women's club, and for all her good-natured patter, Kara could not bring herself to feel fully at ease with her. Her reserve might not have been justified, but it was there, separating Kara imperceptibly from all of their neighbors. Now, with Sam facing the possibility of trouble, the distance she had maintained made her feel less dependent on others. She glanced across the street on the way to her door, taking in Bess Fowler's house. Like the Blooms, the Fowlers were friendly, unaffected, and respected in the community. Just the sort of people who had turned on her family and destroyed them.

Kara looked at the affluent residences surrounding her, and something buried deep inside her memory transformed them, robbing them of their familiarity. She saw the orderly housefronts as facades, propped up like sets for the sake of appearance, but inhabited by creatures who would lose all semblance of humanity at the first scent of her husband's past. This time, at least, she would be prepared for the transformation.

She entered the living room and sat down, putting a hand to her mouth and gazing thoughtfully at the light streaming in from the window. This was America, she reminded herself. The fact that Rowena Bloom liked to gossip did not mean she was capable of throwing stones. But the sense of dread lingered, and she wondered if it were due to more than fear of her neighbors' judgment.

She reached over to the coffee table and opened a magazine, forcing her attention on the table of contents. There was little sense in trying to anticipate reactions to an event that might never take place. She would wait and face whatever happened as it developed.

Later, that determination to remain under control caused her to dismiss the movement she heard in the garage as a product of her imagination. Like her husband, she had been forced to develop a finely tuned sense of danger. But like him, too, her instincts had been dulled by the years of happiness they had shared together, leaving her vulnerable with the passing of time.

The Everglade Lounge was new to the Lauderdale Airport, facing one of the busiest plazas in the narrow, horseshoe-shaped reservations building that separated the parking lot from the actual airfield. Clement was pacing the area in front of its facade by 3:45, scanning the pedestrian traffic from under the brim of a hat he had brought with him for just that purpose. Several times, a glimpse of blond hair flashed among the bobbing heads at the distant reservations counters, but on each occasion, the racing in his blood subsided in yet another disappointment. He had begun to think she might not appear at all when the public phone on the wall behind him came to life. It rang unheeded for a full minute before he rushed to it with a sudden understanding of what she had done.

"Vera?"

"Of course. You're not going to lose me this time around." It was the voice he had dreamt at the hospital, lower than the one he remembered from his youth, with a rasp that might have been in the phone itself.

"You *were* at the hospital, then."

"I work at hospitals, Sam. You met me at one a long time ago, before you got rich on our money. I thought I'd see hospitals for the rest of my life, until your son showed up. He's a nice-looking boy, Sam. I love him already for leading me to what's mine."

Sam shot a guarded look at the oblivious passersby and leaned into the phone, lowering his voice for emphasis. "Listen, Vera, I put that out of my life. Forever. What I have, I got other ways, and there's no part of it I can give you without knowing you'll come back for more."

"Bastard." The word was a hiss in his ear, and he knew that the rasp he had heard had not been in the phone. "Don't you tell me what's mine. I'm not interested in your clean living, although I'm sure the police would be."

Clement had been prepared for the threat. "Don't talk to me about the police, Vera. Turn me in and we'll see which one of us looks worse."

There was a brief silence at the other end of the line. "Well, you've finally grown up, Sam. We'll leave this between us." The voice paused for emphasis, before adding, "Of course, I'll want to include that wife of yours."

Clement tensed in an attempt to control himself. The effort aggravated the soreness in his abdomen, and he slipped a hand underneath his jacket to find the pain, determined not to waver in the face of the threat.

"Are you armed, Sam?"

The question might have been intended to provoke him further: an open declaration of how far she was willing to go. But at that moment, he caught his reflection in the restaurant window, his arm pushed underneath the flap of his jacket, and he knew. Not just from the posture he could observe, his right hand resting lightly on what might have been the comfort of a hidden weapon. He actually felt her presence, something hostile and pernicious not far from his immediate vicinity. The renewal of a sixth sense that had long fallen into disuse helped to heighten his excitement. "I might be," he told her in an effort to fight for time. If she could see him, he knew he should be able to locate her from his position. "I'm not incapable of eliminating you," he offered, running his eyes toward the far end of the hall without turning away from the receiver.

"You'll be the last, Sam. I'll save you until after I've got my money. But your wife—" the voice ceased abruptly. He had found a silhouette that might have been hers, framed by the rectangle of a phone booth. It was separated from him by the facades of three airlines, but he had been leaning out from the phone, peering in that direction when her voice stopped.

Within seconds, he heard a clattering sound in his ear, as though the receiver at the other end of the line had been dropped, and the rectangle he had been staring at lightened, dispensing a figure in a beige trench coat with a blur of blond hair and legs outlined by white stockings.

She threaded her way through the crowd at a pace just short of an open run, and he dropped the phone, shuffling through the crowded airport without taking his eyes from her. Her back was to him, but when he had gained enough on her to think he might overtake her before she reached the distant doors to the parking lot, she darted a quick look over her shoulder.

He caught only the blur of her face, but she must have seen that he was catching up, because her figure bent in on itself, and he could tell from the flicker of her stockings that she was running. He tried to quicken his pace, but he had already pushed past the boundaries of the healing beneath his dressing, and a few sharp stabs of pain reduced him to a halting limp. She was very close to the exit, and he knew she would probably be able to lose herself in the parking lot before he was in a position to glimpse her through the glass of the doors.

He let his glance drop briefly, and for the second time he caught himself thrown back in the plate-glass reflection of a store window. He was sweating, and his face was flushed with exertion. His hat was in his hand, and it swung awkwardly back and forth with the motion of his arms. He had exercised religiously since his mid-twenties, but most of his conditioning had been lost to his convalescence, and he found his situation ludicrous. He saw himself as a parody of what he had been, bent double by age, and locked in a life and death chase that had been reduced to a shuffle.

He remembered Kara then, younger, and with a meaningful part of her life to live. He gasped openly in an effort to rush the remaining distance to the doors, but when he burst through them into the brightness of the daylight, she was already gone.

He leaned back against the building, removing his jacket and loosening his tie while he took the time to catch his breath. The aching below his belt subsided after a few minutes of resting, and it did not resume when he took the first tentative steps in the direction of the parking lot. By the time he was nearing the vicinity of his car, he was giving silent thanks for the thought that he had not undone any of his past healing.

It was then that he saw her, less than a hundred yards away. Her back was to the sun, and she was further concealed by the wrap of a kerchief and dark glasses, but she remained motionless, facing him over the roof of his car, and he knew that he was being mocked, even though he could not see her expression.

She allowed him to narrow the distance between them by another row of cars before she raised a gloved hand and stabbed a finger down in a savage gesture to indicate his Porsche. Then she turned with deliberate slowness and walked toward the center of the lot. He knew that he was incapable of catching her on foot, and by the time he had reached his car, her kerchief had disappeared between the rows of metal roofs. There was no mark on his car, and it remained locked, as it had been when he left it.

As he entered the busy coil of traffic leaving the airport, he continued to look for her, but with little hope. She had shown him the futility of resisting by entering his office undetected, and when he had discovered her presence while they were on the phone, she had not only managed to lose him, but to inform him in a final, defiant gesture that he had been in her observation since he had parked his car. Now she would give him some time to think about the implications of what she had done.

It was not until he returned home that he found out how wrong he had been.

Clement's house was in Plantation, a four-bedroom modern on two acres of land bordered by a lagoon. It was large without being ostentatious, and there were enough grounds for privacy, although certainly not for isolation. To the rear, behind his pool, a twenty-foot inboard bumped against a modest dock, while the house itself faced an affluent suburban street from a distance of some hundred yards. It was not until Clement passed the shrubs bordering the facade that he noticed Kara standing in front of the garage. He brought the Porsche to a halt in front of the driveway and hurried toward her, concerned by the expression on her face.

"There's smoke in the garage," she said.

Clement pressed his face against one of the rectangular windows that lined the broad door. "God, it's like a fog. Have you called anyone yet?"

"I didn't think we should call."

Clement turned from the window and stared at her.

"There was a noise while I was reading in the living room," Kara said. "Some things fell off the kitchen wall." Clement's garage was a part of the house itself, sharing a common wall and an access door to the kitchen. "I think it was a small explosion."

"An explosion?"

Kara raised a shoulder. "I thought I should wait for you," she said. "There were no flames that I could see from the window. No more smoke, even."

Clement nodded and turned toward his car. "Just that cloud hanging there." He leaned in through the window of the Porsche and activated the switch that raised the garage door. Almost as soon as it began to fold away from the driveway, a light curtain of smoke pushed out and streamed up over the roof of the house. There was not a great deal of it, but before it had dissipated Clement could see that it had come from under the hood of the small station wagon parked on Kara's side of the garage.

He didn't permit her to enter until he had cautiously approached the car and raised the hood, jumping back as he did with an arm across his face. But there was not even a residue of smoke, and after peering wordlessly at the engine, he motioned Kara to his side.

"Something small," he said, pointing to a charred rectangle that looked as though it had once been the workings of a transistor radio. "Meant to frighten. We'll need some electrical work, though." It was apparent, even to Kara. The rubber-covered leads sprouting from the distributor, and the distributor itself, had been melted out of shape by the heat of the blast, and the insulation that lined the interior of the hood had been reduced to a gummy nap.

"So, we will have a mechanic, then," Kara said firmly, and her real meaning was betrayed only by her eyes.

Clement gave her a sharp look. "You know what this means?"

"It means you were not so crazy at the hospital." Kara managed a smile.

"She's found me." Clement slammed the hood of the wagon shut, as if to emphasize the statement. "I saw her at the airport. She wants money. What she considers her share. I'll tell you everything later, but that's what you should know now in order to make a decision."

They had walked to the front of the garage, and she turned him toward her with a firm hand on his shoulder. "You told me everything from the beginning, Sam, and I made my decision then, did I not?" There was strength and not a little anger in her voice as she pointed back toward the interior of the garage. "I have seen smoke before, and plenty of fire to go along with it. She can not harm our marriage, because I have always known. She will not hurt us, because we will be stronger, yes?"

Kara's accent always became more pronounced when she was excited, and hearing her speak reminded Clement of what they had endured before they met. He reached out and embraced her. They remained locked together until Todd interrupted them moments later coming up the driveway.

"Maybe I'm more in the way around here than I think," he said, but his tone was light, and Clement looked up to see him flashing one of his rare smiles.

Todd owned a motor scooter. He would have preferred the Honda he had ridden in high school, but the construction of the scooter made it possible for him to mount and dismount without swinging his leg over the obstacle of an engine. He walked the vehicle to a place in the center of the garage, but after he had lowered the kickstand, he paused.

"What happened to the wagon?" he asked, running his hand over the swell of a large dent in the hood that Clement had only just then noticed.

"This afternoon at dancing class," Kara responded before Clement had time to react. "Your father was just forgiving me."

Todd hesitated, but his features fell into his customary expression of indifference and he shrugged. "I won't need it 'til Friday," he said, before nodding and disappearing through the door to the kitchen.

"If anything ever happens to me, you can tell him," Clement said when he was sure that he was gone.

"Nothing will happen," Kara soothed, and they walked arm in arm around the side of the house as if by agreement. "I think he is improving." They seated themselves at a table beside the pool and she smiled at him. "He did not say what you spoke about, but he mentioned that you had been talking. I think he was happy about that."

The irony of the remark brought Clement back to reality, and he massaged his forehead slowly with his hands while he focused on what he should do next. Kara kept her silence, and in minutes, he spoke to her without looking up. "Kara, what time did you get home from class?"

"Some time after three-thirty. The usual."

"So the car wasn't even in the garage until then?"

"That's right." She caught the tone in his voice and put her hand over his.

Clement looked up to face her. "I was with Vera at the airport this afternoon. She couldn't have been near the house, because I saw her. Then I drove straight home, so she wouldn't have been able to get here much sooner than I did." He came to his feet, working his hands against each other. "The odds have changed, Kara."

"Yes?" She looked up at him, expectantly, but without apprehension.

"Don't you see now about the car? If Vera couldn't have done it, it means she's not working alone."

*   *   *

Todd was drawn back again that night. Not to the field, but to the swirling pipe dream of the war that preceded it. Mai was there, his lover then, signaling the beginning of the whole deception. Even on the edge of sleep, he sensed that it was something separate and secret in the life of his father that was intruding on the isolation he had made for himself, and that because of it, he might be led through his own nightmare again, with the end game of the field. There were associations, omens he had learned to identify from his own experience.

Why had his parents lied? As though he could ever forget—even in the confines of his own garage—the smell of sulfur, and the stronger scent of fear, in the aftermath of an explosion. Todd rolled away from the shadows in his room and covered his eyes with the back of his arm. He thought back to earlier in the week, seeing himself in the man he had thought of only as his father. Not just in the revelation of his smoking, but in something gaunt and haunted behind his eyes. The windows of the soul, Mai would have said. Had he brought this home with him, some unseen and vindictive force that had germinated since his return and now threatened the safe and ignorant world of his parents?

When he finally succumbed to sleep, Mai was at him immediately. The pajamas fell away first, the dark delta exposed for him against the pale skin of her torso as she pulled her top over her head in the dim light of the hooch. He had reached for her that first time they made love, but she had pushed him back onto the dirt of the floor, sliding his pants away and squeezing him to a taut erection with a few practiced motions of her hand. He realized then that she was the same as the bar girls, in spite of her French and her quiet ways. The warm circle of her mouth enclosed his penis, and she shifted her position, sliding a leg across his chest so that the fold of her vagina was open to him, inches from his face. He was repelled and driven at the same time, but as he looked into the darkness between her legs, she continued to arouse him, and something rank and animal won out over her lack of innocence.

In his dream, he did as he had then, gripping her by the V of her legs and pulling her into him. But during the act, the sharp smell of sulfur mixed in his nostrils with her woman's scent, and in that moment, he knew that the confusion of another time was being visited on his own home. It was the same unspoken threat he had learned to sense in other surroundings, as though once again, love and destruction could exist vividly and separately in the same place.

Chapter Five

The winter of '42 saw a war that had spread and intensified, but as Christmas approached, there were bright spots on the horizon. Rommel was retreating in Egypt, and America was contributing more planes to the war effort than Germany and Japan combined. The people on the homefront were beginning to pay the price for these victories. Price ceilings were established for goods and housing, tires were limited to five for each driver, coffee was being cut with chicory, and buffalo meat was being sold—and selling out—in Seattle.

The shortage of meat, Sam discovered, was the first and most obvious source of Max's new prosperity. Less than a month after expressing reservations over his new job to Vera, Sam concluded that the blood he had seen on the floor of the DeSoto was not human, but animal. By then, he was making several trips a day for Max, many of them to the better neighborhoods of his own city, and neither Max nor his own customers made any secret of the fact that the tightly wrapped packages he was delivering were meat. The DeSoto was eventually replaced by a 1940 Packard, with hydraulic brakes, a column shift and overdrive. There was also the novelty of air conditioning, which Max pointed out to Sam with considerable pride the day he introduced him to the new car. The back seat had been removed, providing ample room for a full day's deliveries.

Max never volunteered to explain how the meat stored in the cold room of the Essex Pub was acquired, and Sam did not ask. He was relieved enough to know that the bloodstains he had seen had an innocuous explanation, and with the squeeze on gas becoming progressively tighter, it was possible for him to think that Max preferred the use of a car over the unnecessary bulk of a delivery truck.

He had moved in with Vera by then, unwilling to be away from her bed for even a night, and explaining to his mother that he had taken an apartment of his own. Mrs. Clement had received enough extra money from her son to rely on the gifts as a second income, and she interpreted Sam's move as another sign of his growing prosperity, a belief that was shared with envy and admiration by her friends in the neighborhood. Sam might have ignored the misgivings he had over his work indefinitely had it not been for an incident the following spring that confirmed his suspicions and brought about a direct confrontation with Max.

It occurred on a mild afternoon when he was returning from a delivery in the Point Pleasant area of the Jersey shore. Max had told him that the customers were personal friends of his, and Sam had arrived at a sprawling, shorefront home with enough wax-paper packages to fill the entire storage area of the car. Two servants assisted him in unloading the delivery, and when he pulled back down the pebbled driveway, he was looking forward to a leisurely drive that would find him home early enough to take Vera out for dinner.

The trouble began when he had stopped at one of the last intersections on Route 35 before it ran uninterrupted through the undeveloped land stretching north toward the Newark area. He was squinting into a warm sun, waiting for the light to change, when he was brought around sharply by a voice inches from his open window.

"You just deliver some meat to the Walkers?"

The question had the demanding tone of authority, and when Sam looked up to see a large man in sunglasses and a brown suit, his first thought was that he had been stopped by the police. Unsure of himself, unsure even if he had been breaking the law, he kept his tone neutral. "Is that part of your business?" he asked without raising his voice.

"It is when some bastard's moving in on my customers!" Sam saw his own surprised expression reflected in the stranger's sunglasses as he leaned down and reached through the window in the direction of the dashboard. "Pull over," he demanded.

Sam gripped the sleeve of the intruding arm, but before he could react, the back of the hand flew up at him and caught him sharply in the face.

He let out a grunt of protest, but the shock of the blow had turned his fear to anger. He threw his shoulder against the door with enough force to drive his attacker backwards, where he collided with his own car, idling beside Sam's. The man appeared more surprised than hurt, particularly when Sam stepped out of the Packard, facing him with the challenge of raised hands.

"You're dead," the stranger announced coldly, but after brushing at his jacket, he climbed back into the Lincoln and turned it around with nothing more than a final glare in Sam's direction.

Sam gave himself some time to calm the shaking in his hands before he put the car in gear and headed north again. He had no idea of why he had been stopped, but he was certain it had nothing to do with the law. He could not confront Max soon enough, and he would have reached home in record time, but his tank had been close to empty, and five minutes out of town, he spotted the winged horse of a Mobilgas station and pulled off the highway.

He was sitting behind the wheel while the attendant filled his tank when the Lincoln appeared again, braking to a skid just past the station. Sam looked up to see the brown suit behind the wheel, backing the convertible off the road with two additional passengers in the rear seat.

"There he is!" one of them shouted, and he was out of the car before it had come to a halt. Sam started his engine, but the Lincoln had backed up beside him by then, and one of his pursuers was standing in front of his grill wielding what looked like a large pipe. "Shut it down!" he yelled, and he reinforced the order by bringing the pipe down on the hood of the Packard in a blow that vibrated right through to the dash.

"Cut it out!" Sam shouted. He raced his engine in warning, then let out the clutch, forcing the man blocking his path into a rolling dive across his fender that sent him sprawling onto the pavement. There was a second's hesitation as the filling hose stretched to the breaking point and slapped back into the pump, leaving the metal nozzle protruding from Sam's open tank. Then he was out onto the highway in a squealing turn that took him into the opposite lane before he gained enough control to head the car north.

When he finally had the presence of mind to look into his rearview mirror, the Lincoln was already a spot on the road behind him, gaining definition as it steadily narrowed the distance between them. Sam kept his foot to the floor, but the Packard was already vibrating, and he knew it was only a matter of time until he was overtaken. He scanned the sides of the highway for a source of help before he realized bitterly that there could be none. For all he knew, he was as far removed from the law as his pursuers, and he cursed himself for appeasing his conscience over the past year by staying ignorant of Max's operation, vowing again that things would change when he got back to Newark. If he got back.

Minutes separated the speeding cars when the scrub pine fell away from a corner of Sam's vision to reveal sweeping fields of horse corn on one side of the road. There were no buildings in sight, and more importantly, no fences, so he banked the car over the shoulder of the highway and aimed it directly into the crops.

He was squeezing the steering wheel tightly, braced for the shock of a collision, but the stalks offered little resistance, disappearing underneath the nose of the car with a liquid, swishing sound. They were pale and misshapen, but they were well over the height of his car, and there were enough of them to crowd out everything around him except a small patch of blue directly above his windshield. Unfortunately, as well as hiding him, they concealed his pursuers.

Sam had pushed the Packard a full half mile out into the field before he caught the unmistakable shriek of tires against concrete. A quick glance at the solid wall of corn behind him brought him to a sudden halt, and he was out of the car and on its roof before the Lincoln had approached the place on the road when he had entered the field. He thought he saw an empty back seat through the reflection of the sun on the windshield, but he could not be sure. In either case, the heavier car was crossing the shoulder of the road cautiously, allowing him several precious seconds to think.

They could not see him, he knew, but he would be at the same disadvantage as soon as they had entered the field. He glanced at the spoor of broken corn behind him and fought back the panic of a new realization. They had only to follow his trail in order to find him. He peered out toward the Lincoln a final time to see the shiny V of its grill already nosing toward the break he had made in the corn when he entered it. Then he jumped from the roof of the car, crashing into the cushion of stalks and pulling himself behind the wheel of the Packard before he had fully gained his feet.

He drove with the complete abandon of fear this time, aiming the Packard directly toward the center of the field, until he had reached a speed of almost thirty miles an hour. Then he curved the car in a sweeping turn, trundling through the stalks a full minute before they parted briefly when he doubled back across his own path. He continued to push across the trail, circling back on it two more times in the rough pattern of a figure eight, and fearing during the last of it that at any moment he might collide suddenly with the black bulk of the Continental. Finally, he forced himself to stop long enough to locate the highway from the roof of the Packard.

He found that he had driven half the distance to the road, but once he was back inside the car again, he worked his hands against the wheel in an agony of indecision. More than likely, they had followed him. But suppose they had decided to turn back toward the highway and were poised on the shoulder of the road, waiting for him to emerge from the field? He held his breath to sharpen his hearing, but he could not be sure if the distant roar in his ears was from the highway or the unseen Lincoln, tracking him along the flattened path of his car.

At that point, he was frightened and angry enough to consider bolting the field and taking his chances. But he fought for control and scrambled up onto the advantage of his roof a final time. He was glad that he had. The sound that he had heard was definitely their engine, and it was coming from the center of the field where they had obviously lost themselves in his patterns. He felt caught up by a strange exhilaration then, telling himself that he had done some fighting of his own, and had managed to beat them in spite of the odds.

He would have headed for the safety of the highway at that point, but just as he was poised to jump from his roof, a change in the sound of their car drew his attention. Either by accident or through frustration, they had left the trampled paths, and a pattern of falling corn slapping against their grill marked the new direction they had taken. They were moving in a rough slant toward the highway, crossing the original path he had made on his way in, but ignoring it this time and gaining the urgency of greater speed.

They had decided to guard the road after all, Sam concluded, but he was no longer afraid, and he welcomed the renewal of the challenge. If he swerved across the field and traced the path he had made when he came in from the highway, he could beat them with time to spare.

But the calculation had forced him to look ahead of the buckling corn that marked the path of the Lincoln, and he noticed a red rectangle that froze him where he was. In addition to the patch of color that caught his attention, the jutting pipe of an exhaust stack and the crescent of a wheel large enough to top the corn marked the position of what must have been some large farm machinery. There was no doubt in his mind that from ground level, it would be completely hidden by the corn, and he waited in sudden anticipation, watching the swath of toppling plants converge on the obstacle with increasing speed.

They must have seen something at the last moment, because the alley in the corn swerved seconds before the sound of bending metal and the delicate crinkling of breaking glass indicated an abrupt collision. A shout of triumph escaped Sam's lips, and he leapt down from the roof and turned the Packard in the direction of the highway and the certainty of safety.

He had intercepted his former path when he spotted the smoke rising from the direction of the machinery, but he continued to push on toward the road, telling himself that someone would see the smoke and be drawn to the scene of the accident. It was hard to suppress his misgivings. The field appeared all but abandoned by whoever owned it, and summer was still too distant to draw any appreciable traffic to Route 35. Reaching the break in the corn where they had strayed from his path made up his mind for him, and he pulled the car to a halt and backed it up, following the opening they had made in the direction of the farm equipment.

He was half convinced he would be murdered for his trouble, but as he drew cautiously closer, he could hear the sound of flames, and he could not bring himself to retreat. He did stop the car when he was near enough to catch a glimpse of color through the corn, and he crept up on the scene by leaving the track of the Lincoln and approaching on foot from a different angle.

The first object he identified was a large, tractor-like machine with a crib sagging in its wake. It might have been a harvester, Sam guessed, but whatever it was, it had long ago rusted to the reddish color he had caught from the roof of his car. By contrast, the Lincoln shone in the glow of its own flames. There was not much fire, but what there was seemed to be spreading rapidly from the rear of the car to the crumpled stalks around it.

The driver had not waited for his friends after all, Sam concluded. The man in the brown suit had been the only person in the car, and he was rolling on the ground near the open door, a bloody hand clamped tightly to his forehead. He was apparently too dazed to react to the menace of the growing flames, but Sam cringed from their heat, slapping at his clothing once he had dragged the other driver to the safety of his car.

By the time they had driven back out to the edge of the highway, Sam's passenger was sitting up in his seat, drawing deep gulps of breath with an open mouth. Sam stopped the car on the shoulder of the road and walked around to the passenger side, helping the man to his feet with the support of an arm.

"Can you walk?" he asked, peering into eyes that seemed only just then to be gaining the full focus of consciousness.

The brown suit stepped shakily away from the car and nodded slowly. "Yeah."

Sam withdrew his arm, slapping him off his feet and onto the shoulder of the road with the back of his hand. "Then walk, you bastard!" he said.

Then he slid back across the seat of the car, slamming the passenger door behind him and pulling the Packard out into the northbound lane of the empty road.

Max had put on three additional drivers since Sam had first begun to work for him, and one of them nodded amicably when he pulled up to the loading dock behind the Essex Pub.

"Looking for Max?" he asked as Sam approached the rear door of the restaurant.

Something in his tone made Sam feel that he was expected, but he nodded without comment and made his way down a narrow hall to the tiny room that served as Max's office. The response to his knock was immediate.

"*Entrez.*" Max smiled up at him from a stack of ledgers piled haphazardly on the top of a battered card table. "Take a load off your feet," he offered, pointing to a folding chair on one side of the room.

"I'd rather stand." Sam kept his voice under control, but there was a tightness in it that Max could not have missed. "I ran into some bad trouble today, Max."

"You ran into trouble," Max corrected. The wrinkles around his eyes hinted at amusement, but before he went on, he shuffled out from behind the table and opened the folding chair for Sam, patting the seat lightly before he took his own. Sam sat down reluctantly, keeping his eyes on Max's face. "*Bad* trouble is when other people do the telling, on account of you can't," Max announced.

"That might have happened if I hadn't been lucky."

"You weren't lucky, kid, you had balls. But at the worst, you would have gotten away in one piece. No one was out to kill you."

Sam's eyes narrowed with understanding. "You knew about this?"

Max shrugged. "I got a call from Waters. He was the one in the car." He frowned at Sam with open curiosity. "You always punch people out after you rescue them?"

"Christ, he wanted to kill me!"

"He wanted to talk. He's just a little pushy, that's all. But it's okay, what you did. I think he respects your way of doing business."

Sam leaned back against the support of his chair and gathered his thoughts while he looked away from Max at some indefinite spot on the peeling ceiling. When he spoke, it was softly, but his tone was pointed. "Max, what *is* our business? Are we in the black market?"

If the question bothered Max, his expression didn't reflect it. "That's their term," he said, gesturing vaguely toward the city lights outside his window. "I prefer *bootlegging*. That's what we called it during the Prohibition. It means doing what you always did before somebody made up a new rule."

"There are reasons for those rules, Max. There's a war going on."

For the first time since he had known him, Sam saw Max's face tighten briefly with anger before his features relaxed and he assumed an expression of understanding. "I'm going to forgive that, Sam, because you've been through a scare, and because you have a right to find out just how we operate. The first thing you should know is that I don't do a thing I can't live with. As a person, as an American. I sell people things they can afford, knowing damn well that if they didn't get them from me, they'd go somewhere else. That's good business, Sam, not profiteering." Max rose, hitching up the loose waist of **his** pants and pacing a small circle behind his table. "They just finished seven hundred homes for construction workers in Winfield Park, and everytime someone there flushes the toilet, the shit squirts out his neighbor's light socket. That's taking advantage, and that's hurting the war effort, Sam. Not what we're doing."

"It's still breaking the law."

"Not the law. The regulations. And I'll break 'em daily if they don't hurt the boys on the other side." Max leaned over the table and tapped his chest with a finger. "*I* served, Sam. Did you know that? In the war that was going to end them all. And I came back to a city of people who'd done pretty well while I was gone." Max shook his head. "Not this time. Liquor, meat, a few dairy products—all the things I was already connected to through my business. That's what I'm moving. We deal in food, Sam. Food I buy with my own money and sell at a profit. If that's all of a sudden illegal, it's temporary, just like Prohibition." This time, Max's finger found Sam. "You think you're surrounded by people following the rules they're making up? Why do they puncture the tops of the cans and boxes down at Elm Market? So your mother and my aunt can't hoard! Don't be a fool, kid. You did everything you could do to ship out, and you landed up here. Make what you can of it."

"Get rich off the war?"

"Get rich from your own hard work. And stop punishing yourself for it. If every kid was as ready as you were, they wouldn't be setting up these draft boards." Max put a hand on Sam's shoulder and bent down until his unfaltering expression was inches away. "Listen, Sam, anyone can die. Four hundred people went up in the Coconut Grove fire, and they weren't looking for that kind of evening. Don't confuse what you can do with what you have no control over."

"Civilians have obligations."

"Sure, but not always the ones the big deals would like you to believe in. 'Go without, so they won't have to,' right? But don't expect your friend Eddie to see any of that surplus. The people who make all the rules just spent eighty-five million on their new offices at the Pentagon. Truck drivers are pulling in a hundred and fifty a week, Sam, and you're feeling guilty about delivering meat." Max turned away, throwing his hands in the air to signal his exasperation.

Sam considered what Max had said. "And Waters? He and his friends are just like us?"

Max made a point of meeting his eyes. "No. But ninety-nine out of a hundred people we deal with are. Butchers, restaurant owners, packers. People who see an opportunity to even the odds a little without hurting the war effort. Factory people, like you. They've never broken a law in their lives. Waters is a little shady, I'll admit. He's always handled drugs, but with the war on, he's added a few sidelines. We need stamps for gas, Sam, particularly now that they're extending rationing to the rest of the country. Waters knows people who can get them."

"Steal them, you mean."

"In some cases, I'm sure they do. But before you give me more war talk, let me tell you that it ain't the gas the military needs. It's the rubber we eat up with our mileage." Max pointed dramatically in the direction of the loading dock. "And every car out there runs on five tires, regardless of how many I could get if I really wanted to."

Sam allowed himself a moment to think before he voiced his last question. "If you deal with Waters, why did he try to get in my way?"

"You weren't the regular driver. We pay to deliver down there, so it's natural he'd want to protect his profit. Drug people run everything the same way they handle their dope. Territories." Max allowed himself a smile. "Don't worry, though. Waters even asked me if we'd be interested in moving some of his reefer after he saw you in action."

"I'm not worried. I'm not a crook, either."

"Neither are the people who want to work with you. Do you have any idea how many honest businesses in this state were started with money from the Prohibition?"

"I don't really want to know any more than I have to."

"You know that much already. Want to talk it over with Vera?"

Sam shook his head and let out his breath as he came to his feet. "I don't have to. I know what she'll say."

Max stood up to face him. "What do you say, Sam?"

"If you're being straight with me, I'll stay on. I can't see how meat is going to make a big difference."

Max pulled on his battered fedora and grinned, once again the avuncular figure that Sam had always known. "It won't. But don't take my word for it. You've had your eyes opened. You can judge for yourself."

During the course of the following year, Sam learned all of the methods Max used to exceed the price ceilings set for meat by the Office of Price Administration. He had made up his mind to steer clear of the other lucrative fields that he suspected Max might involve himself in, but he had crossed a line as far as the marketing of meat went, and he was determined to educate himself.

One of his first conclusions was that if there were such a thing as integrity on the black market, Max could lay claim to it. Most of the wholesalers got more than the legally permitted amount of money for their meat by misrepresenting their product. Grade A meat would be sold as grade AA, and the seller would pocket two cents more per pound without appearing to have violated the maximum prices permitted by law. A cruder method was simply to sell the various cuts untrimmed, so that the retailer would be paying pure meat prices for what was partially fat and bone. At the more sophisticated end of the spectrum was an agreement Max referred to contemptuously as the tie-in. It was more difficult to detect, because the meat actually changed hands at the sanctioned prices. The buyer, however, was obligated to purchase an additional stock of neck bones, tripe, and other undesirable cuts in order to obtain what he actually wanted.

"It gets people a bit hot," Max commented to Sam after they had reached the point where they could discuss the business openly. "And customers won't appreciate methods like that after this war is over. I didn't gouge anyone when I was running liquor, and when I came out of Prohibition, not only could I buy this place, I kept drawing the same customers. In the open, of course." He looked across the office table at Sam, who was bent over one of the ledgers. "I may have to hide what I rightfully make, but my prices are never unfair."

"Just illegal," Sam muttered without looking up from his numbers.

"By the letter of the law, perhaps," Max grinned. "And what about you? You don't think you hurt the company name by living with Vera out of wedlock? Some rules are made to be broken."

Sam waved off the banter and frowned up from the ledger. "It's these invoices, isn't it, Max? We're billing most of these people for stuff we never delivered."

Max raised his eyebrows in a show of appreciation. "It didn't take you long to find it, but I expected that." He leaned forward, placing his elbows on the table. "That's the only way to do it. You don't shortweight, and you don't sell garbage. You give them top quality, you charge the sanctioned prices, and then you send 'em an invoice that covers your services."

"A phony delivery of meat. That's how you account for the extra money."

"Rather a crude way to express it. But that's the basic idea."

Sam appeared skeptical. "That would work for butchers, but isn't that a lot to cover up with our big retailers?"

"Right again. For that, we—"

"—collect from them on phony loans."

"Is there something about the word phony that appeals to you?" Max asked, but it was clear from his expression that he was impressed.

"Jesus." Sam pulled at his lip. "So it's really only a matter of hiding money? The extra money we charge?"

"Unless you want to doctor the meat. And we're above that."

Sam returned the ledger to Max's side of the table and sat back in his chair. "Well, I guess it's been working okay, but it seems to me there ought to be a safer method. Anyway, I appreciate seeing this."

Max held Sam in his chair with an open hand. "There was a reason for it. First you worked out a better schedule for your own route, then you organized the other drivers. And you did it without making any enemies. That takes some good jaws. Let's see if you can do what I do, and talk full time for a living. I'm hiring a new driver to cover your route. Starting next week, you can help me with the selling. And the collections."

Sam began to dress for the job. He put aside his Regal shoes for a pair that cost close to twenty dollars. He also paid for a new suit, although he never would have been able to part with the money if Max, delighted with his growing success, had not encouraged him. Vera compounded his guilt by surprising him with a top coat that cost more than the suit and shoes combined.

"You're making Max a small fortune," she told him, "so there's no point in walking around as though you're not entitled to some money."

Sam was doing well. He had always been an organizer, starting with his early union work at the plant, but Max's world was one he was uniquely qualified to dominate. Most of the buyers were businessmen who had never deviated from the law before, and there was a wholesomeness in Sam's youth and blond good looks that tempered any misgivings they may have had. Clement was a fast learner, and he was soon initiating deals without having to consult Max, and buying his own clothes instead of relying on Vera.

And yet, with butchers and packers, or an occasional encounter with hardened associates like Waters, he was formidable. He still thought of himself as working class. He knew the neighborhoods he covered, and was at home with the people. He spent time with his mother, he wrote Eddie regularly, and he wore his new role like his clothing, naturally and without affectation.

Vera shared neither his vague sense of guilt nor his quality of reservation. Sam turned over most of what he earned to her, and she spent it without hesitation. She was not an impulsive buyer. In her own words, it was simply that she had known what she had wanted for a lifetime. When Sam was bringing home four hundred dollars a week, she left her job to spend her time buying it. Within months, their furniture was as new as their apartment, and a wardrobe that did justice to Vera's looks hung in the walk-in closet.

"It's *all* going," she told Sam when he entered the bedroom after coming home from work one evening. She gestured toward a collection of underwear gathered in an unruly pile on the bedspread. Then she spun around for him, holding up the hem of her slip so that he could see the matching panties beneath it. "Silk," she said with her eyes shut, "and I've got six more of everything in the drawer." She crossed the room and gathered up the underwear on the bed. "This is really the best place to keep rayon." She dropped the entire pile into a wicker wastebasket on one side of her vanity, narrowing her eyes when she looked up to see his expression. "Relax, darling. You can still put your money into war bonds; I'm only spending what's mine."

Sam shrugged self-consciously. "That's fine. I just thought your sister or somebody could use what you're getting rid of."

She smiled then and approached him shaking her head indulgently. "You know, honey, it really won't help the cause if Laura inherits my slips, and I *would* like the pleasure of throwing something out for once in my life. Just to see what it feels like." She laced an arm around his neck and drew his touch to the silk of her panties. "See. This is what it feels like."

Bodies flew from the ground, fire and fragments were drawn into a vortex of unmolested buildings, and entire armies marched backwards in jerky retreat. Vera was rewinding the *Allied Invasion of Rome* on the Castle Film she had brought back from a trip to Rockefeller Plaza when the phone sounded from the shadows of the dining room.

"I'll get it," Sam said, leaving Vera to the projector. The lights were out in the apartment, so it was difficult for her to read his expression in the flicker of the film when he returned. "It's my Mom," he said thickly. "She's at City. The nurse on the phone said she had some kind of attack."

Vera switched off the projector and came to her feet in one motion. "We'd better hurry," she said, sweeping him along with her. "They called you, so someone must have already taken her history. If we don't get there before she's out of emergency, they'll put her in a ward."

"It's a nice room," Maureen Clement said. She might have been drunk with her slurred speech and the crooked smile of contentment she turned on them. "It seems so different than it was with your father."

"It is different," Sam said tensely. "You're going to come home."

But Vera silenced him with a squeeze of his wrist. "It's a

private room," she said, and the women nodded together in mutual understanding. "They'll see that you have whatever you want."

"Sam's father died here," Mrs. Clement sighed. "Downstairs." She reached over the siderail and patted Vera's hand. "Oh, but this one. This one will take care of you, Sam, just like she did for me. It's all going to be different for you."

"It's different for you," Sam protested. "We're going to take you back to our place." He colored then, with the realization that he'd revealed they'd been living together.

If his mother had understood, she was not affected. She smiled at him through the haze of her medication and nodded. "Oh, I knew, I knew." Then her eyes focused on something they could not see and her voice hardened. "Don't you let them do it, Sam. Every day he went to that plant. Even the day he died. Carl brought me his toolbox afterwards." She took them in with watery eyes. "There was a picture of us inside the cover. A snapshot he must have taped there when we were first married. He never told me. Everything seemed in front of us in that picture. He thought that plant was his first job, but he never had a chance to work things out." Her voice broke on the conclusion, and she reached out, locking hands with Vera in a silent communication that Sam could not fully understand.

Then, without letting go of Vera, she twisted into a position where she could peer at him with her head held away from the pillow. "Don't you let up, Sam. Don't you let them stop you for a minute! You're everything they are now, those people we've worked for. Better. And you're our son."

The thought seemed to comfort her, and she settled back down onto the pillow. Vera continued to hold her hand until she was asleep.

The home he had known was empty and silent. Sam stood in the tiny center hall, glimpsing his past through the open doors of each room. Wallpaper he'd peeled as a child in a ragged strip below a light switch; a chip in the kitchen door frame, knocked away when he had helped his father move in a new table; soiled circles from the back of his head in the corner of his room that had been hidden behind his bureau. A secret place.

"God, you could fit it all into half of our apartment," Vera said beside him. "Your mother would like that."

"My mother's not here," Sam said. "I'm giving it up."

Vera was indignant. "Sam, we can hold the lease and sublet twenty percent above ceiling. That's what she would have wanted."

There was no life in Sam's expression. "She wanted me to have more," he said flatly. "I'm not bucking the OPA for a few extra dollars on this place. There's not enough return for the risk. We want more. I'll get it."

Chapter Six

Francis Langford sang from the windowsill in Max's office, but her words were lost in the buzz of a vibration.

"I gotta get that speaker fixed," Max commented, working at the door of the closet behind his card table. "Vera says you got that F. M. Some sound. Damn, I know this thing's unlocked." The door suddenly swung open, causing Max to pull his head back sharply. The closet contained five shelves, and they were all empty except for the center one, which held a bottle of whiskey and a stack of paper cups. Max tucked them under one arm and turned to find Sam frowning at a poster tacked to the inside of the door. It showed the profile of two figures conversing over a table, and it read: *Loose Talk Costs Lives*. Max nodded at it before he nudged the door shut with his leg. "Sort of appropriate for the business," he explained, seating himself across from Sam and pouring them each a cup from the bottle. "As well as for these trying times, of course." He raised his cup in a salute. "Glenmore Kentucky Bourbon," he announced proudly. "Like all the supposed better things in life, from meat to women. If you can't eat 'em, they're nothin' but show." He pulled at the cup and brought it back down to the table with a noisy expulsion of breath. "Good stuff. How come you're not drinking?"

"In a minute." Sam passed a typewritten paper over the bottle. "This is what I was telling you about. Your own corporation."

"La-dee-da." Max studied the numbers before he began nodding. "Essex Meats Incorporated. I like that."

"You'll like it a lot more when you see what we can hide." Sam leaned across the table and guided Max through the numbers with his finger. "This is just a dummy based on the biggest customers. Each one gets stock in the corporation, and naturally, they have to pay for it. We can assess them for all kinds of additional expenses, and we can sell out the entire offering two or three times over. They're not going to audit every customer we have at the same time, so there's no way anyone gets hurt."

Sam settled slowly back into his seat without taking his eyes from Max, but the older man was already shaking his head in admiration. "Jesus, kid, you've got a very refined sense of dishonesty. That's rare."

"You have any questions?"

"Yeah. You want that drink?"

Sam pushed the cup to Max's side of the table. "We'll need a lawyer, you know. Someone we can really trust, because he's got to know the whole operation."

Max finished his drink and peered into the empty cup. "I'm not the vagabond I seem. We've had one right from the start. I'll set something up with you two. It's about time you met Harry Balfe as it is." He saluted Sam with the drink he'd surrendered and emptied the second cup.

"Max. I want to head this corporation. For more money."

There was no evidence of whiskey in the look of assessment Max turned on him. *"Absolutement.* I've never been fully accepted on Wall Street, anyway."

Harry Balfe was tooth-powder clean. During their initial meeting, Sam eyed him carefully ˌwhile the lawyer's attention was on the proposal in front of him. There was a subtle richness in his appearance, with the subdued color of his suit and the predictable pattern of his tie. It was a look, Sam decided, of money quietly asserted, and it was more impressive in the new world he had entered than all of the elaborate shoes and jewelry that men like Waters exhibited. Sam caught his own reflection in the green glass of the window behind Balfe's desk, and was surprised to find that his appearance was all but indistinguishable from the lawyer's.

"I like what I see," Balfe said when he looked up from the folder in front of him.

Sam colored self-consciously before he realized that Balfe was referring to his proposal and not his appearance. "I'm not claiming it's foolproof," he responded. "I just roughed out what we wanted."

"You've never incorporated one of your companies, then?"

Sam smiled in the face of the compliment. "Not really. In this case, I want everything to hold up to any kind of audit they might throw at us. No matter how thorough."

"I see." Harry Balfe was amused. "Sam, do you have any idea of what the odds of an actual investigation are?"

"Not exactly."

"As near as anyone can tell, OPA has about fifty investigators for each state. In other words, roughly ten for every thousand businesses. If I were you, I wouldn't be overly conservative in taking advantage of your opportunities."

"But if we did come to trial—"

"—*if* you did, we have enough combined staff to throw a hundred thousand dollars' worth of litigation at them in one month. OPA attorneys make an annual salary of about six thousand dollars, and there'd only be one assigned to your case. They'd come away with very little."

Sam was impressed in spite of himself. "Well, it might be rare, but it happens. One of the wholesalers in Boston was just fined forty thousand dollars. Max knows him."

"And did Max tell you what they overcharged to deserve that stiff punishment?"

"You know?"

Balfe smiled. "A matter of public record. As it happens, it was a little over three hundred thousand. I'd pay a forty-thousand-dollar fine for that kind of profit any day, wouldn't you?"

"It's socialist," Max observed when Sam outlined his conversation with Balfe. "All those government people trying to change the free enterprise system for which our boys are dying. Congress isn't even that wild about it, and why should they be? All those guys got where they are through big business, so you can bet they're not going to break their backs going after their buddies. Meanwhile, they organize working slobs like us to inform on each other. That's all these citizen volunteer committees are. Little people going after little people, while the bastards who run things let their friends in industry walk off with whatever they can carry."

"We're not so little anymore," Sam said. He was sharing a table with Max in the Essex Pub itself, and he leaned in toward him so that he could lower his voice. "Anyway, I wouldn't worry about it too much. You picked the right man in Balfe. He knows the OPA upside down."

Max wiped at the corners of his mustache with the back of his coat sleeve. "He ought to. He used to work for them."

Like most of Sam's ideas, Essex Meats Incorporated worked, allowing Max to expand his operation beyond the boundaries he had set for himself in order to avoid the exposure of an audit. The spring of 1944 brought greater profits to an already profitable organization, and Sam's benefits eventually exceeded his substantial salary.

"I just turned down a thousand dollars," he called out as he entered the apartment one evening after work.

"What?" Vera's voice came to him from the bedroom where Jimmy Durante was signing off the air with a final good night to Mrs. Calabash, and Sam smiled to himself as he heard her turn off the radio and hurry into the living room where he was pulling off his shoes. "Did you just say what I thought you said?" She was in her slip, and her fingers worried the embroidery along the hem while she looked at him with an anxious expression.

Sam bent over his shoes to hide his smile, enjoying her discomfort. "A thousand dollars. That's what Max wanted to give me as a bonus. The corporation idea has been working out pretty well." He tucked his lip under his teeth and looked up at her. "I turned him down, of course. I didn't want to take advantage."

"Oh, you fool!" Vera put the backs of her hands to her face and paced the rug in frustration. "Take advantage? Don't you realize, it's Max who's taking advantage of you? The world's worst worker can't get fired with this war going on, even if he tries. And you're the best! Didn't you see that sign Max put up in the restaurant?"

Sam looked toward the ceiling and recited. "'Be Polite to Our Waitresses: They're Harder to Get Than Customers.'"

"And you won't take an extra pencil home from the office!"

Sam held up his hands to restrain her then, grinning openly. "Hold on, lady. It's the money I wouldn't accept. I didn't say anything about extras."

She focused on his expression. "Sam! What are you saying?"

But he was already moving toward the window. It was open, and he leaned out over the ledge, peering down into the street with a knowing smile as soon as she joined him. "It's ours," he said. "And I guess it's about as close as you can come to a new car, since they're not making them anymore."

Vera let her eyes linger on the Packard parked in front of the entrance below them before she turned. "Oh, Sam, it's even better than the money!" She threw herself against him, interrupting the embrace briefly to glance toward the car a second time.

He shut his eyes, enjoying the reaction he had anticipated since early that afternoon. "I'm glad you like it," he said, "but you'd better stop doing that in front of the window. We're going to draw enough attention in this neighborhood with a new car."

He chose a warm spring Saturday morning on which to polish it.

Vera wanted him to hire someone else for the job, but there were certain unwritten laws in the old neighborhood which would have condemned that as pretentious, and he was determined the ritual would take place on Clay Street. He parked the Packard in front of his old building and used the water from Skorski's cellarway to wash it down. His father had talked of owning a car during the hard times of the Thirties, and when he was growing up, Sam had earned pin money by polishing the automobiles of wealthier families who lived outside the Ironbound. It was his turn now, and without envy his former neighbors smiled at him from their stoops, sharing the experience, and feeling some pride in the prosperity that had come to a part of Clay Street.

For them, and for working people across the country, it was a better time than it had been for many years, in spite of the war. Or perhaps because of it. Americans moved closer to each other, as they had during the Great Depression, only this time, the unity created by a nation's determination to survive was accompanied by a new prosperity. There were more jobs than there were applicants to fill them, and after the bitter years of the Thirties, the common workingman found his fortunes swinging from one extreme to the other. The economy had come to life again, and the war that fueled it also did its share in renewing the nation's confidence in itself and the entire American way of life.

Skorski emerged from his apartment just as Sam was putting the finishing touches on the Packard's hood ornament. Some boys had wandered down from the opposite end of the street where they had been gathering scrap metal in return for free admission to a movie matinee, and he stepped over the debris they had stored along the curb, taking in the car with the same open admiration as the teenagers. "Sweet Jesus, kid. I didn't even own a bicycle when I was your age."

Sam looked up from his work and smiled at him. "Why not, Frank? That was before the Depression."

"Maybe so, but they didn't pay plant workers what they do today. Even in good times. You started asking for too much, and there were plenty of others ready to take your place. Plenty." He nodded toward the metal piled along the curb. "'Course, that's all different these days with all this defense work. Labor's on top now. I seen the way some of those guys work, and believe me, they don't have to strain themselves."

Sam had removed his jacket and rolled up his sleeves, but he had performed the entire waxing in his suit, and he straightened his clothing as he talked to Skorski. "Well, I wouldn't work that way myself, but I can understand it after what they've been through for so many years." He made a point of looking up from the trunk where he was storing his cleaning things. "Besides, defense workers run a special risk. Their plants are the first places they'll hit if they come over here."

Skorski's expression darkened, and he nodded an emphatic agreement. "Don't think we don't know it." He took in the upturned faces of the boys along the curb before he crossed his arms and squinted toward the river. "Not that we ain't ready for them."

Sam jerked a thumb upward in a sign of confidence before he climbed into the Packard. "I can believe that, Frank." He brought the car to life, and the boys stood up to watch his departure. "Thanks for the water," he called out through the open window. Others in the neighborhood waved as he swung the Packard away from the curb.

"You're welcome to all you want," Skorski called out after him. "It's still your building, kid."

The car was the first open indulgence Sam had allowed himself, and he realized that he was beginning to enjoy the benefits of his job with less guilt. People who had come close to starving five years earlier suddenly found themselves with enough money for luxuries, but the rationing system imposed by the war gave them few places to spend it. Sam began to agree with Max that there was some justification in supplying a man with a steak if he had waited most of his life in order to afford it. But he still refused to take full advantage of his position in the black market.

Even the gas he had saved for the initial drive with Vera came from the accumulation of his own ration stamps, when he could easily have used the unlimited coupons that Max procured for purposes of running the business.

He picked Vera up at City Hospital. She refused to put any of the money he gave her into war bonds, and she shared none of his zeal for the effort on the home front, but she had given over her Saturday mornings for volunteer work at the hospital. Sam suspected that she had gotten involved only to please him, and he found' her outspoken objections a source of amusement.

"God, it's good to be out of there!" she said, pulling open the door on the passenger side before the car had come to a complete halt. "You were right about one thing, though." She planted a kiss on the side of his face as he swept out into the traffic and nosed the car in the direction of the Oranges. "I'm damned glad I'm doing it."

"Oh? Changed your mind?"

"Are you kidding?" Vera let out her breath in a sigh of exasperation, clouding the dash with cigarette smoke. "It just feels good to see what I've been missing." She rolled her eyes at the sight of Sam's smile. "Listen, you don't know what it's like in there. They've drafted every doctor that's young enough to walk without a cane, and the ones they've got left are more overworked than the nurses. That's saying something, too, because we have to do everything for ourselves these days. Make the beds, take the linen to the laundries, deliver the meals. All the help's gone to the jobs that pay good money."

Sam raised a hand from the wheel. "Maybe you should spend your Saturday mornings in a defense plant."

"I would, if I needed the money." She squeezed his knee. "Anyway, this is the only job I'd work at if I didn't have you. The defense money may be great, but Rosy the Riveter is on her way out as soon as this war is over. And it will be over," she added in a rush, "look at that!" Vera pushed her head out of the window, reading the copy on a series of Burma-Shave signs stationed behind each other along the side of the road. "Let's

make Hitler . . . And Hirohito . . . Look as Sick . . . As Benito
. . . Buy Defense Bonds . . . Burma Shave!" She slid across the
seat in a flurry of excitement and kissed him again, pulling play-
fully at his ear. "God, I'm so happy about this car! You don't
know what it does for me!"

Sam looked away from the road long enough to smile. "Helps
you catch up on your reading, does it?"

"You!" She darted a hand between his legs before she retreated to her side of the car. "It makes me ready for love."

They spent the bulk of the afternoon in Morris County, a rural
area less than an hour's drive from the heart of Newark. Sam
had packed a picnic lunch, and they ate it beside a lake in a
public park. The lake was centered by an island too small to
serve any use other than acting as a base for the slender tower of
a monument erected to the veterans of World War I. Sam eyed
the statue of a doughboy that overlooked the peaceful vista of the
park, comforting himself with the realization that the current
war, too, would end, and he would no longer be an outsider. In
fact, he would have a start on most of the others who had left him
behind.

He considered Vera very much a part of that start, and there
was a special, unspoken closeness between them during the drive
home. Just outside the Oranges, when the sky was darkening
with the clouds of an approaching storm, they pulled over to the
side of the road, enjoying the twilight silence that seemed to
anticipate the coming rainfall.

"You can actually smell the soil," Sam said, drawing in the
scent of the warm air outside his window. "I'd like to have a
yard of my own some day."

"The privacy would be nice," Vera agreed, brushing his hair
lightly with her hand. "I'm not much on gardening, though."
She glanced through the windshield at a sloping embankment on
the other side of the road.

There were several people tending the plantings sweeping
down from the elevation of a railroad bed. Sam watched the
efforts of a variety of amateur gardeners until he noticed an older

woman attempting to move a wheelbarrow up the grade to a storage shed near the side of the tracks. By that time, twilight and the change in the weather had nearly emptied the small lot of the others, and Sam pushed open his door, crossing the street to confront her.

"You look as though you could use a hand," he said, taking the handles of the wheelbarrow without waiting for an answer.

"I guess I don't have any choice," she said, but she laughed and fell into step beside him as he moved effortlessly up the slope of the embankment. The hair that she had tied back with a bandana was streaked with gray, but her skin was a healthy tan, and she walked with the springy, upright gait of a younger woman. "The railroad lets us use their right-of-way for victory gardens, so it's hard to complain. Even under these conditions."

He stored the wheelbarrow and the rest of her tools in the shed near the grading before they slid down the soft shoulder of the embankment, laughing together. Near the street, Sam turned out his cuffs, shaking the soil they had collected out onto the pavement.

"That's too nice a suit to dirty," the woman said, brushing at his pants with the back of her glove.

"I'm sure he's got others." The voice came from the near corner of the lot, where a middle-aged couple had gathered up their folding chairs and was moving in the direction of the curb. "He looks like he's doing well enough," the man went on without attempting to hide the anger in his voice. He paused to look over at Sam with one hand on the door of his car. "Four-F, son?"

For a moment, the mood of the entire day hung in the balance while Sam struggled with a reply, but the woman responded before he could voice his answer. "Why, Albert, how nice to see you here for a change! I guess all that driving you've been doing has kept you away this past month."

The other man cleared his throat awkwardly and made a show of noticing the darkened sky. Then he joined his wife in the car without answering.

The woman watched them drive away with a grimace of disgust. "Don't pay any mind to Albert. He's not growin' his own vegetables to save blue stamps. He's after the extra gas like the others." She pushed a thumb over her shoulder in the direction of the plantings behind them. "They claim they're working a victory garden outside of town, so they get their gas allowance increased. But they don't burn much ethyl coming out here once a month for show." She snorted contemptuously. "That man couldn't tell a carrot from his you-know-what if he bit it by mistake. 'Scuse the language, I didn't see that pretty lady waiting for you across the street."

Sam reddened slightly. "I *am* Four-F," he offered.

"And you're not any happier about it than the others I've met." She reached out and squeezed his arm. "Well, I'll be happy for you. I've got a son out there somewhere, and I wish he was in the same boat as you, although he'd be just as silly about it, knowing him. Like most everyone else, we have our own code for writing, and he keeps tipping me off in his letters that he's still in Australia. Probably just so I'll feel better." She captured Sam's hand in her own and smiled up at him. "You make me feel better, son. Try not to be sorry about not bein' shot up." She turned and waved toward Vera before she walked away in the direction of her car.

Sam gazed after her until the shoulders of his jacket began to spot with the first random drops of the storm. Then he crossed over to the Packard where he shared the encounter with Vera while they watched the rain stream in heavy beads across the newly waxed hood.

Her voice was soft and subdued when she responded, as though she were trying to preserve something fragile about the total experience of the afternoon. "I'm glad someone besides me talked some sense to you." She shook her head and sighed, staring out at the curtain of water being drawn across the landscape. "As much as I love you, I guess that one difference will always be there. You're sorry for what you have, and I'm sorry for what I haven't gotten." She found his eyes. "You'd better get used to it, Sam, because I want enough for life, and I'm going to see that you make it happen. For both of us." She pulled him toward her from behind the wheel, hiking up her dress so that she could straddle his lap. "It *is* happening, you know, starting right with this car." She leaned down and covered his mouth with hers. "And you're getting to like it, aren't you?" She pushed his hands against the front of her dress.

"I like you in your uniform," he said, feeling his breath escape him.

"How do you like me out of it?" she asked, and in seconds, the fastening of her dress came undone. She lifted the halter of her bra to expose her breasts for him.

Sam glanced at the windshield behind her, but the storm had arrived, and the windows were a blur of water, shutting them off from the rest of the world.

Vera managed to undress them both from the waist down, pulling his pants below his knees and working out of her own underwear so that she could mount him where he sat. There was something open and assertive about her appetite for anything she wanted that drew him on, and as she moved against him, the reward of the car and the special gift of her body merged to become part of the same extended exhilaration. He ran his hand over the perfect roundness of her buttocks, and she moaned in appreciation when he let his fingers slip lightly into the fold between them.

The smell of her perfume mixed with a special woman's scent in the close confines of the car, and he remembered the hope and uncertainty that had gripped him the night he had parked with Maura after the attack of Pearl Harbor. Everything he had wanted then had been denied. Yet, for the first time since that fateful evening, he found himself grateful for what he had received in return.

By the middle of 1944, the Allies had invaded France, the United States was extending aid to the Soviet Union on a lend-lease basis, and Sam Clement had managed to save six thousand dollars.

By that time, there was a feeling in Sam's old neighborhood, and in neighborhoods across the country, that the war would soon be at an end. Eddie was not permitted to reveal where he was serving, but from the letters he wrote to Sam, it was easy enough to guess that he was stationed in the South Pacific. Sam had begun to form plans for his own business when the war ended, and he was elated that he had the capital to back them. The money not only gave him a special sense of security, it also appeased his conscience. He had determined that Eddie would have a job when he came back, a partnership, if he would accept it. And there would be other veterans in need of work; Dewey himself had made their jobs a part of his campaign. Sam would be ready and eager to fill that need.

By the fall of that year, everything seemed to be moving in the direction that would make Sam's plans possible. Poland had been freed, the German rear guard was destroyed in the Battle of Mons, and the invasion of Germany itself was on the horizon. But Americans were still dying, and a battle in the South Pacific changed Clement's life as irrevocably as if he had been doing the fighting himself.

The telegram came days before Christmas, and Sam was there when it arrived. Most of the neighborhood witnessed the appearance of the official car, because the Branagans had held a Christmas party in their basement, and people were still leaving when the uniformed driver pulled up in front of the building directly across the street.

The gathering on Clay Street had been a reunion of sorts; not just for Sam, but for parents who had been linked together by the common bond of their sons, only to drift apart when the war brought an end to that association. The last of them had climbed the steps of the Branagans' cellarway that cold December day filled with a special hope that was reinforced by being together, telling themselves that they had just celebrated their final Christmas in the uncertain shadow of the war.

While they were being accompanied out onto the sidewalk by

Joe's parents, the courier was approaching, and they stopped to stare at him with the open-mouthed guilt of revelers who had been caught in the act of violating something sacred. The Branagans had just dismissed Joe's recent failure to write as typical of his irresponsible attitude, and Mrs. Syms had been agreeing with Sam that Eddie was probably in the South Pacific, finishing off the Japanese. Joyce Harms reacted by pressing her face against her son's shoulder. Like Joe Branagan, Greg Harms was in the Navy, but he was home on leave, and while he was safe from the nightmare of the telegram's arrival, the sight of the uniformed driver drew him from the warm associations of the party to the cold uncertainty of his future.

Those who had already reached the stoops of their homes remained frozen where they were, and no one spoke, so that the heavy black shoes of the courier sounded his approach on the slate of the sidewalk even for the women, who were looking away.

"Mrs. Syms?" he inquired, and all of them drew breath again, as if in the wake of an accident that had spared them, but taken one of their number. Sam had wrapped his arm around Eddie's mother, and she leaned into him when she heard her name, trembling against him with birdlike motions. "I don't have my glasses," she protested into the muffle of his topcoat, as if she could prevent what had already happened by turning from the telegram.

"I'll read it," Sam said thickly, and the others came from the stoops and the sidewalks toward the center of the street, converging wordlessly in a ragged circle around him. He read it to himself, but he read it for all of them, and they took the meaning from his face as quickly as it swam up through the blur of his vision from the actual telegram. He wanted desperately to be alone, but he was a leader, and it had fallen on him to pronounce his friend dead.

"He's gone," Sam said, and the circle closed in, taking the weight of the sobbing woman from him and huddling together for warmth.

The Branagans guided Eddie's mother back to her empty apartment. Mrs. Branagan stayed with her in the tiny living room, while Joe's father went back across the street to their phone and did the necessary calling. Both of them were torn between a profound pity and the guilty sense of relief they felt over their own son's survival.

They could not know that he was already as lost to them as if the messenger had emerged from the car with a telegram bearing their name.

Sam was wearing only his trunks, but when he saw that it was Vera, he unchained the door of the apartment and led her into the living room. If she was angry, she gave no indication of it.

"It's been two days," she said softly, taking a chair across from the couch where he had draped himself. When he limited his response to the suggestion of a shrug, she took the time to light a cigarette. "I was worried."

"I figured Max would tell you I was here."

Vera sighed, sending a cloud of smoke across a small table between them. "I'd rather have heard it from you. Where's Max?"

"With a lady friend. He said he knew I'd want to be alone." Sam showed her a tired smile. "I think he was dying for the excuse."

"That's not fair. He really cares about you."

"All right, Vera. I know that."

"But you're quitting him anyway?"

Sam held up a hand of protest, but before he answered, he opened the silver case she had left on the table and lit one of her cigarettes. "Max will do okay without me. Everything's been set up to run itself. Larkin's dying to take over as it is. And it doesn't change anything between us. We can still get married."

"Like hell we can. Not on fifty dollars a week or whatever they're going to sucker you for on some straight job."

Sam brought his feet off the couch and leaned across the coffee table. "Vera. I'm not making any gravy off people like Eddie, I don't care how harmless it sounds." Anger had come into his voice, and he pointed with a shaking hand to a pile of newspapers on the floor near the front of the couch. "You know what's been going on while we've been making our hard-earned profits? All those illegal slaughterhouses that have been supplying us were dumping their carcasses. Do you know what that means?" Vera had the sense to confine herself to a shake of her head. "It means a shortage of animal glands. A spokesman from one of the pharmaceutical companies called it a crisis situation." Sam spread his arms and looked at her intently. "They make medicine from those parts, Vera, and we've been buying from people who waste them." He seemed to catch the intensity in his voice then, and he sank back against the couch with a sigh. "Christ, that's not even it, exactly. There just wouldn't be all that money in meat if we weren't fighting a war, and I'm tired of kidding myself about it."

Vera pursed her lips and nodded slowly. "All right, honey, I understand that, and this isn't any time to argue with you. But I didn't just come to bring you back. Eddie's service is today. I thought you'd want to go."

For the first time he noticed that she was wearing her new boycoat, and beneath the parting of the fleeced collar, he caught the dark purple of her best blouse. "Oh, my God!" He came abruptly to his feet, darting a glance in the direction of the bedroom.

"Don't worry, darling," Vera soothed. "I have one of your suits outside in the car."

Eddie had died on one of the beaches in the South Pacific during an amphibious assault. Instantly, the brief report termed it, but that was a word used to console countless grieving families, and Sam had his doubts. Even the men sobbed openly during the service, but the gathering at Eddie's apartment afterwards was full of the noise of countless conversations, and Mrs. Syms was kept dry-eyed and fretting while she saw that there was enough for everyone to eat and drink.

Sam and Vera stayed until all of the guests had departed except for two of Eddie's elderly aunts. While they moved silently around the apartment conducting the clean-up, Vera patted Mrs. Syms on the shoulder and slipped an envelope under the fold of her hands.

"This is something Sam and I want you to have," she explained softly. "I'm sure it's more of a comfort to us than it is to you, but right now, it's one of the few things we can do."

Mrs. Syms nodded dumbly, and they took their leave. It was not until they were in their car and headed in the direction of their apartment that Sam thought to ask Vera what she had left.

"I gave her a thousand dollars of the money," she answered without looking at him. "The money you put aside for your business." She turned toward him. "Are you angry?"

Sam shook his head. "I'm sorry I hadn't thought of it myself. Do you think she'll accept it?"

Vera slipped an arm along the back of the seat and rubbed gently at the back of his neck. "Returning it isn't going to bring Eddie back."

Gabriel DeFillippo had cut Sam's hair since he was in second grade, and when he spoke to Sam a week later, it was in the capacity of a man who could claim the authority of the neighborhood.

"You just don't know what you did, a thing like that," he announced without warning when he was brushing the residue of a haircut from Sam's shoulders. "That woman had no one after Eddie went. She'd have to have moved in with relatives, and believe me, I know what that means." When Sam rose from the chair, the barber reached up and confronted him with a hand on his shoulder. "Eddie would have been proud of you. We're all proud of you."

Sam reddened in the face of the praise. "I think it's Eddie we should be proud of."

DeFillippo rang up the sale in the register. "No denying it, kid, no denying it." He blocked Sam before he reached the doorway and thumped him in the chest with the back of his hand. "But you did all right, despite your situation. You gave your mother the best, God rest her soul, and then you took care of Eddie's. You keep it up, Sam, and you'll be someone special." He rolled his eyes suggestively in the direction of the factories along the river and put a hand to his mouth, speaking to Sam in the hushed tones of intimacy. "Listen, you don't think every time someone makes it out of those plants and starts to turn over some money on his own it's not good for everyone? Christ, that's what it's all about!"

Sam mumbled his thanks and allowed DeFillippo to pump his hand as he squeezed past him and out onto the street. "You're a credit to the neighborhood, hear me?" the barber called after him.

Wallace Waters planted a shoe against the edge of his desk and pushed back from it until his weight was balanced on the rear legs of his chair. "So, you want to work for *me* now, huh?" he asked with a smile.

Sam kept his expression neutral. "Not you. Max. It's just an opportunity to extend your operation."

Waters was skeptical. "Max never had anything to do with reefer before."

"He doesn't like the idea now. I talked him into it, and I'm the only one who's going to be doing the driving."

Waters let his weight fall forward and planted his elbows on the desk. "You talked him into it. Why?"

"A few reasons. The simplest one is I like making money."

Waters frowned and waved a hand of warning. "This isn't dodging those stiffs from OPA, you know. Drugs means you're bucking the law. There's a lot of risk."

"That's my other reason."

Waters cocked his head, but when he took in Sam's expression, it was obvious that he was serious. "Shit," he said, breaking into a grin, "from the way you cold-cocked my ass in that cornfield, I can believe it."

"Believe it," Sam said. "When do we start?"

The Port of Newark handled over six hundred thousand items bound for the front during World War II, and the warehouses there held goods representing every part of the country. Sam never took the marijuana directly from a ship; he simply carried cargo from the dock that concealed it. Max had given him the Packard as a bonus several months ago; now he had set him up with a car that had scoops under the fenders and an extra hollow space hidden by the hump of the transmission. Most of Sam's initial deliveries went to an apartment in New York, but in time, there were also trips to Boston, and then an occasional run to cities as far as Chicago.

He drove with the abandon of a violator who was indifferent to being caught, risking progressively larger amounts of the illicit drug, until he and Max were splitting close to five hundred dollars a trip after paying Waters for connecting them. Sam was moody, and he neither liked nor trusted the people he was dealing with, but Vera was openly impressed, and she made a point of encouraging him.

"You were born with a head for business," she told him one night when she was counting the cash he had turned over to her on the kitchen table. "The whole meat angle goes right out the window as soon as the war is over, but there's always a market for what you're moving. It just takes guts, that's all."

Sam shook off the praise as he worked out of his jacket in the living room. "I don't have guts, Vera. I'm just a coward who's afraid to settle for a normal living again." He strode into the kitchen and raised a handful of cash from the table. "We didn't get this because I'm smart. I'm just a crook who's switched rackets. And do you know why I changed?"

There was something wild in his expression, and Vera stopped counting to look at him without speaking.

"I changed because I liked the customers." He pressed his lips tightly together and nodded. "See, Vera, the people who buy this stuff don't take a thing from the war effort. Not a piece of meat, not a scrap of metal. Nothing." The anger seemed to go out of him then, and he sank down onto one of the kitchen chairs. "That's my contribution," he added, as much to himself as to her. "I've discovered I can't live without the money, but I won't hurt the cause. So now I'm just a plain crook."

Vera's hands were passing over the table again, shuffling bills into neat piles. "You're not anything of the kind," she said without looking up from her counting. "You even go out of your way to help people."

"I know," Sam said flatly. "I'm a credit to the neighborhood."

Joe Branagan was every inch the drunken sailor. He was home on leave for a short time, and Vera and Sam had surprised him with a party in their apartment. The gathering was a mixture of old high school friends, employees from Branagan's tavern, and any of the young people from the Clay Street area who were not away in the service themselves. The women far outnumbered the men, but Vera had done an impressive job in arranging an elaborate bar and an open buffet, and within hours, the front rooms of the apartment were roaring.

Branagan sat on one side of the living room couch facing Sam, and his tanned complexion took on a deeper glow as he consumed one depth charge after another, dropping shots of whiskey into an open mug of beer. "This is what I've learned in the Navy," he said with a crooked smile. He raised his mug and saluted Sam before he drank. Like his father, he was a short man, but he had a compact body that seemed ideally proportioned by the cut of his uniform. "What else can I say when you ask me what it's like? I sleep with a few hundred guys in an area about the size of your apartment. We eat Navy food from a table that rolls from side to side, and a little later, we all go and shit in the same room. Boy, it's really swell. The only women you see are taped to the walls, and you can't even find a place to squeeze your mickey."

He let his head roll back against the couch and took a long

pull on his drink. "Twice we've seen action, and the only thing scarier than our guns shaking the shit out of the ship is *their* guns trying to blow it out of the water. That's when you pray to Christ for another chance to go back below decks and be bored shitless with all those smelly guys." Branagan stifled a burp with the back of his hand. "As you can see, I sure wouldn't give all that up to be sharing a bedroom with Vera Campbell."

Sam shook his head. "You're doing something I should be doing."

"Horseshit. You're doing what I should be doing." He held up a hand. "Oh, I don't mean with Vera. I'm talking about getting a start for yourself. I'd give a hell of a lot to be in your situation."

"Selling reefer?" Sam drank deeply from his own glass. "It's admirable."

"You don't think it is?" Branagan squinted at him indignantly. "What the hell does my old man do? He sells people what they want. And he doesn't ask whether it's good for them."

"There's a difference."

"Sure there's a difference. *You* wear a suit and do business with special people. He serves up suds to anyone who walks in off the street. And for a lot less money. That's what's waiting for me if I make it through this mess. Joe the bartender."

Sam planted a hand on his shoulder. "You're just down on yourself, Joe. That's not the way it's going to be."

"Sure. I could end up like Eddie." Branagan narrowed his eyes. "Sam, you're not the one who's missing anything, no matter what you think. It's guys like me who want to be where you are." He shrugged then, as if he had embarrassed himself with the outburst. "To Eddie, then," he said, raising his mug.

"To Eddie." Sam touched Joe's glass with his own, and they both drained their drinks.

When they were through, Joe came shakily to his feet. "Well, there's one thing this uniform is good for besides drawing fire." His grin had returned, and he motioned toward the gathering in the dining room. "Stuffing a patriotic woman like Mary McFarland." He put his hands to his chest as though he were cupping breasts and squealed in a high falsetto, "'Oh, Joe, it's so wrong of us, but you could be gone tomorrow!'"

Sam was at war with himself, unwilling to give up the status he had earned during the past three years, and unable to completely rationalize what he was doing. In an irony only he could appreciate, the more he sought the retribution of the law by taking greater chances, the quicker he accelerated his success.

One weekend, his car broke down in Chicago, and he was forced to spend the night. His connection there was one of the few people he liked doing business with, a young man about his own age who went by the single name of Seaver. Seaver walked with a noticeable limp and had also been turned down by the military, although his rejection had been obvious from the start, and he shared none of Sam's bitterness. He put Sam up in his apartment that weekend, and they talked until the small hours of the morning. They also smoked some of Sam's delivery.

After that initiation, Sam began to use marijuana regularly, finding that it relaxed him, particularly during his long hours of solitude on the road. There were times he managed to transform his role completely under the influence of the drug, thinking of himself as a man on a mission of danger and importance. Late at night, he would take in the city lights below the window of his hotel room and assess the chances of completing his run safely, like a pilot attempting to return to base. He grew quieter during the following months, and drew further into his isolation, but the people around him only noticed his growing success.

The final trip, and the one that would change his life, was outlined for him by Vera when he returned from visiting Eddie's mother one night.

"Max just left," she rushed to tell him as soon as he had shut the door to the hall. He could see by her expression that she was barely able to contain her excitement. "Waters wants to send you to Florida next weekend. Right to his source!"

Sam rubbed wearily at the backs of his eyes and crossed over to the couch. "Oh. You mean he wants me to pick up some stuff directly?"

Vera smiled and nodded. "There's a supplier waiting right in Miami Beach. Waters is going to give you the money to buy for him. Do you know what that means?"

Sam shrugged. "No middleman. A bigger profit, I guess."

She had started to move in the direction of the bedroom, but she hesitated long enough to ask a final question. "Will you do it?"

"Hell, I don't care."

"Wait here, then!" She disappeared into the bedroom, returning in seconds with the shoebox that held their savings. "We've got over eight thousand here," she announced. "I want you to take it."

He grinned up at her from the couch. "We're not getting married?"

"We're getting everything we ever wanted!" She sat down next to him, placing the box on his lap. "If they can buy, *we* can buy."

Sam was confused. "Why do we need our own money?"

"For our own profit, dummy. You know people who can sell whatever we buy. Seaver could probably take the whole deal." She trapped his hands between hers. "Can you imagine what we'd make with all that profit for ourselves?" She searched his face while he considered what she was saying.

"What about Max?"

Vera spread her arms. "What about him? You buy whatever he and Waters want. It's no skin off their noses if you want to sell a little on your own."

"Did you ask them?"

She tightened her hands around his, looking at him with a pleading expression. "You know Max will let you if you tell him you want it badly enough. Oh, Sam, this could be your last trip if you can pull it off. You'll be done with it all. Finished. We can get married."

He didn't answer immediately, and when he looked at her, he

made a point of holding her eyes. "You really mean that? We'll be through with it, money and all?"

She nodded her head rapidly in a childlike confirmation. "I really mean it. The last trip."

As it turned out, she was right, but for reasons neither of them suspected.

Part Three: Kara

Chapter Seven

When Sam had Kara's station wagon repaired, he asked the mechanic to fit her hood with a lock. He was reasonably sure that Vera would be unlikely to tamper with it a second time, but they were playing a guessing game, and she might have counted on the car being vulnerable for that very reason. When Kara drove to her class the following week, she left the wagon near the edge of the parking lot, in full view of the bordering street. It never occurred to her that she might be in any danger herself.

Kara was a dancer. She had received only five years of formal ballet before the war caught up with her family and changed her life, taking her parents, and leaving her and her sister in a concentration camp. But years later, and in a new country, she had found herself drawn to dancing again. At the time, she told Sam it was because of him, that the healing had begun and she could turn to things she had known as a child without reliving the loss of her family. She was in her twenties then, but what began as a form of conditioning after the birth of Todd became an avocation that she still found enjoyable and fulfilling in her middle age.

For the past five years, one of the classes she taught had been an adult course at the local high school, leading housewives in a workout to a fast-paced music that was meant to benefit them more physically than aesthetically. Her group met two evenings a week between seven and eight, and by the time she had put her records in order and changed clothes, it was usually close to nine.

That Thursday, the sky had been gray and overcast, so it was dark in the first-floor hallway when she was leaving, even near the windows of the exit doors. Kara pressed against the firebar of the one in the center, but it failed to give way. The doors on either side were equally intractable, and she moved the width of the hallway, shaking the U-shaped brackets a second time before she concluded that they were locked. She paused to recall the nearest alternate exit, and in the silence, she heard footsteps.

She was not always the last person to leave the building, and her first thought was that one of the other women had made the same discovery moments earlier, and was searching the wings to find another way out. But when she concentrated on the sounds echoing in the hall, she realized that the steps were approaching her directly. In a brief moment of alarm, she considered sheathing her hand in the protection of her shoulder bag and pushing out the thick glass in one of the doors, but she rejected the impulse almost as soon as it occurred to her. For one thing, it was almost July, and unless there was one of the occasional softball games being played on the adjoining athletic field, no one would hear her. More importantly, she wasn't sure she was in any danger.

She decided to compromise between being cautious and over-reacting by chancing the stairway behind her in the darkness. It would take her to the second floor, away from the footsteps, where she might find an open classroom window. The echoes in the hall rang in her ears with the exaggeration of her concern, but she skirted the short distance in one continuous rush that brought her clattering to the top of the stairwell. When she had shut the door behind her, she leaned back against it and attempted to catch her breath.

Before she was fully under control, the sound of renewed

movement in the hall below caused her to clamp a hand to her mouth. She heard the door to the stairs swing slowly open, and then the sound of the steps resumed, tracing her path. She pushed away from the door, twisting toward the dim light at either end of the hall before she realized that she was trapped.

She could either try the classroom doors fronting the corridor, hoping that one of them was open, or she could rush in the opposite direction and descend the far stairwell. Rejecting the idea of returning to the dead end of the first floor, she kicked off her sneakers and padded quietly toward the short end of the hall, pulling at each locked door until there were no more to try. By then, she could hear the door to the stairwell being opened, and she could only flatten herself against the wall.

The same steps hesitated near the entrance to the hall before they resumed, moving unmistakably in her direction. Kara had the sharp handle of her comb raised in a shaking fist over her head by the time a small figure came dimly into view. The rectangle of his T-shirt told her that it was a man, and as he approached her, she could see the tangled profile of a mop in his free hand.

"These your shoes?" he asked, holding out the white blur of her sneakers.

"Yes." He frowned at her reaction, a frail man who looked as though he were in his late sixties, wearing blue work pants that were rolled at the cuffs. "Thank you," she whispered, and the relief in her voice made her gratitude seem strangely out of proportion. She reached out and took the sneakers from his outstretched hand. "You are working here?" she asked when she had slipped them on.

He rubbed at the back of his head. "Well, I don't work here ordinarily. I'm at Governor Jackson, but we rotate in the summer to cover vacations. I snapped them doors shut and the damn things locked on me. Pardon the language."

Kara laughed as she rose from tying her sneakers. "My God, you scared me."

The white hair bobbed in a nod. "You had me worried your-self. Any place we can get at a phone?"

Kara was already moving in the direction of the stairs. "In the room I use for my class."

When she had unlocked the door to her studio, she pointed to the outline of her desk. "The phone is over there. I'll put on the lights."

"No lights." The voice was the same, but it had assumed the edge of command.

Kara felt a sinking sensation in the pit of her stomach. "But you wanted to call."

"I wanted a phone. You're going to use it. To call Sam."

She made a move toward the door, but he checked her with a sharp tap against the blackboard where he was standing. His arms were extended in her direction, and something metallic glinted in the grip of his hands. "You won't get past me," he warned, "and all the doors are locked if you do."

Todd had last tried Winslow's over a month ago. He deliber-ately rotated his visits to the singles' bars in order to remain anonymous, although occasionally he would meet an old high school friend. That Thursday, he had established his usual pat-tern when Jon Chaiten surprised him. Todd had been on his way out of the men's room, and it was impossible to pretend he hadn't heard his name called with Chaiten standing at the bar, close enough to put a hand on his shoulder.

"Hello, Jon," Todd offered. His tone was casual, but he real-ized the feelings Jon Chaiten evoked were still difficult to control.

Chaiten was openly warm. "Christ, it's good to see you." His hand remained on Todd's shoulder as he turned away to signal the bartender. "Two Scotch and waters, please." He called out the order before Todd could protest, and when he turned back to him, he was smiling. "I hope that's still your drink."

"It is, but I have to make it a quick one." Todd tempered the request with a smile. "I was talking to someone over there."

Chaiten followed the direction of his nod to one of the tables near the rear of the room. "I'll say you were. Well, I'm here with a buddy myself." He grinned. "Can't play your game anymore. I'm married."

"So you told me on the phone." Todd took the glass the bartender slid in his direction. "That was a few years ago. I guess that means it's worked out." He raised his drink in a salute.

Chaiten's Scotch remained on the bar. "Everything's worked out," he said meaningfully. He waited until Todd put down his glass. "I had a little help from other people, of course. People who'd been through the same thing." When Todd continued to look away without responding, he touched him lightly on the arm. "Maybe I could give you a little help."

Todd glanced past him to the table where the girl was waiting. "Not unless you've grown a pair of tits since Nam."

Chaiten's laugh was perfunctory, and he made no effort to lighten his expression. "I haven't done that, but I have grown." He tightened his grip on Todd's arm. "Why don't you stop fighting it? Try one of the meetings they've been holding. I'll go back with you if you want to get started."

Todd met his eyes. "Why don't you forget it, Jon?"

"I can't forget it, any more than you can. But I can learn to live with it."

"I'm living."

"So you say." Chaiten sipped at his drink. "You look like you just got off the plane. Any reason you never returned my calls?"

Todd pushed his empty glass away, as if to end the discussion. "It's been five years. People change."

"Wait." Chaiten stepped away from the bar to detain him. "You were the closest friend I had over there, and I'm not the only one who might not have made it without you. I'd just like to return the favor, that's all. You're entitled to your own life, but it might be a lot easier to live it if you talked things out the way some of us have."

"No thanks, Jon. Being there was enough."

Chaiten shrugged. "Well, you know where to find me if you change your mind. You can always pick up the phone."

"I'll do that." Todd patted him lightly on the arm before he turned away. "Thanks for the drink."

Chaiten watched him work his way across the room, noticing the slight limp barely visible below the line of the tables. Then he returned to his own seat where a man a few years younger frowned up at him.

"So who's the guy throwing moves on Marilyn?" he asked.

"Just a good friend." Chaiten settled into his chair with a preoccupied expression. "He was part of my unit in Vietnam. A big part."

Chaiten's companion watched over the rim of his glass for a few minutes. Then, when the couple on the far side of the room began making their way toward the door, he pushed back his chair and came to his feet.

The movement brought Chaiten out of his thoughts. "Where the hell are you going?"

The younger man nodded in Todd's direction, slapping an open palm with the ball of his fist. "Marilyn's pretty tight with one of my friends. I think I'd better show pretty boy over there it's not such a good idea to move in."

Chaiten stretched a leg under the table and kicked back his friend's chair, waving him into it with a shake of his head. "Sit down, Conway."

Conway was indignant. "Why the hell should I?"

Chaiten leaned across the table, lowering his voice for emphasis. "Because you can't count the ways that pretty boy over there could tie your ass in a knot."

The skin around Todd's knee was white and puckered in the dim light of the bedroom, and the girl ran her hand over it with a sharp intake of breath. "You poor man. Were you in an accident?"

Todd laced an arm under her breasts and swept her gently back down onto the bed. "I burned it as a child," he said. Then he covered her mouth with his, rubbing lightly between her thighs with the fingers of his free hand.

"Oh, God." She shut her eyes, opening her legs slightly against the motion of his hand. "I can't believe I'm doing this."

"Marilyn," Todd said, remembering her name. Then he shifted his weight and entered her, increasing the tempo of his movements in time with her response. He had no difficulty in remaining hard, but he envied the pleasure reflected in her open moaning. It had been five years, but there was still a second woman in the room every time he made love.

A clock with a luminous dial stood on her night table, and he saw that it was still early evening. If he hurried, he realized he could be home before ten. Sleep would be difficult enough without allowing himself the luxury of resting a few hours in her bed.

Clement reached his home around nine-thirty. On the nights that Kara taught, he preferred to work late himself so that both of them could eat a meal together. It was close to ten before he began to feel at all apprehensive, and he put down the paper he had been reading in the living room and climbed the stairs to knock on Todd's door.

"Todd? Where did your mother say she was?"

"She's going to be late. I left you a note." Todd's voice came to him through the additional barrier of his bathroom door.

Clement leaned into the room. "I saw the note. But what did she say on the phone? Just that she was going to be late?"

"Oh." Clement heard the rush of the shower as Todd opened the door to the bathroom, and then his voice rose above the water in a shout. "She said that dinner was in the oven. Just heat it up with the gas on low."

"That's all she said?"

"That's all."

Sam remained in the doorway. "We don't have gas," he said.

"What?"

He raised his voice to the level of his son's. "Was she calling from school?"

"I guess. Why?"

But Clement was already moving toward the kitchen. He opened the door to the oven to confirm what he suspected. It was empty. Then he leaned back against the counter and put a hand to his face. It was possible for Kara to be late, but it was unlikely. And the only reason she would deliberately leave instructions that made no sense would be if she were being held against her will. He glanced anxiously in the direction of Todd's room where the sound of the water had stopped. Then he turned and hurried toward the door to the garage.

When Kara put down the phone, the old man remained behind her, and she could feel the pressure of a gun in the small of her back. He placed a hand behind her head, and she bent down obediently until her head and shoulders were pressed awkwardly against the top of her desk. "Put your hands behind your back," he ordered, and when she responded, he looped them tightly together with something he must have produced from his pocket.

Then, still keeping a position directly behind her, he drew her into an upright position by the back of her hair. "I'm going to turn you around," he warned, "and when I do, I want your eyes to be shut." Kara nodded, and when she was pulled around, she heard a small tearing sound before his touch moved across her face, pressing an adhesive covering of some kind over her eyes. His hands were away long enough to push into his pockets a final time, and then they were brushing against the sides of her hair. There was a brief pressure against the bridge of her nose, and then he stepped away.

"Those are sunglasses," he announced. "No one can tell you can't see, but it's a good thing to keep in mind." He pulled the flap of her blouse from her waistband, and something cold made brief contact with her skin. "There's a knife if you yell for help. I could be away before anyone even knew what happened." Kara responded with an exaggerated nod to show that she understood. "Good," he said. Then he put an arm around her and pushed her in the direction of the door.

*   *   *

Sam arrived at the high school less than forty-five minutes after Kara had been led into the night. As he hurried toward the main entrance, he saw the wagon parked near the street, and he wondered if he had overreacted. A black man with the uniform of a maintenance worker was just approaching the center door.

"Excuse me," Sam called out, hurrying up the steps behind him. "Have you seen my wife? Her class ends at eight, but I think she's working late."

"I'm late muhself. Damn doors was locked, so I had to fetch a key." He pushed into the building, motioning for Sam to follow. "Know where her room is?"

Sam was already moving down the hall. "I can find it," he called out over his shoulder, and he trotted the short distance to her studio. It was the only room marked by an open door, and the darkened interior immediately renewed his fear. When he located the lights, the orderly appearance of the room told him nothing, so he made a brief survey of her personal items, checking the closet to see if her street clothes were missing.

It was not until he was standing over her desk that something grated under his heel, and he stooped down to find her ring. It was set with the small diamond he had given her for their engagement, and it confirmed everything he had feared from the start. It was the most obvious reason for a robbery, but if Vera had been waiting for her, Kara might have managed to slip it off before being taken from the building.

"Find her?" The maintenance man peered at him from the darkness of the hallway.

Sam shook his head. "No, but I'd like to look around. Her car's still in the parking lot."

"Mm." The janitor snapped off the lights and accompanied Sam in the direction of the entrance. "She coulda' been stuck. Some lady was gettin' into a car when I come the first time. Maybe she got ride from a friend."

Sam stopped and turned, resisting the impulse to shake him

by the shoulders. "That might have been her. Did you see what she looked like?"

"Couldn't tell from where I was. Couldn't see neither of them."

Clement worked his hands against his sides. "What about the car. Did you happen to notice that?"

The janitor grinned. "Shit, yeah. A white Camaro, same as my old lady's."

Kara counted to herself from the time they left the high school. He had put her on the passenger side of the front seat and locked the front door, but except for asking her to sit normally, he kept silent for the entire ride. He might have deliberately confused her by doubling back on parts of the trip, but from the time that Kara calculated, as well as the unmistakable sounds of a major highway, she felt that they had taken a fairly direct route to Miami.

That made sense. There were innumerable places in the city for Vera and her accomplice to live inconspicuously, and if they planned to take her even further, Miami provided more than a few alternate means of transportation. Kara focused on the most obvious ways they might exploit her kidnapping, preparing herself for resistance or possible escape. She had put her fear aside the minute she saw the gun and realized what was happening to her. Fear was useful as a warning device; it had no place in the coming test of wills.

They would want what Sam had buried in his past, and they would threaten to kill her in order to get it. She doubted that they would. Vera was amoral, but there was nothing to be gained from Sam by committing murder except revenge, and if she sought that at all, it would wait until she had what she wanted. Kara could only hope that Sam would not weaken and give it to her. She knew that she herself would not.

When they had been on the road for what seemed to her roughly an hour and a half, a series of turns indicated that they had left the highway, and less than fifteen minutes later, the tires of the car made a crunching sound on the shoulder of a road that jolted her with the undulations of uneven pavement. The car came to a halt, and Kara's door was opened from her side.

"Not a word," the driver warned, and Kara nodded as he guided her over the curb and onto the sidewalk. She felt the rise and fall of slate beneath her feet, and off in the distance, there was the sound of a dog barking and the occasional drone of a passing car. Kara reasoned that they were probably in one of the poorer sections of the city, and the brush of an undergrowth against her ankles as they left the sidewalk confirmed her suspicions.

She envisioned the ramshackle homes of the black neighborhoods she had seen so many times from the advantage of the highway, wondering if she was in casual view of people lounging on porches less than a hundred yards away. Then there was the sound of a door being unlocked, and after a few tentative steps across a hardwood floor, four flights of stairs with the hand of her captor guiding her on the small of her back.

Kara changed her original guess from a private home to an apartment building, but her concentration was broken when she was pulled to a halt and her hands were freed, only to be bound again in front of her. Then she was led through another door and nudged onto the softness of a mattress. The old man gripped her by the legs and shifted her weight to a horizontal position. "Lie down," he ordered, and her arms were drawn over her head and bound to a metal support. He did the same to her feet, until she was secured along the length of the bed.

For a moment, Kara thought of her sister under the body of the German soldier, but the man rose from the end of the mattress and his footsteps receded into the hall. She reminded herself then that there was a point to her captivity this time, a logic beyond routine brutalization. It was an advantage she found difficult to comprehend. Another set of footsteps sounded over the shuffling gait of the old man in the hall outside the door. Then the door itself was thrown open, and a woman's voice came to her, nearing the edge of the bed.

"So this is what Sam found himself? Something young and eager for my money?" Her hands closed on the collar of Kara's blouse and tore it open. Against the silence of the room, a button hit the wall and bounced across the floor. "He says he still has it, Mrs. Kara, so you should be able to tell us where it is. Right?" A finger hooked the halter of her bra, and the back of the knife squeezed tightly against her chest as the blade slit the binding cleanly in two. Vera yanked it away, cupping a breast in either hand. "Does he love you, dearie? We love you, too." She clawed deeply into the white skin, twisting her arms sharply at the same time.

Kara's mouth opened in the agony of a scream, and she arched against the binding of the bed. "Please, no!" she wailed. Pig, she thought, you should have started with the knife.

Todd was sitting on the living-room couch in his underwear when Sam returned from the school. He looked up casually from the magazine that was open in front of him, but his eyes never left his father's face. "Find her?"

"No. Her car was stuck, so she left with some friends. They must have stopped off for something to eat on the way home." He had prepared the lie carefully on the drive back. "There haven't been any calls?"

"Not a thing." Todd rose and stretched. Then he disappeared down the hall in the direction of his bedroom.

The moment Sam heard his door close, he hurried into the kitchen. While he heated enough water for a large thermos of coffee, he systematically searched the drawers and cabinets for a weapon of some kind. He finally settled on a large kitchen knife with a plastic handle, cursing his failure during the past week to make the final commitment of a gun. He had never deluded himself into thinking that Vera would simply go away, but he had counted on the warning of another contact before she was driven to the point of violence. He had not been prepared, and Kara, not he, was paying the price for it.

When he had finished preparing his coffee, he wrapped the

thermos and the knife in a brown supermarket bag and carried them out to the car. He had transferred the home phone to his answering service, planning to call in every half hour, although he doubted that Vera would contact him until morning at the earliest. She would want him to weaken under a night of uncertainty before making her demands. If she did call, he would know about it almost immediately, and Todd would not be in a position to intercept the message at home.

But Todd surprised Sam before he backed out of the driveway.

"She's not coming home, is she?" he demanded, appearing suddenly in the rectangle of the car window.

Clement noticed that he had dressed. Todd rested both hands on the door of the Porsche, peering down at his father. There was an alertness in his expression, a quality of concern that Sam had never seen before. "She's fine," he persisted. "I told you, she's with some friends."

"The same neighborly crowd that blew up the wagon, right, Dad?" Todd walked purposefully around the front of the car and slipped into the seat on the passenger side. "Can I know where we're going?" he asked as he swung his door shut. "We'd stand a better chance if we both had some idea of what to expect."

Clement stared at a pistol Todd placed on the seat between them. It had the square profile of the handguns he associated with the military. "I didn't know you had that," he said.

"I didn't know there were people out there who wanted to kidnap my mother."

Clement dropped his gaze. "There were things we wanted to keep from you," he said in a voice just above a whisper. "Things that were over. We didn't think anything like this would ever happen."

The driveway hummed with the sound of a thousand insects. For a moment, the two of them sat there and listened to the night, profiled against the sweep of the headlights. Then Todd put a hand on his father's shoulder. "Will she be all right if we find her?"

Clement let out his breath with a sound of resignation. "I

don't know. I don't think they would do anything . . . final. But
I never dreamt they would do this." He reached up and covered
the hand on his shoulder with his own. "I found her ring at
school. I think she was taken from there in a white Camaro, but
I can't even be sure if it was them that the janitor saw." He
shifted his weight and twisted the ignition key, bringing the car
to life. "You can come, but it's unfair to you. There's so much we
have to tell you to make you understand. I wanted your mother
to wait until I had died."

"You can wait forever," Todd said with feeling. He smiled
tightly, thinking of his own furies. "I fought a whole year without understanding why; I can get through a night."

Clement put the car in gear, twisting around in his seat to
back them down the driveway. "I'm glad it's out," he said, as
much to himself as to Todd. Then his tone changed, and he
looked to either side of the street without committing the car to a
direction. "It's a woman," he announced. "She's down here
from up north, and she has at least one helper. You should know
that much before we begin. Not that I have any idea of where we
should start. Any suggestions?"

"Well, if they're from up north, they probably aren't keeping
her in Plantation. Let's try some of the back streets in Lauderdale."

Sam nodded, turning down the corners of his mouth. "We
don't have a chance in hell, but it's better than waiting at
home." He raised his watch to his face. "Ten more minutes and
we'll check in with the service to see if they've called. We won't
waste more than a few hours on this effort. Then we can alternate shifts by the phone back home. Unless, of course, we get
lucky."

The guards at the camp introduced a game the children
learned to imitate, and eventually to play among themselves for
the privilege of enough to eat. Kara had not thought back on it
for many years, but lying there in the night with her breasts still
swollen and throbbing from the savaging of Vera's hands, the

association was inevitable. Ingrid's face came back to her first, before her name did. Then the gray outlines of the camp, and finally the numbing state of existence that was necessary to survive those years.

Alone in the darkness, Kara smiled bitterly at the secret knowledge she shared with a handful of people, the ones who had lived to make the camps a part of their past. There was no longer anything that could be experienced by her that would shock, nothing that could break her will in the arena others called the real world. For over three years, she had lived in hell itself.

The road there had been paved by the good intentions of a world that normally protects children from emotions and events they can not possibly hope to understand. In 1938, the English and the French stood by while the unthinkable happened, beginning with the German annexation of Austria. Kara's father had been a prominent doctor in Vienna, and within months of the occupation, he was no longer able to practice medicine, except to treat fellow Jews in a limited and restricted capacity. In time, a program of Aryanization was instituted, and the businesses of their friends and relatives were taken over by self-appointed representatives of the Nazi party, many of whom had been colleagues or even neighbors.

Each time her family had accepted the latest decree as the final indignity, the hatred would flair up again, feeding on itself until the city they had known for a lifetime had become a different place, unfamiliar and menacing. In the end, it struck out at them directly, and there was killing and looting in the streets, as though the last of the old order had finally been reversed, and citizens were encouraged to destroy to satisfy the new laws.

Sam's face materialized behind the binding over her eyes, and Kara thought of his guilt in the agonizing perspective of her memory. His were such small sins. They paled to the point of disappearing in the light of what she had seen, and she loved him again for the man he had been. Every circumstance that surrounded her husband gave him ample opportunity to justify what he had done, but he focused on what he knew to be right, refusing the comfort of changing his standards.

As a child, Kara had learned in months what others realize after the truth of a lifetime. She was on the earth alone, and those that surrounded her would only help her as far as the borders of their own self-interest. But not Sam. He would have been one of the few coming out into the streets during the horror to stand with the victims, becoming a victim himself. That was the tragedy of her man. To consider himself evil when his life had shown that at worst, he could only bend in that direction, ultimately straightening with the force of his own humanity. Unless he broke in the process, she admitted to herself, remembering the struggle she had now come to share.

The thought put Ingrid before her again, this time more vividly than before. She was standing with her feet planted firmly apart, a scowl of obstinacy on her mottled face, her fists raised in readiness. A visitation to remind Kara that there was yet another barrier to be broken.

In 1939, the Nazis established the Central Office for Jewish Emigration, and for the first time since the occupation, her parents allowed themselves some hope. A few Jewish leaders were released from detention, helping to run a program that promised to deliver Jews from Austria and other occupied countries that were no longer considered their native lands. Her father applied, and they were accepted, boarding a train in a matter of weeks with their few remaining possessions under their arms.

They were transported out of Vienna as promised, but their particular group eventually found themselves outside Munich instead of crossing the border to one of the free countries. In time, they learned that they had been delivered to a concentration camp. It was the first to be established in Nationalist Socialist Germany, and the guards that separated her and her sister from her parents called it Dachau.

For almost a year, Kara's eighteen-year-old sister bought them time and the privilege of subsistance food by leaving the barracks at night with one of the guards. That arrangement ended with his transfer, and by that time, her sister's looks had been worn down by the effects of camp life, making her indistinguishable from the other women. One morning, after Eleanor had managed to arrange a meeting with two soldiers from another part of the camp, Kara woke to find her sister still missing from her cot. When she had not returned by that afternoon, Kara knew that she would never see her again.

Kara had the well-shaped limbs of a dancer, and she had always been strong beyond her years, but she was thirteen at the time, and not yet fully developed. If she were to survive, she knew she would have to find a different method than the one chosen by her sister. She eventually saw that opportunity in the hitting game, which the older children of the camp had adopted from the guards. Two soldiers would agree to exchange blows, each one progressively harder than the last, until one of them was knocked from his feet. There was a place between the fence and one of the barracks where the older children gathered when they were not working, and as they came to reflect the brutality surrounding them by playing the game with increasing severity, the guards, and even some of the officers, began to wager on the contests.

The girls' circle was dominated by Ingrid, and as the months went by, she actually managed to grow fatter and more formidable from the food bestowed on her by the admiring Germans. She looked no older than fifteen, but she was close to six feet tall, and she had the thick arms and heavy shoulders of an athlete. Kara watched her batter challengers into the mud of the circle for weeks before she felt prepared to make her move. A few of the contests had been close in their outcome, and in each case, she noticed that the larger girl was out of breath when she met the next challenger. Kara decided her chances would be greatly increased if she could manage to enter the circle during one of those intervals.

She also broke each game down into a series of blows, and in time, she began to see patterns in Ingrid's movements, as though she were studying the choreography of a new ballet. When the barracks were busiest, or where she would be ignored in a corner of the busy yard, she planted her feet firmly and shifted her upper body in a series of maneuvers designed to avoid imaginary blows.

But the game was not a ballet, and the afternoon that Kara decided to play, Ingrid had come close to killing her opponent. It had been a long contest, with the champion faltering slightly at the start. For that reason, when she began to gain the edge over the tall blond who had challenged her, Ingrid prolonged the contest with a series of slaps that sounded across the mud of the yard, numbing the other girl to the point of a stupor and provoking the cheers of the guards. When the blond could do no more than maintain her balance by holding out her arms, Ingrid balled her hand into a fist and caught her in the nostrils, sending her backwards into the mud with a crunching sound that could only have meant the breaking of bone.

Psychologically, it was the worst time to step into the circle, but Kara knew she might never again have the same physical advantage, and when the cheering had died down, and the other girl had been dragged senseless from the ring, she placed herself across from Ingrid, where the champion looked at her with a mixture of surprise and contempt. When Kara held her ground, the gathering fell silent, and after Ingrid had shrugged in the direction of the smiling guards, she delivered a sweeping blow that missed Kara's bobbing head with enough force to send the heavier girl off balance. Kara countered with a sharp punch to Ingrid's exposed ribs, and with a scream of outrage, the champion just managed to gain her balance, responding with a rain of punches that eliminated any real chance for a response.

But Kara had no desire to hit back. For close to five minutes, she feinted and ducked, kept on her feet by sheer adrenalin whenever a random blow made contact with her head or shoulders. The cheering died down, and in time, only the sound of Ingrid's breath could be heard, punctuated by grunts as her frustration caused her to expend more and more of her energy. The pattern of a blow for a blow had long been forgotten when

Kara suddenly bent her knees and landed a punch to Ingrid's neck that carried the leverage of her entire body.

Kara had used fear to sustain the frenzy of motion that had been her defense. She put it aside when she landed that first blow, exactly as though she had changed weapons. Her sister's face was before her then, and the painful image of her parents. The anger came on cue, and a murmuring went up around the yard as the smaller girl bent her opponent with three sharp jabs to her temple. Ingrid managed to catch her in the breast then, but her punches had lost their power, and the ineffective blow merely served as a reminder.

When the older girl brought back her arm a second time, Kara went for the swelling beneath her smock, driving into it with a force that caused her opponent to call out in pain. From that point on, Kara was relentless, making Ingrid pay for her age with a vulnerability she herself did not yet have.

In the end, when the other girl had resorted to holding her arms in front of her breasts, Kara was ready. She split Ingrid's lip and bloodied her nose before she managed to center in on her jaw, but when she did, she caught it with the full force of her fist, and her opponent lost consciousness immediately, toppling face forward into the mud.

The onlookers were delirious, and Kara smiled in response to their cheers, making a point of limping as they helped her out of the ring. If she faked an injury, she knew that they would allow her a few days' rest before she would have to fight again. Her well-being was now more important to them than it had been only minutes before.

While she would never be considered human, she had at least managed to achieve the status of a highly valued animal.

The old man came into her room some time during the small hours of the morning. She knew that it was him from the sound of his footsteps. It was a halting gait, one in which he dragged his feet; not like Todd, whose handicap was physical, but as though he had some inner weakness brought on by the infirmity of age.

Kara pictured him again in the dim light of the school hallway. His skin had been white enough to outline his arms, and his face had the sort of unhealthy pallor that suggested he led an existence that was completely hidden from the sun.

"I hope you decide on helping us," he said softly. "Not so much for me, but mostly on account of Vera." At first, Kara had envisioned Vera standing silently in the doorway while the old man tried a different approach with her, but there was an absentminded quality in his tone that made her sense the visit had been his idea alone.

"She's been hard at it the last few years," he went on, "and I think she's getting tired. She shouldn't have to work, you know. You can tell from her looks that she's different from most women. She got—" He hesitated, searching for a word, and as he did, he slipped a hand tentatively under the hem of her skirt, "—majesty. She's always been special, so you can't blame her about being angry about working as a nurse. We used to talk about the stash after the war." The hand moved with a light rubbing motion over her thighs. "And years later, we'd always bring it up when things weren't going too well. Leave it to Vera to find Sam. And you."

Kara flexed her buttocks against the cushion of the mattress and considered what she would do if he continued to touch her. One of the new arrivals at Dachau had been taken for a prostitute, but she had been returned the same day with a change of assignment. When Kara asked her how she had managed it, she told her that while the first soldier was on top of her, she had opened her bowels in the middle of the act. She had taken her life into her hands, but the men in line behind him had exploded with laughter, and since she was only fifteen, she was spared that duty indefinitely. Kara considered that alternative as she felt the edge of her skirt being pushed up toward her waist, but the quickened breathing she heard as he exposed her gave her another idea.

"I've had the good life," he was saying, "so of course, it doesn't bother me as much. Not that I wouldn't want to take care of her better than I do. But I'm disabled." For a moment, the hand stopped its motion. "Not that you can see it. There's a lot of damage done that you can't see. The guns can do that, without even hitting you."

His voice grew softer, and the words came haltingly during the recollection. "Sometimes the whole deck moves if there are enough of them going off, and you can't even hear what's coming in at you. It's not like it is on the shore. There's no place to go on a ship, and the fools that you're shooting at don't even care. You can't stop them when they *want* to die, their planes coming right down on top of you half the time, even after they've been hit. You can't fight craziness like that, except by getting away from it."

Kara moaned appreciatively, and the sound brought his hand to life again, the fingers slipping briefly over the V of her panties. "I could have had it all when things were over, if I hadn't left. The store. In time, a whole string of stores. I was young then, and able to handle a business. The same as Sam. I don't hate him the way Vera does, but she's right, you know. He owes us." Kara controlled the urge to struggle as he pulled back the band of her panties. She knew that he was looking at her. "That's all we want, is what he owes us."

He fell silent, pulling her panties in a roll over her hips. She raised her weight from the mattress, allowing him to slide the underwear down around the binding of her ankles. "It's so warm, being young," he said, running his hand along her legs until it had settled between them.

Kara parted her knees slightly and let her breath escape in a sigh. The hand was withdrawn then, but seconds later, she heard the working of his zipper, followed by the sound of a belt buckle hitting the floor. He mounted her awkwardly, grunting against the barrier of her upraised knees.

"Please," Kara whispered, working her legs in an attempt to part them. "I can do nothing with the rope." She felt his weight shift off the bed before he hesitated. "Just the legs," she persisted. "For you."

It had not been a tight binding, and when he removed the rope, she stretched gratefully, finding that her limbs had retained their full range of motion. The action provoked him, and he lowered himself onto the bed, covering her naked body with his until the buttons on his shirt pushed against her swollen breasts and his breath crashed in her ear.

She wanted both his hands to be free, so when he reached down to enter her, she was forced to make her move at once in order to avoid trapping his arm. In a sense, the binding of her arms was an advantage. She used the anchor of the headboard to shift her weight suddenly, pulling her legs out from under his in one continuous motion. It was critical to squeeze the air out of his lungs before he could cry out, and she grunted with exertion as her legs scissored around his waist, locking shut against the clasp of her ankles.

There was a brief choking sound forced from his mouth, and then his face fell against hers, growing warm with the rush of his blood. "You will die," she announced, and she arched further into the mattress, closing tightly on the softness of his middle with the full power of a dancer's quadriceps. "You will die," she repeated. Then, in a voice of command, "My hands, give me my hands!"

His head moved away from her, and she knew that he was looking behind her at the rope. She could feel the strength draining from her body, and she realized that she would weaken if he continued to delay. She had only the use of her head, and she brought it up from the mattress, finding his neck and capturing the skin there between her teeth. He made an animal sound of protest somewhere in the back of his throat, but his hands shot forward, pulling frantically at the rope behind her. He worked with the speed of desperation, but even after she felt a release in the tension holding her arms, she continued to flex her legs. The use of her hands seemed to renew her strength, and she tore the tape from her eyes, blinking at the shock of an early morning light.

Then she began the process of shifting her position, and they rolled like lovers across the shadow of the bed until she was on top of him, allowing the weight of her body to share some of the pressure being applied by her muscles. She used the same rope that had bound her hands to gag him, pushing a section of her severed bra into his mouth before pulling the knot tight enough to force his lips apart. Only then did she relax her legs slightly, allowing him to draw breath in hoarse, sniffling sounds between his nostrils.

Her breasts fell against the open flaps of her blouse and her skirt was still rolled into a bulky band around her waist, but she lashed him firmly to the bed that had held her before she thought about her clothing. When she had rolled down her skirt and fastened the remaining buttons on her blouse, she located her sneakers in a corner of the room and crossed over to the window.

She knew from the surrounding buildings that she was right about having been taken to Miami. But she was wrong in guessing that she was in one of the poorer residential neighborhoods. The immediate area was older, but most of the buildings had several stories, and toward one end of the street below, she caught the rectangle of a loading dock. Everything she saw was from over the obstacle of a lower roof, and she realized that the room she had occupied faced some sort of a courtyard. She saw the obvious last of all.

Breaking her view into a series of wrought-iron rectangles was the guardrail of a fire escape, and without hesitation, she pushed at the window, relieved to find that it slid open without any resistance. She thought of locking the door behind her, but a glance over her shoulder revealed no way to fasten it from the inside. In any case, she knew she might have very little time. Vera might have been as close as the next room, or returning to the building with the growing light of day. She stepped out onto the platform of the fire escape.

The structure was shaky, and in places it actually pulled away from the stucco of the wall, but it carried her safely down to the next platform before presenting any problems. Kara had counted four flights of stairs when she entered the building, and she assumed that she had stepped out of a second-story window. But after she descended to the next floor, she found that two more rows of windows separated her from the overgrown courtyard below. The platform she stood on held the sliding ladder and fulcrum that terminate most fire escapes, but she was not sure if the mechanism still functioned, and if it did, whether the ladder would slide into place on the ground or simply fall away from its corroded fastenings, dropping the remaining two stories below.

A glimpse of public sidewalk between the buildings that made up the courtyard decided her, and she leaned out from the platform, pulling at the rails of the ladder in an attempt to launch it toward the ground. Either the cable that held it to the framework of the fire escape had rusted to its pulley, or she was simply too light to overcome the resistance of the counterweight. In either case, the ladder remained where it was. She looked up at the window of the room she had just escaped and resigned herself to taking a chance. Settling down onto the metal floor of the platform, she pulled on her sneakers and allowed herself a few moments' rest.

Then she came to her feet and swung her weight over the guardrail and onto the ladder before she could hesitate. The downward jolt she had braced against never came, and she continued to cling to the ladder, desperately searching for an alternative. Finally, she tightened the grip of her hands and lifted her feet from the rung she was standing on, coming back down on it with the force of a jump. There was a brief scraping sound, and the ladder suddenly slid into motion, throwing her against the rungs with the force of its descent. Her eyes were tightly closed, so she could not see the ground rushing up to meet her.

Todd woke up screaming under Sam's touch. He had fallen asleep on the couch by the time the call came, and when Clement put down the phone, he expected to find Todd awakened by the ringing. But Todd's eyes remained shut, although his lids were fluttering. When Sam crossed the room and bent over him, he could hear him murmuring vaguely, as though he were arguing with someone in his sleep. He shook him gently by the shoulder, and then the body flew up at him from the couch. Sam found himself with his arms around Todd's shoulders, as much to prevent himself from being thrown backwards as to restrain his son. Todd ceased struggling in that position, and as he did, the screams quieted, changing in pitch as he came gradually to tears.

"It's all right," Sam said softly. He had not held his son since his early childhood, and he made an awkward job of patting his back. "They just called. She's all right."

"She's dead. I saw her die."

He continued to shake in Sam's arms, and Clement shifted his position, finding his son's eyes wavering on the edge of opening. "She's alive, son. Wake up, you've been dreaming."

Todd gradually became aware of where he was, wiping at his eyes and stepping back to orient himself with a shake of his head. "It wasn't a dream," he said thickly. He focused on his father and blinked his eyes. "Did you say you heard?" he asked in a voice that was suddenly normal.

Clement watched the awareness come back into his expression and nodded. "She's fine. The Miami police called. She turned herself in."

"She turned herself in? Is she all right?"

"She sounded fine over the phone, but there wasn't much she could say under the circumstances. I think she told them her car had been stolen. The important thing is that she's alive and well. We'll have to wait until we bring her home to find out what really happened."

Todd swallowed and sank back down onto the couch. "Thank God." He stared at the floor, lost in his own thoughts until he noticed that Sam had gathered his wallet and keys from the table by the phone. "I'm going with you," he demanded, coming to his feet and hurrying toward the door.

Clement looked at him, remembering what he had seen in his face only a few moments earlier. Then he laced an arm around his shoulders, pressing against him in a brief embrace. "I want you to," he said.

"You bastard."

The old man rolled his eyes to find Vera standing in the doorway.

"She hasn't been gone ten minutes, and you're already dead to the world. She must have given you some workout on that bed." She crossed the room and leaned over him, yanking roughly at the rope holding his gag in place.

When she had removed the clot of moist material from his mouth, he drew his breath in gasps before he found his voice. "She's gone! I heard her leave through the window!"

"I know she's gone!" She glared down at him. "I *wanted* her to escape, even if I hadn't planned on your little game." Her glance shifted to the open window. "We weren't going to get anything out of that one. I could tell that after the first ten minutes. But you, you got a few things from her, didn't you?"

He looked away from her. "She caught me off guard," he muttered.

Vera grimaced as she rifled through the contents of her pocketbook. "Oh? Did she take you from behind and pull your pants off you? That must have been quite a trick, sneaking up on you like that while she was tied to the bed."

"You never want to make love," he said sullenly.

"Make love?" She crouched down to his level, whispering hoarsely inches away from his ear. "In another hour, that bitch is going to be home again, and Sam is going to know we're in this thing for keeps. Do you realize what that means?"

The old man shook his head.

"That means he's going to make his move. We're a day or two away from a million dollars, and you want to squeeze someone's ass!"

"You think he's going to give it to us?"

"Either that or he's going to take it and run. The important thing is that he has to get it from wherever it's hidden. And when he does, I'll be there to collect."

He saw her take the car keys from her handbag. "You're not leaving, are you?"

She turned and strode to the door. "I have to watch the house. He could go for it as early as today. I'll be back when I'm sure he's not up to anything."

"What about me?" he called after her, straining to raise his head from the bed.

She paused, looking in at him from the hall. "If he makes a run for it, we're both in for a hell of a fight, so you'd better remember to keep your mind on what you're doing. For now, you can lie there and think about that with your pants down."

She turned and disappeared in the direction of the stairs without shutting the door.

While Kara lay asleep in her bedroom, Sam and Todd remained downstairs in the living room, unable to sleep after the ordeal of their long wait. Sam stayed inside himself, but his eyes were narrowed, and his hands opened and closed on the arms of his wing chair. It was the first time that they had been alone since the drive back from Miami, and Todd surprised himself by finding that he wanted to break the silence.

"Are you angry?"

Sam looked up at him without changing his posture. "I'm furious. Do you know what I thought about all the way back? Your gun. You can't know how much I want to use it."

There was an edge to his voice that Todd had never heard before. "She said they didn't hurt her."

"That's what she said. If they did do anything, she won't let me know about it until she feels I can accept it. The war was over for five years before she told me everything that happened in that prison camp."

"I didn't know that." Todd shook his head. "How could she have kept all that inside for so long?"

"Are we any different?" For a moment, Sam seemed as surprised by the question as Todd. Then he pushed to the edge of his chair. "You could have lost your mother last night, and you wouldn't have even known why. Because I couldn't face telling you. You still don't know why, but that's going to change along with a few other things I've delayed for the last forty years." His eyes remained locked on Todd's. "Do you hate me?"

Todd had already been unsettled by Clement's tone, and he literally drew his head back in the face of the question without offering an answer.

"Last night I told you we couldn't go to the police because of some of the things I'd done in the past. Did you hate me for that?"

Something relaxed in Todd's expression, as though he had begun to understand the openness of his father's questioning. "No, I was almost glad." He found Clement's eyes. "I don't mean about the trouble. It's just that all my life I'd always thought you'd never done anything wrong." He smiled tightly. "God, I couldn't even think of a thing you'd done to *me* that I could complain about."

"Is that bad?"

Todd shook his head. "Hell no, of course not. It's just hard to live with sometimes. It made me feel pretty bad about myself."

"About the war, you mean."

Todd looked away from him. "I didn't say that."

"You didn't have to. That's the only thing you could feel bad about. I was around for the first twenty-two years." Clement lowered his head to find Todd's eyes. "I asked you before if you hated me because I'd broken the law."

"I told you I didn't."

"But I can't feel that way about you? No matter what you've done?"

Todd's body tensed, and he folded his hands, pressing them slowly against each other. "You don't know what went on over there."

"And you didn't know why we couldn't call the police last night, but you gave me the benefit of the doubt, didn't you?"

"You're my father, for God's sake!"

"You're my son. Were you dreaming about the war when you woke up screaming?"

Todd looked into the fold of his hands. "I'm not sure. There was a lot on my mind."

"I know. I put it there." Clement crossed over to the couch where he was sitting. "But that wasn't what you were seeing in your sleep. Something's working at you from the inside, and you'll never be yourself again if you can't let it out. I've learned that these last few days, at this end of my life. I'd like to be around long enough to see you free of it while you're young."

The warning startled Todd into looking up. "Be around? What are you planning on doing?"

"I'm going to face something I've been looking away from. I wish you could know how that feels."

Todd pressed his hands to his head. "God, what do you want from me?"

"Nothing for me. I thought we'd lost something between us, but I found out last night that we haven't, and that makes everything I'm going through a lot easier to take. Now all you have to do is settle with yourself."

"It's not that easy."

Clement's expression softened. "I know. It's taken me forty years. Just realize you're loved, and with reason. That was the beginning for me. Now I'm ready for whatever's coming."

For a long time Todd remained silent. "I'll be all right," he finally said in a subdued voice. "I just don't think my problems are important now. This thing isn't over yet, and you're not going to face it alone."

"I have to."

Todd ignored the comment. "Are these people trying to kill you?"

"They might, if they don't get what they want."

"What do they want?"

Clement came to his feet. "I think it would be harder on me but easier on you if I started from the beginning. Could you use some coffee?"

Todd nodded, following him into the kitchen. When they had warmed the remnants of the previous night's coffee and seated themselves across the table from each other, Sam lifted his shoulders in a shrug. "It's hard to begin after all these years, especially with your own son." He raised his eyes to meet Todd's attentive gaze. "I guess I should start by saying I lied about what I did during the war."

Chapter Eight

Miami did more than separate Sam from Newark. In a dreamlike sequence of events, it separated him from himself. Away from Max and Vera, away from the area that had made up the landscape of his entire life until that time, he was isolated from everything except the business he was conducting, and in the end, he was unnerved by what he had become.

In the fall of 1944, the end of the war appeared imminent, even to the enemies of the Allies. The Germans had lost their grip on Poland, and in the Pacific, newly won bases in the Marianas allowed B-29 bombers a long enough range to bring the war directly to Tokyo. But with Eddie's death, Sam had ceased to orient himself toward that ultimate victory, moving deeper into the underground of drug dealing as a refuge from the war as well as a means of making the money he found he could no longer live without. As it turned out, he found the war in Miami, too, haunting him in a different form, and adding just as directly to his sense of guilt.

He had taken a hotel room on the outskirts of Miami Beach, and since he was not due to meet his contact until the early evening, he indulged himself by smoking in his room. He was

165

determined to curb his growing use of marijuana, but he was nervous about the impending deal, and he counted on no longer being high by the time he met Dick Cato.

Sam did not know what sort of person to expect. He was no longer working with butchers and businessmen who were merely bending the law, and Max had told him about some of the people operating in Miami as well as the places. Many of the names he mentioned were already familiar from the newspapers of the Thirties: Lansky, Costello, and the most famous ground-breaker in the thriving area, Al Capone. "I drew the line," Max said. "They took what they learned during Prohibition and ran it into big business."

Sam looked over at the bed in his room and wondered if he were any different from the mobsters. A leather money belt lay on the linen coverlet with six pouches evenly spaced around its circumference. Three contained the payment for Waters' delivery; the others were packed with all of the money he could raise for the first and final deal he would make for himself. He was also wearing a gun: a short .35-caliber strapped to the small of his back that would be concealed by the drape of his jacket. Waters had told him it would be a good idea simply because he would be carrying large amounts of cash, but Sam wondered if Dick Cato, his contact, would also be armed, and if guns were common among the men around him.

For the first time in his experience, the reefer did nothing to lessen his misgivings, although another anxious glance at his watch confirmed the fact that he was heavily under its influence. He had been in his room less than an hour, but the convoluted sense of time that affected him when he was smoking made him feel as though he had been waiting for the better part of the afternoon. He worked slowly to his feet and crossed over to the bed. He would get dressed and explore the Miami Beach that Max had described to him. If he couldn't keep from worrying about the coming evening, he was afraid he would change his mind before the dealer arrived.

He drove cautiously to Miami Beach, remembering the concealed gun as well as his own impaired ability to control the car. What he found there left him in a state of paranoia that suggested he was the victim of a conspiracy involving nothing less than an entire city.

The first disturbing indication wavered at him through the heat rising from the borders of the sidewalks. A long column of soldiers in perfect marching order emerged suddenly and incongruously from the ornate facade of a luxury hotel. Sam pulled the Packard over to the curb, wondering why others in the crowded business district hadn't been attracted by the sight. For a moment, he thought that it might have existed only in his imagination. Then a jeep pulled up in front of him, and as he watched two Air Force officers climb out, he became aware of what was going on around him.

The streets were alive with men in uniform. Sam pulled away from the curb and drove slowly toward the center of town, staring at people in khaki who outnumbered civilians to the point where he felt his gray suit made him a conspicuous intruder. The military had moved in, he learned from one of the few women he saw who was not in uniform, and everything he observed that afternoon confirmed it. The White House Hotel was a school for cooks and bakers, the Evans served as an office for clerks and typists, while the Breakwater and most of the other resorts were merely posh barracks.

Sam looked numbly at men his age who would be moving on toward the war in a matter of weeks. An entire town had been converted for their purposes. Expensive shops had been closed, or had changed their contents to items that were within the means of enlisted personnel. The doors of a theater opened, only to let out a stream of cadets with notebooks under their arms. Sam guessed that they had been undergoing some kind of testing inside. Soldiers had their feet examined on Collins Avenue in offices that still displayed the markings of a local brokerage house, and officer candidates filed into cafeterias where the food had once been five dollars a plate.

Even away from the streets of the business district, he was

unable to escape the sight of men preparing for war. The swimmers in the pool of the Roney Plaza Hotel were arranged in rows, taking instructions from an officer overseeing the class from a diving board, and the beach itself was lined with soldiers in bathing suits performing calisthenics. From his car, Sam saw the greens of a local golf course dotted with uniforms surrounding some sort of demonstration, and when he reached Flamingo Park, where Max had told him the Phillies had once held their spring training, the grandstands had become a gallery of faceless recruits, staring mutely over the snouts of their gas masks at an instructor lecturing from the infield below them.

In the fading light of the day, Sam found it easy to believe they were staring at him. He turned from the sight and stepped back into his car, heading for the motel and the appointment with the dealer. Before he was clear of the area, he passed a final column of soldiers marching along the side of the road. They were singing a song he knew from his high school days but could not name. As he passed them, he remembered the sound of "The Star Spangled Banner" coming to him from the plant as he walked down Raymond Boulevard toward the enlistment station, and once again, with renewed bitterness, he realized that he had been deprived of the only experience that could possibly make him feel right about himself.

By the time he had reached the motel, he knew that something inside him was changing, that the guilt he had felt at Eddie's death had not been eliminated by his success, but merely obscured by it. He sat on a bench in front of the crescent-shaped driveway that fronted the motel office, remembering the person he had been when he and Maura had first learned of the war, and the sort of man he had become three years later, waiting for a contact with a pistol strapped to the small of his back.

A red convertible pulled up to the lobby, and Sam caught the tanned face of a young officer behind the windshield. As the man emerged from the car and crossed the driveway, there was enough resemblance between the two of them for Sam to reflect

bleakly that he might have been looking at himself if the circumstances in his life had only been slightly different.

The officer paused to survey the people around him before he
caught the color of the handkerchief that Sam had made a point
of putting in his lapel pocket.

"Sam?" he asked, breaking into a grin.

Sam hesitated before he came to his feet, momentarily taken
back by the greeting.

"Dick Cato," the other man announced. Still smiling, he displayed a neatly pressed blazer that lay draped from a hanger
over his shoulder. "Mind if I take a minute to change before we
leave? I've been running my tail off in this soldier suit all day."

Dick Cato was also blond, although he wore his hair brushed
back tightly against his scalp, and he was slimmer than Sam,
with a profile that seemed suited for the stylish outlines of his
clothing. He wore a handkerchief in his breast pocket that
matched the design of his tie, but there was nothing slick about
his appearance to suggest that he was involved in anything related to a life of crime. On the contrary, there was an openness in
his smile that seemed to epitomize everything that was positive
about being young. During the course of their ride, Cato discussed the opportunities in the Miami underground as though
he were no different than any other rising young businessman
with an eye to the future.

"This party is going to give you a chance to see some of the
people behind this town," he told Sam without taking his eyes
from the road, "and believe you me, there's a lot going on. You
know what the population's done down here in the last ten years
before the war? It's doubled." He turned off the main road and
the vegetation hung a ragged border around the arc of their
headlamps. Through the darkness of the trees, Sam caught rectangles of light, suggesting the windows of a large house.

When they emerged in a clearing the size of several city lots,
Cato banked the convertible behind at least forty other cars

clustered around a U-shaped driveway. The house they approached was built on a small rise of land, and its Victorian outlines reminded Sam more of the homes along the Jersey shore than the wealthy residences he had seen from his car during his drive through Florida.

"Chicago money," Cato announced, nodding meaningfully in the direction of a stuccoed facade with a sweeping front porch. "They don't build 'em like this anymore down here. I wouldn't mind owning the land, either, after the war."

"Has the war changed things down here?" Sam asked.

They were close enough to the porch lights for Sam to catch Cato's grimace. "Temporarily, but nobody's worried. Early on, the U-boats really fouled up the shipping in the straits. It was still boom city down here until the wreckage started washing up on the beaches. Not just oil and boats. I mean bodies, for Christ's sake, some of them burned as black as a crisp. We got one report after another that the Germans were landing. It didn't matter that they never came. The rumors were enough to play hell with the tourists. Anyway, the fly boys are here now, crowding the trains and just about filling the beachfront. Hell, it's a war, but we've adapted."

From the appearance of the people Sam saw arriving in the hall, it seemed to him that they had. Most of the men were older than Cato, and none of them were in uniform, but the vogue of the military touch was well represented among the women. Hats were everywhere, and many of them were velvet versions of berets or sequined copies of Army caps. As Cato led Sam through the crowded living room toward the bar, Clement noticed the patriotic design of eagle wings sweeping prominently across the low-cut fronts of more than a few dresses.

"This punch is the second best stuff they have here," Cato said, turning from the bar to supply Sam with a drink. "I'll be back with the best when I've found someone I want you to meet. Look around if you want." Sam thanked him and moved away from the bar in the opposite direction, anxious to examine the people around him while he was unobserved.

There was nothing sinister about the gathering, he concluded. The men were well turned out in double-breasted suits, although some of them wore their collars open over their lapels instead of knotting them with ties. The house itself was lavish in the Northern style, with stained wood, scrolled molding and flocked wallpaper. Only the potted palms at the foot of the staircase added a tropical touch, and there was nothing to betray the source of the owner's obvious wealth.

Sam was sure that he had found the owner a short time later, when he had left the crowded hallway for the relative quiet of the den. A fire glowed unneeded and unattended in an immense fireplace, and over the mantelpiece hung three large portraits done in pen and ink. The style of the art was contemporary, and the family looked down at him in the clothing of the day. Sam stared at the trio, moving his eyes from the daughter to her mother, and finally stepping back to study the middle-aged face of the father. Like the people surrounding him, they appeared normal, and for the first time since he had arrived, Sam realized it was their ordinary appearance that made him ill at ease. He retreated the distance of one large square on the black and white pattern of the tile floor, studying the picture centered over the fireplace as though he might learn something about himself.

"He's very big in S. and G.," someone whispered softly in his ear.

Sam turned abruptly to find a woman smiling behind him. She was wearing a crepe blouse with high shoulders that was pulled in at the waist to imitate the lines of an Eisenhower jacket, but her dark hair was long and flowing, unlike the shorter styles around her. She took in Sam's startled expression with obvious amusement.

"You are Sam, aren't you?" she asked. She was almost as tall as he was in her narrow heels, and she seemed a dark version of Vera's flawless looks. He had been angry with Vera since he had arrived, resenting the prodding behind the commitment of this last trip, but he felt a wave of physical longing sweep over him, and for the first time since he had left, he missed her.

"Do I know you?" he asked.

"You will." Dick Cato had come up behind him to squeeze his arm. "This is Loretta," he said. "I sent her to find you so we could get the show on the road. Loretta, this is Sam, my contact from up north."

The openness of the introduction surprised Clement, but Loretta merely arched an eyebrow before she turned to move away from them. "It's nice to meet you, Sam." She threw Cato a meaningful look over her shoulder. "Dugan's eating now."

Cato grinned. "Isn't that funny, I was just feeling hungry myself. A very big connection," he told Sam as they followed Loretta into the dining room.

The heavily laden buffet could not have been produced with ration stamps. A profusion of cold cuts covered an entire table, and there were several side bars offering a variety of salads and more fresh vegetables than Sam could remember seeing since the beginning of the war. Many of the guests served themselves and left the room for other areas of the house, but Loretta guided Sam toward a long table set up near the French doors that bordered the terrace.

"I keep an eye out for the right people," she said when she had seated herself beside him. "When they eat, I let Dick know. The rest is up to him." She glanced toward Cato, who was laughing with a heavyset man at the far end of the table. "He's got a real way with people, don't you think?"

Cato rolled an eye in their direction without interrupting the stream of his conversation. "Is he going to join us?" Sam asked.

"Probably not." Loretta brought the high shoulders of her Eisenhower jacket up in a shrug. "I usually end up eating alone. You have to make sacrifices to get ahead."

When he wasn't speaking with Loretta, Sam listened to as much of the conversation going on around him as he could without being obvious. It was the usual small talk, laced with references to people he had never met. He did notice that when business was brought up, it was always in abstract terms, without the mention of any specific occupations. Only one incident the least bit out of the ordinary occurred, but it left Sam inwardly shaken, as though a tiny crack had opened in the facade of respectability, hinting at something savage and corrupt underneath.

At one point near the end of the meal, his eye was drawn to his left. An attractive woman was doubled up over her plate, the curve of her bare back obscuring her place setting, while her long blond hair actually brushed the tablecloth. Sam turned to Loretta, but she was facing away from him, and when he looked back toward the woman, even those on either side of her were talking in a normal manner. At first, Sam thought it might have been a polite way of ignoring a lady who had too much to drink, but seconds later, a hand reached out, pulling the woman back into an upright posture. From the corner of his eye, Sam saw an angry red blotching on one side of her face, as though the same man who had pressed her back against her chair might have slapped her a moment earlier. The only acknowledgment she made of her pain was to bite down on the edge of her lower lip while the other diners continued to look past her. Later, when she had composed herself, she joined the conversation again, leaning against the man beside her as though nothing had happened.

After the meal, Loretta wrapped her arm tightly around Sam's and introduced him to several couples in the room. She referred to him as a friend from up north, and all of the people Sam met seemed to have ordinary occupations that would have been represented at a similar gathering of wealthy people. When the windows of the room were dark enough to throw back the reflection of the noisy gathering inside, Loretta placed her face against the glass before steering him over to Cato, who was alone at the bar for the first time that evening.

"The pool appears to be all ours," she said, putting a hand on his shoulder. "I think Gwen just got here, so it might be a good time to get your business out of the way."

"Beautiful. We'll grab a few drinks and join you. Always pushing," he told Sam with a smile as Loretta disappeared into the fold of the crowd. When they each had two drinks in hand, Cato shouldered open one of the French doors in the dining room and stepped out onto a slate patio. Sam saw Loretta and another girl in a yellow strapless gown occupying one of a dozen empty tables surrounding a distant pool.

"People keep mentioning S. and G.," he told Cato when they were far enough from the lights of the house to be out of earshot. "Does that have anything to do with us?"

Cato shook his head with a knowing smile. "Not yet, but it could if we learn to play our cards right. The real action down here is on betting, not drugs. S. and G. is really four smart bastards in like Flynn with the Miami Beach City Council. Anyone else who takes book in this town gets raided." He broke off the conversation as they neared the table. "Sam, this is Gwen." Cato exchanged winks with the girl in the yellow gown. "She's been Loretta's sidekick since high school, and she's lots of fun."

"I always love their friends," Gwen said, pushing her chair to one side to indicate that Sam should take the place next to hers. Her short blond hair was bobbed, and the tops of her breasts swelled above a push-up bra, but even wearing heavy makeup, she gave Sam the impression that she was still in her late teens. She took her drink from him without interrupting what she was saying, and she spoke as though she had always known him. "I'd of been here earlier, but I couldn't get a ride. Lucky for me, there was a shift dance tonight, and a lot of girls at work went." She tamped out her cigarette, holding it between her thumb and index finger. "I'm a carhop, temporarily, and I got some guy to take me home early. I told him I lived here, and brushed him off at the driveway." She looked over at Cato with a hand to her mouth. "I hope that wasn't mean."

This time, Cato winked at Sam. "As long as you got here, right, Sam?" He rubbed his hands together over the table. "You three do the talking. I'll set us up with a sample of this reefer."

It was a moonless night, making it difficult to see beyond the borders of the pool. Gwen gave Sam's hand a playful squeeze while Loretta looked at him over the light of a single candle she had placed in the center of the table. "Waters tells me you have quite a name up north," she said with open interest. "I hope this isn't the last time you get down here." As if to complete the thought, she dropped her gaze, wetting her lips with her tongue while she watched Cato unwrap a cellophane packet he had produced from inside his jacket.

"Bucks," Gwen whispered softly.

Sam followed her eyes to the table, where Cato was emptying the packet in front of them. "Bucks is the word," Cato agreed, exchanging a smile with her. "This is the same reefer you're taking up north, Sam. Try before you buy is the way we do business down here."

Loretta took it on herself to roll the first smoke, and watching the supple motions of her fingers, Sam was once again reminded of the same decisive manner that touched everything Vera did. When Loretta had finished, she leaned back and lit the reefer, adding something stylish to the gesture by waving out the match and sending it hissing into the pool behind her. Sam accepted the joint when it was passed his way, although the smoking he had done that afternoon gave him serious misgivings. Taking it from Gwen, he noticed her fingernails were painted in shades of red, white and blue.

For the better part of the night, the four of them sat around the dimly lit table, listening to the droning sounds in the bordering undergrowth and the laughter coming from the distant house. They also listened to Cato, who went on with uninterrupted enthusiasm about the fortunes that would be made in Bal Harbour and North Bay village when the war ended.

"It's all gold north of Seventy-first Street in Miami Beach," he told them, and Loretta nodded, enthralled by the drug and what he was promising. "After that, it's all of southern Florida, with enough time. And enough smart money. If they put through some of the canals they're talking about, the inland areas are going to be worth almost as much as the beachfront." He frowned in reflection. "Sam, we take chances. It's not easy, but it's the only way to get ahead."

The women bobbed their heads in silent agreement, looking out into the night as though they had already caught the sight of something glittering in the darkness beyond them. Loretta rose from the table and stretched languorously, pulling at the ties of her blouse. "I want to get wet before we go," she told Gwen. "What about you?"

"I'm game." Gwen came to her feet and gave Sam a smile before she hurried after Loretta. As they moved into the shadows at the far end of the pool, Loretta was already baring her shoulders.

There was something calculated in the departure that Sam resented, and he lost himself in the flicker of the candle, deliberately forcing Cato to speak first. "You want to get that business out of the way?" he asked.

Sam nodded. "If you tell me how you want to handle it."

"Nothing to handle," Cato said, and his smile returned. "Just leave the payment in the morning, and our people will load your car." He busied his hands with the preparation of another reefer. "You mentioned something about a double order," he said without looking up.

Sam watched the girls come out of the water. Gwen immediately slipped her gown over the white outlines of her underwear, but Loretta drifted closer, sorting through her clothes near the edge of the light from their table. Like Gwen, she had kept her underthings on, but her bra was clinging to her breasts and the dark suggestion of her pubic hair was visible through her wet panties.

"You don't know what that woman does to me," Cato said, turning to follow Sam's gaze.

"I think I do," Sam replied softly. But he was speaking to himself, and the meaning was lost on Cato, who was smiling at him expectantly. Sam looked up to wave away the joint. "I've got enough to cover Waters' deal in cash," he offered. "I'll let you know about the extra order when I make the pickup in the morning."

Cato's smile was gone for only a moment. "Suit yourself," he said, coming to his feet and giving Sam a firm handshake. "Personally, I think you've got a shot at a real opportunity."

"So do you, if we get moving." Loretta had come up behind Cato, and she let her head fall against his shoulder before she looked over at Sam. "Mind driving Gwen home?"

"Not at all." Sam felt Gwen tuck her arm underneath his.

"Then we're off," Loretta announced, nudging Cato in the direction of the house. "I won't say good-bye," she added over her shoulder, "because I know we'll be seeing a lot more of you."

Gwen sank down onto the dampness of the lawn as soon as the other couple had stepped through the rectangles of the French doors, signaling their final good-bye with a wave. "God, what a beautiful night," she said, stretching out on the grass and folding her hands behind her head. "I was actually swimming under the stars."

Sam settled down beside her, aware of the way her breasts pulled away from the edge of her gown with her breathing. "Do you come to these parties often?" he asked.

She pushed up on an elbow to face him, rubbing absently at the back of her leg. "This was only my second time, but that's changing. I'm getting to know the right people, thanks to Loretta." As if to include him in that category, she smiled, but when she reached out for his hand, she pulled her breath in sharply, holding her fingers up to her face to examine them. "Christ, I don't believe it!" She sat up, raising her gown above her knees. "My makeup ran. Damn, I should have remembered before I went in the pool!"

"You look fine to me," Sam said, squinting at her in the darkness.

She looked at him and laughed. "Not my face, silly. My *legs*. I painted them. You know, to look like stockings." Gwen pulled her dress still higher, and Sam could see a streaking where the border of color met the white of her upper thighs. "If this stuff rubs off on my gown, I'll never get it out."

He took her foot in his hand, wiping at her ankle with a napkin he pulled from the edge of the table. "It's coming off," he said, peering at an area of her skin that was growing lighter with his efforts. "Just don't move around so much."

"Oh, God, I have to!" She fell back onto the lawn with both hands to her mouth in an attempt to stifle her giggling. "It tickles."

Sam raised the hem of her dress. "Just give me a few more minutes," he said.

But she gave him a full half hour. When his hands moved above her knees, she fell silent, parting her legs slightly, and gradually, he let his touch drift higher. When he finally brushed the V of her panties, she lifted her hips for him, and he pulled the underwear the length of her legs, putting it aside with the crumple of the napkin. She waited quietly while he worked out of his own clothes and covered her body with his own. Just before he entered her, he remembered Vera and the first time that they had made love. He had been helping her with her stockings, too, and he wondered in that moment if her surrender had been as calculated as Gwen's.

He had decided not to go through with his own deal by the time he dropped Gwen off at her apartment. She had pressed against him just before they parted, reminding him that she would be available during his future trips, and asking him to bring her some real stockings. The openness of the request made him wonder if his relationship with Vera was any different. Reflecting on it during the drive back to Miami, it seemed to him that they had been using each other, and that Vera's love had been related to his success from the very start of their relationship.

In any case, he decided that he had come to the end of his compromising. He might continue to sell for Waters, but he would draw the line at dealing for himself and becoming a part of the world he had just seen. There might be hell to pay when he reached home, but if Vera couldn't live with his decision, he would know that he had been wrong about her from the beginning.

The thought was disquieting, and he shut the possibility from his mind, remembering that it was more than the resemblance between the women that had given him some insight into what he had become. If Loretta and Gwen were an unnerving reflection of Vera, it was even more disturbing to look at Dick Cato and see himself so clearly.

Sam was less than three hours out of Miami when he saw the soldier. The Packard was weighed down with Waters' delivery, and he had been running his eyes along the sides of the road since he had left the motel, alert for any sign of the law. There were no hidden compartments under the fenders of the car this time. Cato's people had been forced to use the entire trunk, and when that had been filled, they had jammed three packages of reefer the size of laundry baskets into his back seat, covering them with the loose drape of a blanket. If Sam had followed through on his own deal, there would not have been room in the front seat for a passenger.

But there was room, and the man moving along the side of the road was dragging his feet, as though he had been exposed to the hot sun for hours. When he swerved closer to the broad shoulder of the road, Sam saw that he was wearing an Air Force uniform. He had expected the soldier to turn as soon as he was even with him, but he continued to walk with his head down.

"Going north?" Sam called out through the passenger window.

The soldier jumped to one side and confronted him with a startled expression, as though he had been unaware of the car moving beside him until Sam had spoken. "A ride?" he asked, and his eyes narrowed as if he were struggling with the term. Then he smiled. "I live on a farm, now. Six miles up the road."

Sam reached across the seat and pushed open the door. "Hop in," he said.

He was really a boy, Sam decided, glancing at him once they were under way. He could not have been twenty, and there was a certain vulnerability in the way he held himself, sitting upright without making contact with the back of the seat, his arms wrapped tightly against his sides.

"Home on leave?" Sam asked in an effort to put him at ease.

The boy shook his head emphatically. "For good. I was in bombers."

There was a shaky lack of control in his voice that bothered Sam, and he dropped the conversation, making a show of concentrating on the road. They drove the next few miles in silence, but Sam's initial uneasiness returned when the breathing of his passenger gradually became louder, until in a matter of minutes, he was doubled up over the fold of his legs, drawing in air with an effort that made the back of his head shake.

"Feeling a little sick?" Sam asked lightly when it was no longer possible for him to pretend he hadn't noticed.

The boy turned a bloodless face to him. "It's the road," he said. "This kind of road makes a noise."

Sam frowned and concentrated on the sound of the car. They were traveling down a concrete highway, and the only noise he could detect came through the floorboards of the car each time it passed over one of the tarred seams between the segments. "Is that what you mean?" he asked immediately after the tires thudded over the next border.

The boy's face was in his hands, and he nodded without lifting his head. "It's flak," he whispered through his fingers. "All over again."

Sam understood then, and he pulled the car over onto the graveled shoulder of the road, finding that if he drove slowly, he could just manage to straddle the unpaved strip while making only occasional contact with the highway.

Gradually, his passenger raised his head, finally slumping back against his seat. "It's okay to drop me off," he offered.

Sam shook his head. "It's only a few miles," he said. He wanted to go on, but there was nothing he could allow himself to say. You've ridden through skies that were exploding, he thought, while I've been working my deals down here. He jerked angrily at the wheel, continuing to cut a swerving path between the concrete of the highway and the slapping overgrowth of the bordering farms.

They were two miles from a distant rise in the land that the boy identified as his turnoff when Sam caught sight of the police car in his rearview mirror. It was coming up on them, but slowly enough so that he could not be sure if he had anything to do with its movements. Sam bit down on his lower lip, realizing that in either case, he would be attracting attention to himself with his driving. He glanced over at his passenger, who stared into the glare of the windshield, oblivious to the car behind them. He was also relaxed, Sam noted, and something perverse made him decide to hold his position on the shoulder of the road.

You want to get caught, he thought, but he realized that his feelings were not that simple. As he watched the police car grow larger in his mirror, he knew that if they did pull him over, he would do everything he could to divert their attention from the bundles that filled the back of his seat. His resistance to pulling back onto the highway was related more to his recent resolution than any feelings of guilt he had. He was going to direct his life without compromise, and that meant giving his help to someone who was entitled to it.

The car that was about to determine his fate had just gained enough acceleration to overtake him when the boy pointed to a break in the fields less than a hundred yards ahead of them. "That's our road," he said. "You can leave me right here."

Sam eyed his mirror and pushed an arm out of his window to signal. "It's no trouble to drop you at your place," he said.

As soon as he had turned on to the unpaved access road, he moved to the center of the lane, straightening tensely behind the wheel in an exaggerated effort to communicate by every means possible that he was a normal driver. He fought an overwhelming urge to twist around in his seat to see if the police were still behind them. Instead, he asked the boy where he lived.

"Here," he said, spreading his arms. "Everything on both sides is our land." Something tightened in his expression, and the tremor came back into his voice. "Can't work it no more, but it's ours." He caught Sam's stare with a wild roll of his eyes. "Tough run, McCall, but we're almost home."

The shaking had moved to his hands, and Sam wondered if he would get violent. "Is this your place?" he interrupted, pointing out a driveway that led up from the road to a house on a small rise of land.

The boy smiled. "You know it is," he said, and he turned away laughing quietly to himself.

Sam caught the police car in his rearview mirror as he pulled off the highway, and he felt the blood drain from his face. With the boy safely home, he would have allowed himself to make a run for it, but the narrow trap of the driveway had eliminated that possibility. I won't use the gun, he promised himself as he pulled up to a small farmhouse standing to one side of the driveway.

A thick-waisted man in faded coveralls frowned at him from the railing of the sagging porch, moving curiously down the steps as Sam brought the car to a halt.

"A milk run, Dad!" the boy called out in his overly bright voice as he pushed his door open. "Captain McCall brought us in!" He bounced up the wooden steps past his father, disappearing through the screen door behind him.

The old man looked at Sam. "You bring Jody?" There was the softness of resignation in his voice.

Sam shrugged. "I was glad to help," he said.

"Mister, I surely appreciate it." The man nodded his thanks. "I guess you don't want to stick around for a cold drink?"

Sam pushed open his door immediately. "I can't think of anything I'd like better," he said.

The old man grinned. "Good enough, then. Get in here and take a little rest for your trouble."

Sam climbed the steps, but before he could take the farmer's outstretched hand, it flew up in a wave. Sam turned and looked over his shoulder in time to see the police car pulling away from the driveway.

They shook hands, then, and the old man led him toward the

screen door. "Police here don't have much more to do than check on strangers," he said, "but I guess they saw you was only helping Jody." He ushered Sam into a small parlor with a shake of his head. "I guess most people here know Jody."

The bottle on the table was half empty, and the supper dishes lay rinsed but unwashed in the basin of the kitchen sink. Seated across the table from Sam, the farmer pushed a thumb over his shoulder to indicate the flag hanging in the window behind the tie-back curtains.

"I still keep it there," he said, "even though he's not really in the service per se. Just so people who still don't know have some way of understanding how he is." He reached for the bottle and raised the level of whiskey in his glass. He had strong hands, Sam noted, thickly corded behind the knuckles and splayed with calluses at the fingertips. "Of course, he's a good worker, or at least, he always was. He showed that in the service well enough. Six missions over Germany before the guns rattled him. Even now he's almost normal. Some of the time."

"I can see that," Sam said.

The old man took a mouthful from his glass and swallowed it with a grimace. "Still, he's not good for ten hours' work in a week on this farm. I'd soon as sold it the day he came home. We're gonna lose it, one way or the other." He worked a thick nail against a black chip in the porcelain of the table. "I could get a defense job up north, which is the only place they have enough help for people like him. You couldn't find those mind doctors down here even if you could pay for them."

"You should get a good price when you sell," Sam said. He dropped his gaze to the glass in his hand. "I have . . . some friends in Miami who say this whole area's going to be worth a lot after the war."

"*After* the war, maybe." The old man frowned at him from the other side of the table. "In the first place, we can't hold out for however long that is. Secondly, my neighbor's got a farm and two grown sons with all of their senses. They put in a drainage system that makes three quarters of their land prime for farming, and they can't sell it for anything near what they think it's gonna' be worth. Not with fighting going on." He emptied his glass and slammed it back down to the table. "This place here is shit creek for the duration."

But Sam was already ignoring him, leaning back in his chair with the fold of his hands pressed tightly against his mouth. They sat there in silence for several minutes, each lost in his own thoughts, and the tiny kitchen was filled with the night sounds coming from the swamps and fields that surrounded them. Finally, Sam looked up.

"I'll buy it," he said.

The old man made a scraping sound in his throat and squinted at him.

"The farm," Sam said. "I want to buy your farm."

"You're drunk."

Sam nodded. "A little. Not that it matters." He straightened his chair and put both elbows on the table. "I'd want to stay tonight, of course, to look things over in the morning. And you're not even going to get an offer until I have some idea of what land around here is going for. I've got cash, but I want everything registered and legally binding."

The farmer remained looking at him with narrowed eyes, his arms laced across his thick chest. When he spoke, there was a tightness in his voice. "We don't want any charity around here," he warned, "no matter how much money you might have."

Sam rose from the table and met his gaze. "I don't give charity," he said with an edge of his own. "You need money and I need a place to put mine. If your land triples when the war's over, it's still mine if I buy it now. I won't give you a high price, but I won't give you a low one, either, knowing you want to sell now. That's as fair as I get. And there's nothing that says I'm going to buy."

He strode over to the window and brushed the flag aside to look out into the night, pushing his hands into the pockets of his suit pants. "And another thing," he added sharply. "You can count on introducing me to your neighbor as part of the deal. I might just buy his place, too. And I can't see any way you could call that charity."

The old man came to his feet then, grinning. "I guess not, mister, if you're really serious."

Sam withheld his smile. "I'm always serious when it comes to business," he said. "Where can I take title if this goes through?"

The farmer spread his arms. "Right where you are. In Fort Lauderdale."

The flat, muddy land fell away from the sides of the road, and in five minutes' time, more and more homes dotted the landscape. Even before the farmer signaled to him over the rattle of the pickup's engine, Sam caught the smell of salt water, and he knew the blue behind the crest of the next hill was part of the limitless horizon stretching over the ocean. The old man pulled the truck onto the shoulder of the road as soon as they came in sight of the shoreline.

"Well, that's part of town we went through back there," he said, fishing a pack of cigarettes from the bib of his overalls. "And this here, of course, is the ocean. Something you want to do now that we're here?"

Sam declined the offer of a Chesterfield with the same shake of his head. "Not really. I'd like to go back, now that I've seen how far we are from the water." He gazed thoughtfully through the window. "My best friend served in the Pacific. He said the water was bluer down there, but it's hard to imagine."

"Well, you take a good look at it." The farmer pulled on his cigarette, looking curiously at Sam from the corners of his eyes. "Then we'll go right back, if that's what you want. Now that we're here."

But the comment was lost on Sam, who was reviewing the observations of the morning as he moved closer to making a final decision. Several cars swished past on the highway, sending a light movement of air through the cab of the truck, and Sam remembered the cool of an evening, and what Cato had said by the pool two nights ago. Land values would rise after the war if Florida continued to develop. As nearly as Sam could tell from his tour of the area in the pickup truck, Fort Lauderdale seemed to be developing westward as the population moved inland from the beachfront of the coast. The old man's farm was a good five-mile drive from the shore, but if the boom Cato had predicted moved north from Miami, the land was still close enough to double in value.

Sam turned away from the window and faced the farmer. "Your neighbor said this morning there was talk of an intercoastal waterway. Is that true?"

"That's what they say." The farmer leaned toward him across the seat. "Listen, I told you we don't want any favors in this deal. If they do build that canal, the water's gonna' be salt. You won't be able to irrigate with it."

Sam shook his head. "It's not the water I'm looking for the intercoastal to bring. It's people. And even if that doesn't happen, I still think this area's going to be worth money."

The farmer peered at him while he digested what he had heard. "You mean you're gonna' use the land for something besides farming?"

"In time, yes."

"Well, shit." The farmer slapped his leg. "Then I can tell you right now, you couldn't buy a better farm for not farming." He turned away and stared out of the window in the direction of his land. "I been fightin' that place for years, and truth to tell, I felt a little guilty about passing it on to you. What are you plannin' to use it for besides growin'?"

"Plain old real estate. I think people are going to need room to live once this area starts filling up." The explanation sounded shaky, even to Sam, but he had an intuitive feeling that he was right. He had been right about the black market, and he had been right about drugs. Now, for the first time in his life, he wanted to see if he had a good head for legitimate business. If the money he was using was tainted, at least it was better than investing it in drugs. And although being unfaithful to Vera continued to haunt him, spending his savings on land was a risk he felt entitled to take, in spite of her predictable disapproval. It was also another way of asserting his independence. "I'll take the whole deal," he announced, without looking away from the shoreline in front of them. "That means your neighbor's land as well as yours."

There was no way the farmer could suppress his grin, but before he reached out to take Sam's hand, he held up his palm in a gesture of hesitation. "Mister, I need this sale more than you can know, but I got to warn you one more time, particularly the way you been to Jody. If this area don't start growin' people instead of crops, you're gonna' lose a lot of money."

Sam captured his hand and shook it. "Easy come, easy go," he said. And in that moment, he knew he meant it.

Vera stood with her back to him, working her hands against the sides of her skirt. A complete meal lay steaming on the table in the next room, but she made no move toward it. Sam took in the perfect contours of her body from behind, unable to forget how much he wanted her, even while they were arguing.

"It didn't seem right," he repeated softly in an attempt to bring her out of her angry silence.

"It didn't seem right!" She turned on him. "There was nothing that wasn't right about it!" She raised a hand, throwing out one finger after another to emphasize each point. "You had Waters' connection, you had his same price, and you had the protection of his name behind you. For Christ's sake, they treated you like one of them!"

"But I'm not one of them," Sam said quietly. "I may not be much better, but there's still a difference. You weren't the one who had to do it."

Vera narrowed her eyes. "Don't you think I wouldn't have!" she said, biting down on her words. "Do you really believe you do anything I couldn't do myself? You'd know it soon enough if those bastards weren't too stupid to take a woman seriously. Every smart move you've ever made was because of me!" She turned away from him again as her voice grew louder through lack of control. "Christ knows I'll never get any of the credit."

Sam shook his head. "It's not credit, Vera. It's blame. And I'm putting it all on myself. I just had to draw the line somewhere, and I did. There'll be other opportunities."

"Other opportunities? Damn you! They're moving through France and Belgium. With our luck, this is the last Christmas of the war!"

He reacted without thinking, spinning her around by the shoulders. "How can you say that?" he demanded.

"I didn't. Somebody on the Blue Network did."

"You don't want to see it end, do you?" he said, suddenly as angry as she was. "You don't care how many people like Eddie never make it back!"

"Don't be a fool!" She pulled his hands from her shoulders with a grimace of irritation, but when she spoke, her voice had softened, and she looked at him with an offended expression. "I'm not just thinking of us. You might consider Eddie's mother. And what about all those veterans you were going to help with your business? Big plans take big money. Or were they all wet, like the deal in Miami?"

He looked away from her. "Maybe that idea died with Eddie. Things change."

The edge came back into her voice. "They sure do, Sam," she warned. She turned and stalked over to the hall closet, pulling at her coat with enough force to bring it away with the hanger. "You might think about the fact that I could get ideas of my own," she said lightly. "And while you're at it, you can eat for both of us. I'm too sick to hold anything down."

Before he could respond, she was at the door, slamming it behind her with enough force to shake several ornaments from the Christmas tree. They shattered against the hardwood floor of the living room with a soft tinkling noise, and then there was only the sound of her heels striking angrily at the hall linoleum as she made her way toward the stairs.

Sam sat back on the edge of his valise, which was still by the door where he had left it. He decided he would wait for a better time to tell her that he had spent the money on undeveloped land.

During the following months, the two of them maintained an unspoken truce. The balance between anger and forgiveness was made easier by the fact that Vera had returned to work, taking an evening shift that brought them together for a limited time in the late mornings, and then only if Sam were not working. He was still driving for Max and Waters in his limited role, and he was still making good money, but he knew that Vera would never again be content with what he had achieved before he had left for Miami.

It was their first prolonged quarrel, but during their previous arguments, Vera had kept him from her body, lying in a tight wrap of blankets on her side of the bed. She acted differently this time, but the coolness she displayed was something he found more disconcerting than an open show of hostility. She would submit to him several times a week, placing herself on the bed before she had dressed in the morning and waiting without comment for him to react to her.

She never responded to his efforts to arouse her, and Sam would listen to his own labored breathing when he was on top of her, feeling as though he were exposing his most intimate act to the cold observation of a third party. He attempted to match her indifference by staying away from her, but his will to resist broke down under the slightest provocation.

"You're driving tomorrow, so we'd better do this before I leave for work," she would announce evenly, and he would look up from the newspaper to find her standing naked near the entrance to the living room. She would turn before he could answer, waiting for him on the bed with an arm across her face, as though she were taking advantage of the time it took him to undress by resting. When he was done, she would swing her legs over the edge of the mattress and busy herself with dressing the instant he rolled away from her.

It was the sort of situation he would have attacked with an open discussion years earlier, but he had learned some things from Vera, and he fought a natural tendency to expose his real feelings. He moved through the winter of the new year with a cold determination, maintaining his neutral attitude and resigning himself to the ordeal of her mechanical sex. He did confide some of his feelings to Max.

"Vera's working at City again," he explained when Max questioned his new habit of lingering at the Essex Pub after his work was done. "She says someone has to pull in more money if we want to get anywhere."

They were sitting in the back room that served as Max's office, and the bottle was moving between them. "You'd better not remind her of what she's actually making, or you'll be wearing your ass for a hat," Max chuckled. "She's just trying to keep you from forgetting what she wanted. But you stick to your guns. Otherwise, a woman like that's going to control you if you give her the chance."

Sam looked into his drink. "You think she'll give in, Max?"

"I'm a realist, kid. That's why I break the law. With Vera, I honestly don't know." He rubbed thoughtfully at the side of his face. "Her father used to come in here, before his drinking put him on his back. He was a boozer, the old man. Did she ever tell you that?"

"She never mentions her parents."

"Yeah, well, I think he roughed them up a little, his old lady and the girls." Max closed one eye and poked a finger at him. "Now Laura, her sister, is one of the sweetest kids you'd want to meet. All softness. Vera didn't go that way." He smiled in recollection. "One night—Christ, she couldn't have been more than fifteen—she comes in to take the old man home, and he's stinking. Oh, he doesn't want to go for nothing, and he pushes her away kind of rough until a few of us step in and break it up. I take Vera in the back room for a soda and a cigarette, and I have Tony slip the old man a mickey. Boom, five minutes later, he's so gone, he can hardly walk! She holds him under one arm, not even coming up to his shoulder, mind you, and they start out the door together." Max took a pull on his drink and grinned over at Sam. "She ever tell you this?"

"She never talks about anything in the past," Sam said, leaning forward in open interest.

Max touched his glass with the tip of the bottle and added to his drink. "Well, as soon as they're out the door, I start thinking that's quite a load for a girl her size, particularly since Tony can get carried away when he's passing a mickey. He thinks being rowdy at his bar should be a capital offense. Anyway, I go to the door and lean out to see how they're doing. Sure enough, they're not twenty yards from the bar and the old man leans into the side of a building and slides down onto the sidewalk. Out cold. I duck in to get my coat, and by the time I'm back, that little girl's standing over him, and sweet Jesus, if she doesn't haul back with her foot and give him one right between his legs. I swear it!"

Max threw back his head and laughed. "Really, she kicked him so hard he must have slid six inches on the sidewalk." He lost control again before he could deliver the end of the story. "'Vera,' I said as soon as I came up to her, 'why the hell did you do that?' 'Because I couldn't find anything to hit him with,' she says, and she steps back and does it again!" Max wiped at the corners of his eyes with the back of his hand. "You should have seen her back then, Sam," he sighed. "She was such a tiny thing. And so damned pretty."

Sam was smiling, but he continued to shake his head thoughtfully. "Do you really think that did it, Max? Her father? Is that why she acts the way she does?"

Max dismissed the suggestion with a wave of his hand. "Partly, maybe, but you don't see that in her sister." He nodded to himself as he reached for the bottle. "Listen, Sam, as much as we both love her, there are times when I think that girl's just naturally mean." He raised his glass in a salute. "Watch your ass, kid."

There were decisive changes in the war that spring. Iwo Jima fell in March, the British were pushing forward in Burma by the middle of April, and the Americans and Russians stood an equal distance from Berlin. On May 4th, German forces in Holland and Denmark yielded to Montgomery's command near Lüneburg, and on the 9th, a general surrender was ratified in Berlin.

There was a change in Vera, too, although Sam had difficulty relating it to anything that was different in their lives. The warmth gradually returned to her voice when she spoke to him, and she began to respond to him in bed, initiating their lovemaking on mornings when she ordinarily slept late. Sam was relieved by her new attitude, but it had never been in her nature to give in first, and he wondered if the impending end to the war had affected her more than she cared to admit. He didn't consider the possibility that she was merely acting until one evening in May, and even then, his suspicion was the result of an accident.

They had come home late from an afternoon in the park that was touched by the special magic of spring, and they had made love until the very last moment Vera could allow herself before she left for work. When she was gone, he watched the light leave the sky as night came to the city, missing her. She had refused to allow him to meet her when she was done work, insisting that he get his sleep, and Sam was too delighted with their reconciliation to risk offending her. Instead, he thought of the phone.

It was still a novelty for him to have one, and he was surprised that he had not thought of it earlier, when he had begun to spend his evenings at home again. The switchboard at City Hospital transferred his call to her floor, but the voice of an older woman answered, informing him that Vera had left earlier because she was feeling ill. Sam was surprised that she had gotten sick in the short time since she had left him, but he was happy to know that she would be arriving home momentarily.

When she opened the hall door several hours later, he said nothing about the call or the time he had spent waiting for her. Instead, he asked about her work, and when she shrugged the evening off as routine, he remained silent. The following night, he called again, acting as though it were the first time, and her voice came over the line immediately, warm with surprise. It was not a comfort, though, and he wondered what she had done behind his back that could cause her to lie.

"I'm no expert," Max said when Sam asked his advice, "but when a woman acts as sour as Vera has, it usually means she's looking around."

"But lately, she's never been happier."

"Which means she's found someone." Max tempered his judgment with a smile. "Don't worry, though. You're a long way from knowing anything for sure."

"But you think I should tell her? About knowing she left the hospital and all?"

Max grimaced. "Sometimes I have to remind myself that you doubled my business instead of turning it over to the O.P.A. You're too straight for your own good, Sam. Follow her, for Christ's sake! If she's stepping out, she's not likely to tell you to your face, and you're only going to warn her by asking questions. You've been dodging cops up and down the coast for three years. You should be able to shadow your own honey for a few blocks."

The first two nights that he followed her were uneventful, a result he anticipated when he saw her leave work at the normal time. But the third evening he positioned himself across the street from the hospital, she surprised him, emerging from the entrance a full hour early. He was in his car, and he allowed her to enter a taxi before he pulled the Packard around in a wide U-turn and followed her toward the center of town.

She left the taxi at Market Street, and he was lucky enough to find a parking space while she was paying her fare. Everything worked in his favor, including a moonless night that allowed him to follow her down the wide avenue by moving from storefront to storefront, and he began to feel certain that he was being led to some fatal confrontation.

He was not reassured when she disappeared into the Grant Hotel. He waited outside the double doors until he saw her walk across the blue carpeting in the lobby and take the first few steps of the stairs behind the reception desk. Then he went in, tracing her path quickly enough to hear her on the flight immediately above him. He kept the same distance between them until she entered the hall on the third floor.

At that point, he held his breath, leaning into the door from the stairwell and keeping it ajar until he heard the sound of knocking further down the corridor. He stepped out into the hall just in time to see her disappear through a doorway less than twenty yards from where he was standing. He wanted to push his way into the room immediately, but he retreated to the stairwell instead, waiting until he had finished a cigarette. If she were fooling around with someone, he wanted to know the worst, and that meant giving her some time alone with whomever she was seeing.

When five minutes had elapsed, he pushed back into the hall and approached the door. He had no intention of using the pistol he had brought with him, but he patted the bulk at the small of his back to give himself a sense of reassurance. Then he rapped sharply on the door in front of him. It was Vera who answered, opening it immediately and stepping back with a look of mild surprise when he pushed past her and entered the room.

The man standing in front of him was neither naked nor a stranger, and it was Sam's turn to show surprise, putting a hand to his mouth instead of speaking.

"What's the matter, Clement, don't you talk to the common people anymore?"

Sam shook his head, breaking into a grin before he found his voice. "Joe Branagan," he said, and they embraced while Vera looked on in satisfaction.

Chapter Nine

J oe sat on the edge of the couch in the hotel room. His voice was husky, and it seemed to reflect the fatigue Sam had seen in him as soon as they had recovered from the surprise of their meeting. As he spoke, Branagan's fingers worried a patch on his uniform that said U.S.S. *Mississippi*. "You couldn't believe what a pounding we took in the Lingayen Gulf. In a way, I feel guilty about it, because if it wasn't all that bad, we wouldn't have come in for repairs, and I'm goddamned glad to be through with it. For a while." He dropped his glance to the floor. "We lost a lot of guys."

Sam shook his head sympathetically, taking in Joe's drawn looks when his friend turned away from him. "Well, it's almost over," he said softly. "You'll be home for good."

Joe narrowed his eyes. "It's all over in Europe," he said. "There's still plenty of time to buy the farm in the Pacific." His voice became bitter. "You don't know those bastards. They'll never surrender. I talked to a marine who took part in mopping up the Bonin Islands, and he said they were unbelievable. One Jap was surrounded by a whole company, and he still went for them. He wasn't even armed; he just picked up a rock and charged the closest marine." Joe's fingers skirted the front of his uniform until they found a pocket. Sam and Vera waited, exchanging glances without speaking while he lit a cigarette with a shaking hand that caused him to use a second match.

"Anyway," Branagan went on, "I saw it for myself on the water. They came at us with suicide planes, aiming right for the ship. Even if you get them on the way in, they can still hit you with enough momentum. They're goddamned crazy! They don't even take off with enough fuel to get back to their bases. I mean, how can you fight that? It's almost impossible to keep someone from killing you if they don't care about living through it themselves."

"You'll live through it," Sam said reassuringly. "Look at the fix you've already come out of." He made a point of lightening his tone. "Did you surprise your parents, too?"

Branagan's head snapped up in the face of the question. "I don't want my father to know anything!" He took in Sam's startled expression and lowered his voice. "Look, Sam, I can talk to you, but things wouldn't be so easy with my folks. What am I going to say? 'I'm home for a week, but I might never see you again?'" He shook his head. "I'm not putting them through that. They said their good-bye on my last leave. Either I'll be home for good, or I won't. Anything in between isn't fair to them. That's why I'm staying here."

Sam saw his expression change, as though he were making a conscious effort to shut off the train of thought. "Anyway," Branagan concluded, allowing himself a smile, "I understand you're doing pretty well. I figured things couldn't have been too bad if you were turning down deals in Miami."

Sam felt Vera touch his hair lightly from her position behind his chair. "I guess I've been lucky all around," he said, coloring slightly. "I sure haven't been doing much compared to you."

"Anyone can die," Joe said, almost as though he were speaking to himself. Then he met Sam's eyes, leaning in toward him suddenly and speaking in a rush. "I could use your help, Sam, if you'd be willing to think about it. You never even told me about

what you did for Eddie's Mom. I had to hear it from Vera. So
this time, I—"

"Never mind about that," Sam said, waving a hand to inter-
rupt him. He was still having trouble reconciling the man in
front of him with the boisterous person he remembered. He took
in Joe's expression and smiled in order to hide his concern. "You
know I'd do anything I could to help you," he said emphatically.
"You should have gotten a hold of me right away."

"He wasn't ready right away." Vera pushed away from the
back of Sam's chair and moved to one side of it where she could
confront him. "He called me during the day to find out if he
could get in touch with you. He wasn't about to go down to the
Essex Pub with his father's store a block away. And besides—"
she met Branagan's eyes as he glanced up at her from the couch,
"—he didn't know if you were still hooked into Max's operation.
He's got a deal, honey." Vera reached out and captured Sam's
hand, stooping down by his chair so that her eyes were on the
same level as his. "He wasn't even sure if he should bring it up,
but I told him that the least you'd do was listen. He still hadn't
made up his mind tonight, but you followed me, and that settles
it." Sam frowned with curiosity and looked over at Branagan,
who was watching him anxiously.

"Something fell into my hands, Sam," he explained in another
nervous rush of words. "We did some ship clearing on the way
back into port after the attack. A lot of the things we were
supposed to dump were medical supplies. A whole bunch of stuff
had gotten soaked down pretty well, and I was on the detail that
sorted through it. Anyway, I managed to put aside something I
thought was still valuable."

"Valuable?" Sam asked.

Branagan pressed his lips together and nodded. "Yeah, pretty
valuable." He looked directly at Sam. "I took some morphine. It
was soaked with salt water, but I found out later that it doesn't
make a lot of difference. It's still good, Sam, and it's worth a lot
of money."

"You mean as a drug," Sam said. He struggled with what

Branagan was telling him. "Look, Joe," he finally answered softly, "I meant what I said before. If you need anything to help you along, I'd be happy to give—"

"I don't want any money!" Branagan raised his voice for the first time. "Not from you, or my parents, either!" He leaned in toward Sam, gesturing with both hands. "Look, you did a great job at home, but at least you had the chance! You've got a good woman and a good start. I'll be fighting armies for a job when I get out, if I live through this next campaign. And there's a good chance I won't. I just want to know that while I'm over there, I have something to come home to. Besides tending bar, or minding the old man's store." Joe sank back against the couch, lowering his voice. "I told you before, these are damaged goods the Navy didn't want. If I live to make something out of this, it's not going to be as if I owe them anything."

Sam broke the silence that followed with a sigh. "You know they make heroin out of that stuff?" he said.

"For coloreds and trash," Vera put in, coming to her feet and looking at him expectantly. "There's no help for those people anyway."

Sam took them both in before he rose from his chair. "I'll keep it for you until you come home," he said without smiling. "I think I can line up some people for a sale when you're ready."

The tight lines around Branagan's face relaxed and he rose from the couch to pump Sam's hand. "I can't tell you what this means to me," he said with a broad grin. "I want you to have half of whatever we make after things work out."

"There's time to talk about all that later," Vera said, throwing her arms around both of them and leaning up to plant a kiss on the side of Sam's face. "Right now, we've got something to celebrate."

Sam knew the waterfront well from his dealings with Waters. He chose to meet Joe near one of the railroad cars that served the rows of warehouses lining the docks. It was late at night, but even in the darkness, Sam could see that Branagan was not wearing his uniform beneath his open topcoat.

"I thought you were leaving tonight," he said, taking a suitcase from Branagan that was a good deal heavier than anything he had anticipated.

Branagan grinned, once again the confident person Sam remembered. "In the morning. That means the kind of night where you fit in everything you still have time for."

The thought seemed to remind both of them what lay ahead, and Sam reached out impulsively, pressing his friend against his chest, and hoping that by willing it, the war would end before Joe came to any harm. Driving home that night, he remembered that he had hugged Eddie before he left.

On May 8, V-E Day had been declared, officially ending the war against Germany, and toward the end of that month, Sam turned his attention along with the rest of the nation on the final conflict in the South Pacific. Joe's visit had given him a new sense of purpose, and he began to follow the war for the first time since Eddie's death, gleaning the pages of the local paper for the latest reports, and checking the casualty lists apprehensively for the appearance of Branagan's name.

On June 21, the battle of Okinawa ended, with 6,990 Americans reported dead, and on July 5, the Philippines were liberated. It was the following day he saw the item that shattered his faith, throwing him into a state of disbelief, and eventually leading him to question everything that had occurred during the past few weeks. It was a brief summary next to the casualty list in *The Newark Evening News*, significant only to him.

It stated that the U.S.S. *Mississippi* had returned to duty on July 1. It had left Pearl Harbor after undergoing repairs for damage sustained during an attack in the Lingayen Gulf, which had killed twenty-two of its crew and injured eighteen others. Sam read the item again after his initial shock, but the facts were clearly stated, and there was no way for him to deny to himself that Branagan had been lying. The ship on the shoulder patch of Joe's uniform *had* been attacked in the Lingayen Gulf, but it had gone back to active duty a day ago, and not several weeks earlier, when Joe had parted with Sam on the waterfront. And if Branagan were not with his ship, it could only mean he had deserted.

Seaver emerged from one of the back rooms in his spacious apartment, limping across the thick Oriental rug to take a seat beside Sam on the living-room couch. Unlike Sam, he had exploited his early beginnings in the movement of drugs, and his apartment was a penthouse where the city of Chicago was visible as a vast network of lights winking through the picture window behind them. He cleaned his rimless glasses on a corner of the white lab coat he had thrown over his sleeveless sweater, reminding Sam of a chemistry teacher he had known in high school.

"That stuff's never even been damp, much less soaked with salt water," he said, rubbing at his eyes. He licked a residue of crystalline powder from his fingertips. "This is a first-rate product, right off the shelf. For medical use."

"What's it worth?" Sam asked tightly.

"Shit." Seaver grinned. "It takes ten times the amount of opium to come up with this form of morphine." He put on his glasses and allowed himself a moment to think. "I'm no expert on moving this stuff, although I could put you in touch with people who are. Off hand, I'd say you might be looking at a potential of about a half million."

"A half million?" Sam's voice rose with surprise.

"At least. You've got enough in this bag to use for ballast. Your buddy must have gone through a whole storeroom, because he sure as hell didn't get it in one place." Seaver shook his head and grinned. "A happy little sailor."

"I can't believe it."

"Believe it. What you don't believe is that he stumbled on it by accident. No one even vaguely connected with medicine would dispose of damaged supplies by calling in a fucking work crew, much less trust them around morphine."

Sam let his head fall back against the couch, placing his hands over his eyes.

"Look," Seaver said, softening his tone, "the pharmaceutical companies have trouble keeping this stuff from walking, and they don't have it stored on ships during wartime. Your buddy's not the first sailor to take advantage of a good situation, if it's any consolation."

"It's not," Sam said.

Sam struggled with what he had learned, but the only believable conclusion he could draw was that Joe Branagan had jumped his ship, most likely when it had docked at Pearl Harbor for repairs. The name of the distant port brought back the sting of his own rejection from the service, and he realized that even if he could forgive his friend for stealing, he could never understand how he could desert. He remembered the look on the face of the boy he had picked up in Florida, realizing that it was the same fear he had seen in Joe's expression when he related the odds of his survival in the hotel room. But Branagan had not cracked under the strain: he had made a calculated effort to remove himself from danger. And he had financed his plan with a drug that had been vitally needed at the front.

Once Sam began to question what he had been told, one disturbing thought followed another. Joe could have planned his desertion around the theft of the drug, rather than stealing it when he was already on the fringe of desperation. Sam remembered discussing the reservations he had about his work with Branagan when he had been home on leave last year, and being surprised by Joe's open encouragement. That would also explain why Branagan had contacted Vera first, knowing that he might need her support to overcome any reservations on Sam's part. And there was a final question, one that disturbed him most of all. Had Vera known that Joe was lying from the very start?

He had told her that his savings were in war bonds when she

finally questioned him about the money after his return from Miami. But recently he had been planning to confess what he had actually done during that trip, including his evening with Gwen as well as the purchase of the land. Now, with reason to question her own honesty, he was glad that he had kept part of his life from her.

He maintained his silence during the next few weeks by using the sort of discipline that had now become a part of him. He even refrained from visiting Joe's father to confirm his suspicions. Instead, he resolved to wait until the end of the war, knowing Mr. Branagan would more than likely try to hide something as painful as his son's desertion until the last possible moment, when all of the troops were due home.

He dealt with the morphine itself by sliding it under one of the rusting storage tanks on the outskirts of the plant where he used to work. It lay there, concealed and waiting, like the secret knowledge of betrayal he carried inside himself.

July drew to a close, and Vera began to spend as freely as she had when his trip to Miami had been on the horizon. The day after she quit her job, she bought a black muskrat coat for 250 dollars, explaining that she was taking advantage of a summer sale. Even then, Sam could not bring himself to make a final judgment. That moment came a week later, as they sat together in the darkness of the newsreel theater, watching films that showed Japanese kamikaze pilots sending their planes into suicide dives over the decks of the U.S.S. *Nevada*.

"I hope Joe makes it," Vera whispered. There was a quality in her voice that might have told him enough, but just then the screen lit up the theater with another explosion, exposing the unguarded expression on her face, and he knew that she was lying.

"I think he'll be okay," was all he said.

On Monday, August 6, the atomic bomb exploded over Hiroshima, killing 70,000 of its inhabitants and literally flattening a broad circumference of its buildings. Three days later, after a second bomb had devastated Nagasaki, the Soviet Union formally joined the war against Japan. By the 10th of that month, the papers were reporting that the unconditional surrender which the Allies had been demanding was imminent, and Sam decided there was no longer any reason to postpone his confrontation with Mr. Branagan.

The Branagan establishment was only separated from the Essex Pub by the length of a block, and Sam visited it that same night after he had finished work. The liquor store was closed and darkened, but the adjoining bar was crowded with local people, already celebrating the end of the war on the basis of the growing certainty conveyed by the news. Mr. Branagan himself was working the counter with two of his men, and Sam knew the moment he saw his face that he had been right about Joe.

Branagan's Tavern was a fixture in the neighborhood, but although Ed Branagan earned the highest income on Clay Street by selling liquor, he seldom drank himself. He was slightly built, a short, light-skinned Irishman with thinning hair, but that night, he was flushed and sweating, sipping openly from a glass he filled for himself between sales.

He looked away when Sam pushed his way through the press at the counter instead of extending his customary greeting. As much as he wanted to leave then, Sam could not allow himself any lingering doubts. He waited patiently until Branagan had served the noisy customers on either side of him and there was no longer any excuse to avoid his eyes.

"Hello, lad," Branagan said in a flat voice, placing a cardboard coaster on the bar in front of Sam. "What will you have, then?"

"Nothing to drink, thanks," Sam answered brightly, hating himself for what he was doing. "I guess I just wanted to find out when you think they'll be sending Joe home, now that it looks like it's over."

Branagan's eyes clouded over, and he swayed slightly behind the bar, causing Sam to give silent thanks for the numbing effect the liquor had obviously had on the older man. "Joe ain't comin' home," Branagan finally said, and he turned away, renewing his own glass at the spigot behind him until it spilled over.

One of the revelers slumped beside Sam shook his head at what he had overheard. "What's that, Ed? You haven't lost a son, have you?"

"I have," Branagan said without turning to face them, and the bitterness in his voice came through his drinking. "I've lost a son." Sam saw his shoulders shaking under the damp clinging of his T-shirt before he pushed away from the bar and headed for the door, managing to save his own feelings for the darkness of the street outside the tavern.

Sleep was difficult for him the next few nights, and he was awake when the time arrived for him to make his final decision. It was close to 4:00 A.M., and Vera lay motionless beside him, oblivious to the noise in the street below that caused Sam to sit up in bed and drew him to the living-room window.

There was a car outside, moving slowly between the alley of darkened buildings while a young girl on the seat beside the driver reached between his arms and sounded the horn. It was a convertible, and as well as filling the front and back seats, passengers lined the running boards, locking hands with those who were already seated, or jumping down to exchange places with others who were running to join them. Most of them were still in their teens, Sam noted, realizing that he had been close to their age when it all began. He took them in a final time as they drew past him, heading toward the center of town. The blare of the car radio was lost in the excitement of their voices, but he knew what it was saying.

It was telling them that they were survivors, although they could never understand it, in spite of the casual facts they would recite for the rest of their lives. A whole generation had been irrevocably changed by something which had missed them by the narrow margin of a few years. Staring at windows that were suddenly filling with light under the impact of the news, Sam was happy for those who would be coming home, but a part of him was especially grateful for the ones who would never have to face going.

He turned from the window, relieved that the increasing noise in the streets hadn't wakened Vera. Then he carried his clothes in from the bedroom so that he could dress without disturbing her. He had taken the car keys from the hook beside the front door and was about to write her a note when he shrugged, dismissing the idea and shutting the door quietly behind him. He had forgotten that it no longer mattered if she were angry.

He knew that the four corners of Broad and Market would be the natural gathering place, and as he drew closer to the area, the streets grew progressively more crowded with cars. All of them were moving in the same direction, blowing their horns. Finally, when the traffic had slowed to a crawl and there were people streaming past his windows, Sam pulled the car over and parked it, leaving it straddling the curb with two wheels on the sidewalk.

By the time he had arrived at Broad and Market, the business district was nearly filled to capacity. What little traffic there was came slowly to a halt as it was blocked by the crowd, and bewildered drivers emerged from their cars, only to join the celebration once they had been informed of the news. The morning papers, bound and stacked in front of the stands and stationery stores, were torn from their wrappings and passed from one hand to another, declaring that peace was imminent, and heightening the exhilaration of the readers, who knew that it had finally come.

"Three years and eight months," someone in the crowd observed, and others around Sam counted on their fingers, calculating the exact number of days. In less than fifteen minutes, the gathering had filled the entire street, and by 5:00 A.M., buses of detectives and civilian employees began to arrive, called in by the city to control the crowd. But even the authorities were exuberant, and uniformed police stood side by side with the others, cheering a few daring teenagers who climbed to the over-hang of the light poles, still in their pajamas. Later, an effigy of the Japanese emperor was lowered from one of the apartment windows, provoking jeers and then laughter as its unseen creator yanked on the rope around its neck, causing it to dance jerkily against the front of the building.

As morning arrived, buses that were halted by the jammed streets opened their doors, and passengers who had been headed for work were greeted with the news. Some of them turned back in the direction of their homes, anxious to share the moment with their families. Others headed for the bars, which had opened at seven o'clock in honor of the occasion.

Sam spent over an hour in one that fronted Broad Street. At first, the realization that he would have to avoid Branagan's brought his spirits down, but the eager familiarity of the people surrounding him did as much as the alcohol to relax him, and in time he realized that he was happy for the world in general, even if there was nothing left for him to celebrate himself. The thought stuck with him when he left the bar, stepping out into the street to blink against the combined effects of the daylight and the four beers he had forced on an empty stomach.

In a sense, Vera had done him a favor, confronting him with another decision when he was already approaching the cross-roads marked by the end of the war. He walked the distance to his car thoughtfully, deciding once he was in it that he would drive to Raymond Boulevard. When he had parked less than a block away from his former plant, he skirted its borders, slipping through a break in the chain-link fence near the storage tanks and crawling under the one nearest him to emerge with the suitcase.

It represented one of three questions he would have to answer before he made up his mind, but he threw it carelessly into the back seat of his car, leaving it to fate to determine if it would still be there when he returned from the Essex Pub. He was reason-ably sure he would find Max at his bar, and he was determined to tie up any loose ends in his life before he changed it. The third confrontation involved Vera, but he had decided to leave that for last.

The Essex Pub was roaring, and Max was seated at one of the tables in the restaurant area fronting the bar. It was too hot for him to drink in his coat, but his gray fedora was planted firmly on his head, and one of the tiny American flags they were selling on the streets was jutting from the hatband. He was drinking with some of the regulars, and there was a waitress seated next to him, but he sent her in the direction of the kitchen as soon as he caught sight of Sam approaching, patting the empty place beside him with a welcoming smile.

"Ain't you glad you got into something as wholesome as drugs?" he whispered hoarsely, throwing an arm around Sam's shoulders. "People are eating meat just like it was meat these days." He threw back his head long enough to laugh at his own joke.

Sam took in Max's reaction with a smile of relief. The older man was as close to drunk as he had ever seen him, but it was obvious that he was as happy about the news as any of the people surrounding him. Sam seated himself at the table. "I guess I just know how to pull out of something at the right time," he said with a smile. Then he leaned in toward Max, lowering his voice. "And speaking of that, got any idea as to what's up with gas?"

"The same disgusting story. They're gonna flood the market, just like they did with meat and liquor. A guy can't even make a dishonest living anymore." He was about to laugh again when he noticed Sam's expression, and his smile faded. "Word is, they're ending rationing tomorrow. Why? You planning a trip?"

"It's a possibility," Sam said. Then he lightened his tone, pointing to the pitcher at the center of the table. "Right now, I was planning to get drunk."

Max held his eyes for a moment before he grinned, reaching out and sliding the pitcher in his direction.

They drank until the late afternoon, celebrating something

that had grown between them as well as the end of the war. The radio behind the bar was on, and all through the day, reports from the rest of the country were shouted from table to table, often bringing customers to their feet in spontaneous cheering. In San Francisco, people were riding through the streets on the tops of cable cars, and in Salt Lake City, thousands of soldiers and civilians stood shoulder to shoulder, singing in the rain. Someone who'd driven out from New York said there were over 100,000 people in Times Square.

"Must have been a hell of a day to be in the service," Max said toward the end of the afternoon. "I saw one G.I. actually running from a bunch of girls when I was on my way to work this morning. Just a few hours earlier, it would have been the other way around."

Sam rubbed at his eyes and nodded. "Yeah. A lot of things have changed now." He looked up at Max, taking in the familiar rumple of his tie and his unshaven face before his eyes came to rest on the tiny flag still hanging precariously from his hatband. Everything was at an end now, he realized, and with the loss of his mother and his friends, the man seated next to him was the only person he could honestly say he loved. "*You* haven't changed," he said, pushing to his feet and shaking Max affectionately by the shoulders.

"Who me? Hell, no." Max covered Sam's hands with his own, looking up at him to show that once again he understood a good deal more than he was revealing. "I'll always be here. For the next war."

"I can believe that," Sam said.

They shook hands, smiling, and Sam headed for the door without looking back, but both men knew they had said good-bye.

The apartment was filled with cigarette smoke when he got home, and he knew that Vera's anger had grown as she waited for him during the course of the day. But for once he was indifferent. He walked through the dining room and into the kitchen, where he found her seated at a table, nursing a drink.

"The Christian Rescue Mission on Washington Street is giving free calls to servicemen," he said before she had a chance to speak. "Maybe Joe will phone from wherever he is, and we'll find out when he's coming home."

If she heard the sarcasm in his voice, she gave no indication of it. "Where the hell have you been?" she said tightly.

"Out getting drunk. The war's over, and I've been celebrating with a few of the people who've been following it. I just came home to pick up a little more money." He turned and entered the bedroom. "That's what's important, isn't it? Money?"

He stood in front of his bureau and counted eight hundred dollar bills in his top drawer, tucking five of them into his shirt pocket before he slipped the pile back underneath the box that held his cuff links. There was still time to stuff a pair of socks and a change of underwear into the fold of his jacket before he heard her chair scrape against the linoleum of the kitchen floor. "We're all agreed on our values," he said, turning to find her in the doorway. "Lots of money all around. You, me . . . and Joe."

For a moment, she faltered. The light from the kitchen found her face at an odd angle, and he caught something brittle behind her expression, as though it might suddenly shatter. The blue in her eyes appeared washed out, and everything that was slim and feminine about her seemed merely frail. Then she drew color from her anger. "What does that have to do with not calling me? And why is Joe Branagan any excuse for getting drunk?"

"Because he was my friend," Sam answered, planting himself close enough to her so that she couldn't avoid his eyes. "And I found out he deserted. Not only that, but my own girl knew about it, and lied to me in the bargain."

"The hell I did!" She turned her back on him with an expression of indignation. "I may have let him say whatever he wanted without interfering, but I never lied."

"And you never counted on any money. From his desertion."

"He didn't even know what he was sitting on until he'd lugged it across the country!" She turned, deliberately meeting the challenge of his eyes. "Your buddy was a mess when he first called me. That's why he quit. Not because of any money."

"But you put him back together." Sam shook his head and stepped around her. "Did you rehearse your little routine?" he asked when she followed him into the dining room.

"There was no rehearsal needed." She sensed the extent of his anger, and she reached out and held him by a shoulder. "Listen to me, Sam! He saw a man cut in half during the first attack! Did I tell him we'd help him? That it was right to run? Of course I did!" He turned and crossed the living room, but she hurried around him and blocked the door. "I told you from the start that you were a fool to want to get killed, and I wasn't going to say anything different to him." He lifted her to one side, pulling back his head to avoid the swipe of her hand. "You can drink until you're blind," she shouted at him, "but you still can't look away from this opportunity! It's for all of us, not just Joe!"

He was into the hall by then, and he continued to ignore her, even when the door slammed conclusively shut behind him. It opened once more, just before he reached the stairs. "Think about this, when you're out there drinking your beer and passing judgment on everyone else." She spoke in a whisper this time, moving her lips without opening her mouth, and her voice came to him in a hiss down the empty hallway. "You can turn your back on your friend for what he did, but there's one thing you can never forget. At least he went! That's more than you can say, you righteous bastard!"

In the dimness of the hall, she burned at him with the light behind her, and the fact that what she said was deliberately calculated to hurt him did nothing to diminish the pain of the accusation. She was the first woman he had ever made love to, and the only person outside his family he had ever lived with, but that last image of her—glaring at him from the blaze of the doorway—was always the one he remembered.

* * *

Clay Street took on the warm, sepia tones of another summer twilight, and Sam let his eyes linger on the familiar buildings, standing in the shadow of Skorski's cellarway like a stranger. It was a different place now, even though it held the comfort of its old appearance for him. Gradual change was a part of every neighborhood, Sam realized, but the war had reordered entire lives in a matter of years.

For a moment, he allowed his mind to touch on the existence he had known such a short time ago, but too many of the voices he heard had been lost to him, and the memories were still too fresh to be indulged without pain. What had they been thinking of that evening, when he and Maura had celebrated the news of Pearl Harbor along with the others? Eddie was dead, and there would no longer be any noisy gatherings in the Branagans' basement. He touched a hand to his face and wondered if he could ever bring himself to return, even in his memory.

He emerged from the shadow of the cellarway then, and walked back toward DeFillippo's shop, where he had parked the Packard. When he got there, he noticed that somebody had soaped the barber's windows, spelling out V-J in four-foot letters. He caught his reflection there: a tall, well-dressed man stepping into a stylish car. He looked as though he were going someplace.

And then, because the land was the only possession he was not leaving behind with Vera, and because he could think of no other place that might offer any sense of renewal, he drove south toward Ferry Street, in the direction of Florida.

Part Four:
Final Reckoning

Chapter Ten

"I think what I miss most are the leaves." Sam gestured in the direction of the shadeless sidewalks, and Todd followed his motion, gazing through the tinted windshield of the Porsche at invisible trees. "Fall is one of those seasons you begin to feel special about near the end of your life."

Todd took in his father's distant expression from the corners of his eyes. "You're only fifty-eight," he said.

"Well, that's nearly forty years I've been away from where I grew up. This . . . trouble brings a lot back. A different life."

Todd was disturbed by the direction of the conversation. "It must have been something, starting all over down here," he suggested. "It's still a new area to people up north. I can imagine what it seemed like then."

Clement smiled without taking his eyes from the road. "In most ways, it was ideal, although not everyone was sure about it at the time. If they had been, I guess I wouldn't have been sitting on all that land when the war ended. That was a real piece of luck."

"More than luck. You helped people out by buying it."

"I did all right by myself, too. As it turned out, the war had

helped to develop this state in a way most people hadn't fore-
seen. By 'forty-five, we had airports, pilots, air traffic controllers:
everything people needed to fly. It was just a matter of shifting it
all from military to civilian use."

Todd looked out at the affluent homes lining both sides of the
street Sam had chosen. His father had taken him on a tour as far
south as Miami while he finished the confession of his past.
"And all this was farmland?" he asked.

Sam shook his head. "Not really. Some of it was under water,
depending on what part of the area you're talking about. But the
boom came later. I sold one farm and bought into Miami almost
as soon as I arrived. People thought the values had topped out,
but I saw one more change I thought would make a difference."

Clement's voice had warmed to his subject, and Todd relaxed
slightly as his father began to come out of himself. "So there *was*
more than pure luck involved," he said lightly.

"Well, that Packard helped. I think I told you, it was one of
the first air-conditioned cars. Anyway, when you could open up
a beachfront to tourists without using space to keep them cool, it
meant a hell of a lot more people. I still prefer those wide porches
and high ceilings, but air conditioning did mean a lot more small
rooms in each resort. And that meant more paying customers."
He shrugged behind the wheel. "They were good times. Delta
and National created those first package tours, the boom in cars
brought even more people, and we were off to the races. I was on
the Chamber of Commerce during the Fifties. We figured the
population of the state went up eighty percent in ten years." He
drove the next few blocks without speaking, and Todd saw the
focus of what he had been saying leave his expression. "I could
have done fine down here without the bootlegging," he said
softly enough to be talking to himself. "There was plenty of
opportunity back then."

"You did fine," Todd said. "And without any help."

"I started with money I made under the table."

"You left a fortune on some beach. And you never touched it."

"Yes, I left it." Sam pulled over to the side of the broad street they had been driving and stopped the car. "I left it in case I failed." He looked at Todd with the directness of a confession. "I could have destroyed it, but I never did. All those years. That would have been the real test. Knowing I could never go back to that life by living without that security."

Todd shook his head in disagreement, but he gave up the argument before it began. "Do it now, then," he urged. "We'll dig it up and destroy it! Holding it back hasn't done anything to get rid of her."

"Oh, I'm not going to hold it back anymore," Sam said, and once again, Todd felt isolated from him by the preoccupied tone of his voice. "I'm glad I have it now. I need it to find them."

The buzzer on his console sounded almost as soon as he had entered his office. Clement took the time to remove his jacket and make himself comfortable behind his desk before he responded. "Yes, Tanya."

"There's a Miss Campbell on the line. I told her I wasn't sure you were in yet, in case you were busy."

Clement surprised himself with his calm. "Thank you, Tanya. I'll take the call." He thought back to the day before and his conversation with Todd. She had contacted him even sooner than he had expected.

Then the voice was in his ear. The new voice, and one that he had come to identify only with the immediacy of the threat it implied, devoid of the other associations that might remind him of a girl he had once loved. "Hello, Sam."

"Vera, I've been waiting." He released his breath with a sound of resignation directly into the receiver. "I can have it for you."

"How soon, Sam? You said you didn't have it. Now you say you do. I don't want to be kept waiting. I've waited too long."

There was a smugness in her voice that belied her claim of uncertainty. Clement hunched over the phone, encouraged by her sense of confidence. "Two days," he said in a rush. "It's

Monday. You can call me early Wednesday afternoon to arrange a meeting."

"I'll do that, Sam. And you better not cross me again."

"Vera! Don't hang up yet. Please."

"Yes?"

"That man with you. The one who . . ." Sam's thoughts went to Kara, and he left the sentence unfinished. "Is that Joe?"

She was amused. "Who else would it be? This is strictly business, Sam. He *is* the third partner. Of course, there's only two of us now," she added as an afterthought. "You don't mind parting with your share, do you? For interest? Thirty-five years is a long time."

"You can have it all. But I want one condition met."

"You're in no position to dictate conditions."

"I want my wife left out of this. If I don't deliver, you still have the opportunity to try whatever you like. But for two days, I want you to stay away from my family."

"She's lovely, Sam." Once again, the rasp broke through to scratch the speech. "Do you like taking her from behind, the way you had me? I told Joe that was the best position, since she was probably used to it."

Clement shook under the impact of the truth that Kara had spared him. He gripped the armrest of his chair with his free hand in an attempt to supress what he wanted to say, and the effort brought the blood to his face in a rush that made him dizzy. But even in that painful moment, he knew that the final piece had fallen into place, setting the mechanism of his anger in motion with a drive as irresistible as his own fate. "Two days," he managed tightly.

"Just see that you deliver. We'll leave your precious wife to you."

Sam silenced the voice the moment she agreed, slamming the receiver back against the cradle of the phone as though it were something alive. Almost at the same time, his left hand came away from his chair with a sharp tearing sound. He pushed to his feet with the thought that he had hurt himself, but except for the shaking in his arm and a few small cuts where the wood had broken his skin, the hand was uninjured. The chair behind his desk was made of heavy oak, and he had torn away the armrest in his effort to control himself, leaving a ragged line of spindles jutting up where the support had been.

In a brief moment of panic, he slipped his hand over the area of his operation, moving out from behind his desk and pacing the rug experimentally in front of it. There was not even an indication of soreness. He smiled then, and in spite of the circumstances, there was no trace of bitterness in the expression.

The strength that had been with him all of his life had returned, and he was fully healed from his surgery. After one final confrontation with his past, he would achieve something he had not enjoyed since that December day in his distant past, something that coincided with his revenge for Kara's treatment, but went far beyond it. He would be whole again.

Vera, too, had the feeling that fate had brought her back to Sam. She had come to miss him over the years, not as a person, but as the agent who had performed functions indispensable to the ultimate success that had eluded her all of her life. When he had failed to return to her after their final quarrel, she had eventually taken a job with Max.

His operations were limited to the legitimate management of his restaurants after the war, and he paid her only slightly more than she would have earned in nursing, but in the long run, she saw a greater opportunity in working for him. Within a year, she was managing the waitresses and keeping his books, but Max himself remained more like the uncle he had always been, without responding to her efforts to interest him in her as a woman.

The war had been over for five years before she eventually made her way into his bed, and she knew then it was only because enough time had passed to convince him that Sam would not return. For many years, it proved a comfortable relationship for both of them. As an older man, Max was less demanding of her body, while allowing her a welcome freedom from the attention of the males she dealt with in managing his business. In time, he offered to marry her, but Vera declined the proposal. She had a different sort of partnership in mind, and she waited for her opportunity, enduring a merely comfortable living by keeping her eyes fastened on the bright promise of the future.

By the end of the Fifties, Newark had begun to change, as most of the middle- and upper-class residents deserted the city for the landscape of the predominantly white suburbs. Business at the Essex Pub declined with the neighborhood, but Max was in his late sixties by then, and his flair for finding opportunity under the most adverse circumstances was part of a different era. He sold his restaurant in Boston rather than deserting the old neighborhood, and lived without concern from the rapidly declining proceeds. By the middle of the decade, it was clear that the area could no longer support his business.

Vera was excited by the prospect. Age had dulled Max's ambition, but she knew the necessity of finding a new income would draw him back to the world of dealing. Like many cities in decline, Newark had become a prime market in the movement of drugs, and Vera envisioned an operation that would exceed anything she had known with Sam during the war. This time, she would be working with Max herself, and they would be selling from the cover of the restaurant in their own city.

She did not tell Max that they would deal with drugs far more profitable than marijuana, and she kept him from any direct contact with the sort of people who would be supplying them. She simply made it clear from her bookkeeping that they had very few years left to live off their current assets, and she did so at a time when Max was old enough to give his indifferent approval. Unfortunately, he was also old enough to die, and he passed away in his sleep only weeks later. She woke to find him cold and smiling, as though he were amused that, like Sam, he had deserted her on the eve of her long delayed triumph.

Most of his money went to a community organization on Ferry Street, but she was surprised to learn there was a provision in his will that left her enough to live on for many years. She might have played it safe then, investing in a fairly comfortable lifestyle, but she was bitter about having been thwarted once again, just when the ultimate deal was within her reach. She took what she had and entered the underworld on her own.

She lasted five years. She was as ruthless as the people she dealt with, but she was a woman, and her limited resources were not enough to even the odds by hiring the kind of help she needed. Branagan had called her years earlier when she was with Max. He had been living off a series of menial jobs in New York, alone and alcoholic in the wake of his family's rejection. She had little use for him then, but she contacted him when she found herself faltering on her own, and he came to her immediately with a promise of unconditional obedience.

But Branagan was not Sam, and he did nothing to inspire either the fear or respect she needed to survive in the underground of the drug world. The last roll of the dice failed, and she was left at fifty to start where she had begun so hopefully thirty years earlier. In the end, she was forced to send Branagan back to his drinking and accept a job as a nurse in the nearby Oranges. She still might have married if she put enough energy into it, but she was too bitter to give up her independence to any man who was less than wealthy, and by that time, too much of her life showed in her face to make that a likely prospect.

For seven years she worked the wards of the veterans' hospitals, without the comfort of hope or the indifference of resignation, enduring her frustration much like the veterans around her tolerated their infirmities. And then, in an improbable meeting that could only have been dictated by fate, she entered a ward where one of the patients was Todd Clement.

She had seen the name on a clipboard before she was aware of the boy himself, but when she sought him out, she could tell she had at long last been rewarded the minute she caught sight of him. She saw a peculiar justice in it all, as though she were looking at young Sam himself, with everything erased and the opportunity to start where she had begun so many years before.

She did not want to risk getting the information she needed directly from the boy himself, but she found it impossible not to smile at him from across the room.

She was smiling when she hung up from speaking to Sam, and the expression lingered as she stepped away from the pay phone and raised a hand to her forehead to squint across the water. The marina she had called from was separated from the back of Sam's home by two lagoons lined with other residences. Vera found that she could see into his garage through the distant square of a rear window if she placed herself in the proper position between the intervening buildings.

During the day, a portion of either car was visible, taking some color from the window when it was removed from the garage. At night, surveillance was even easier, since the bulb activated by the garage door isolated the interior in a flood of bright light. She had been able to predict when he would reach his office that morning almost to the minute.

Like the miraculous appearance of Todd, Vera considered the ideal observation point an indication that her reckoning had been preordained by forces beyond her understanding, and she was warm with faith in an ultimate justice that seemed about to compensate her for the sacrifice of an entire lifetime.

"I could only hear your side. Did he say he was going to give it to us?" Branagan's voice brought her out of her reverie.

"Of course he did. I told you he would." She turned a sharp look on him. "I'll take the night watch myself, since that's most likely when he'll go for it. But I want you here during the day. And I'm going to check on you to make sure of it."

Branagan swallowed, blinking against the brightness of the sunlight. "You know I hate the water. Besides, you said he was going to bring it to us."

"He'll be doing it on his terms if we wait for that. You just make sure he doesn't slip away when we're not looking, or we're both going to regret it. I'm through with things falling apart at the last minute. The only way we can be sure of him is to be there the minute he puts his hands on it."

Todd entered the small room his mother used for sewing without bothering to knock. It was another hopeful sign, and it comforted Kara at a time when she needed it most. The reserve that Todd had used to keep himself from them was falling away, and they were becoming the family they had been before he had entered the service. There was a particular irony in the timing of the change, but Kara kept the thought to herself, afraid that it would show on her face. When she looked up and smiled at him, though, she realized it would be impossible to keep anything from him very long. He was too intelligent for that, and he was already troubled.

"He's talking about the war again," he said, standing by the chair next to hers without sitting down. "My war. Where did he hear that routine about 'talking through Nam?'"

"Your father called some veterans' groups. Right here in Miami. Talking about what you did during the war is something they say has helped many of the boys that were there. People like you."

"Why didn't he tell me about it?"

"He was going to, of course." She reached out and squeezed his hand. "Todd, he just wants to make sure that there are people you can tell about how you feel, yes? People who will understand."

Todd settled into the chair behind him. "We've already talked about it ourselves."

"Of course." Kara smiled. "And that has made him very happy. But he wants to know that there are others. Did you realize there were groups of men, veterans, meeting here in Miami?"

Todd kept his eyes on the floor and shrugged. "People in my unit live right here in our area. So what?"

"You could call some of them."

He rolled his eyes and shook off the suggestion. "It's only been a year since they stopped calling me. Look, I went over there and I'm back, okay?"

"Are you back?"

Todd fell silent.

"Your father loves you."

He leaned toward her then, shaking his head. "I know that, but that's not the point. Nobody's threatening me, are they? He's the one who needs the help. I've lived with myself since I got back. Why the hell is he so worried about my problems?"

Kara hesitated before she decided on her answer. "Because he thinks he's going to die."

Todd pulled back in the face of the response. "What? He's fifty-eight. The operation—"

"That is only one kind of cancer." Kara allowed herself to continue, expressing thoughts she had kept vague and incomplete for her own protection as well as his. "For all of his life, what your father did when he was very young has been at the back of his mind." She smiled wanly. "He has always been such a good person. From our beginning together, he told me about what he had done during the war. How he had gotten his start." She looked into her son's eyes without faltering. "That is one kind of honesty, and he was rewarded by it when these pigs came back, because I knew everything they could threaten to tell." The anger left her voice then, and she looked away from him. "Now your father sees the chance to face something inside himself. That is a very special honesty only few men have. It would have been very terrible to lose him to disease—" a shaking began in her shoulders, but she laced her arms across her chest, blinking to maintain her control "—but I know that it would be better for him to be dead than look away from what he feels he should do."

"Christ." Todd pushed out of his chair, raising his arms in frustration. "I know what he did! He sold drugs. He made money. Did that kill anybody? He's lived a whole different life since then."

"He wants to pay for that happiness. And he wants to be rid of those people."

Todd shook his hands at her. "He's got a million dollars' worth of morphine if he wants to pay for it! Let him give them what they want. He'll be done with drugs, he'll be done with them, and he can go on living the life he deserves without talking about seeing the goddamned leaves fall just one more time!"

Kara shook her head slowly and came to her feet, working at the ties of her bathrobe. She was wearing a slip underneath, but the purple area rose above it, running in ugly blotches from the tops of her breasts to cover most of her skin from her shoulders to the base of her neck. The hands Todd had been waving clenched in on themselves.

Kara's face betrayed the tears she had been working so hard to hold back, but her voice was under control when she spoke. "Can't you see that he'd rather die first?"

Todd slept with Mai that night. There was trouble in the back of his mind when he made love to her, just as there had been that last time over there, but the sheer exhilaration of the moment pushed it from his thoughts. She was not the first girl he'd made love to, but she was his first lover, and he had become as open as she was in pleasing both of them. When they finally broke away from each other, they continued to lock eyes without speaking, and he was sure that no matter what she might have done with other men, she had allowed him to see a very private part of herself that went beyond the simple act of coupling.

When he told her that he had to go almost immediately, she protested by reminding him how little time they had left together, and she refused to dress until he was fully clothed and pulling on his clutch belt. He couldn't bring himself to tell her that he had a choice in leaving, that he was entitled to be relieved by the rotation the members of his own company had established. If he had, she would have made too good an argument for his staying, and he would have listened.

But they had been hit lately, five times out of six in his particular company, and even if he headed only the handful of men that made up his patrol, he felt an obligation to be with them during a time when they were drawing an unusual amount of fire. It was a war where the territory of the enemy changed daily, and the only clear goal the average grunt could cite was to survive his twelve months and make it back home. But there was one current of concern that went a long way toward compensating for the lack of any universal ideology, and that was the feeling most of them had for each other. There was no call to duty that kept Todd from avoiding that last outing. He simply felt an obligation to be with his people.

Chaiten stood outside the hooch calling his name, and he spent his last few moments trying to console her. They were moving into a nearby village that had recently been retaken after being overrun by the N.V.A. All of the fighting was over, he told her, and they would be doing nothing more than securing the area. Everything he said was true—he had never lied about what he might face each time he left her—but the impending action worked at his insides with a special fear, above and beyond the normal state of mind it took to fight that war.

For one thing, he was short: only weeks separated him from the end of his tour. More importantly, he thought he might be in love, and he didn't know what to do about Mai. The military discouraged any involvement with Vietnamese women, and he knew it would be impossible for him to extend his tour in order to get her out of the country, even if they were married. Mai herself wanted nothing from him, refusing to discuss the possibility of even seeing him once his time was out, much less becoming his wife. Earlier in their relationship, before the day of his departure loomed so near, her attitude had been a comfort to him, even though he was determined to change her mind. It had assured him that she loved him for himself, and not any opportunity he might have represented.

Each time he touched on that last meeting with her in his dreams, it was always worse than the reality, because he acted out everything they had done together, with the simultaneous knowledge of what was about to happen. Todd had not been at the end of the dream since the hospital, and the dread that pulled at him from his insides brought a clenching to his entire body, from the lock of his jaws to a tightening deep inside his bowels. Finally, he forced himself to see her as she had been when he kissed her good-bye, and he remembered the way he had tried to preserve that last moment in his mind, knowing that he might not return to see her again.

The dream always ended there. But that night, Todd sensed the approach of something unexpected and threatening. The nightmare continued, and he turned away from that unnerving farewell with Mai to find a figure standing in the doorway of the hooch. "I never go on from here," Todd protested, and the plea sounded in his bedroom as he called out of his sleep.

But the figure remained in the doorway, and Todd sensed that it was only a question of time until he was irresistibly drawn by it to the place he had been avoiding for the last five years of his life. He woke then, screaming from the pain of memories that had come dangerously close to exploding full blown in his mind.

Sam brought him back to himself, leaning into his room and calling out from the light of the hallway. Todd hesitated, frowning at his father before he assured him that he was all right. For a moment, he had been uncertain as to whether he was still dreaming, since the figure peering at him from across the room was the same one that had stood waiting for him in the doorway of the hooch.

Clement left home at ten-thirty the following night. Kara was in their room, already in bed with the evening paper, but Sam regretted not being able to see Todd. He had called in earlier to excuse himself from dinner in order to spend one of his rare evenings out. Sam had told Kara he was on the way to the airport, where he would fly to Tampa on business. It provided a reason for the brief ceremony of a parting, and even if he were given the option, he had always felt awkward during prolonged farewells.

Earlier that afternoon, he had put all his papers in order at the office, and as he passed through each room of his home, he looked hungrily at the interior. In the garage, he touched a bicycle that Todd could no longer ride, running his fingers over the handlebars and remembering his son at an earlier age. For all of his awareness, he realized that he had never before fully appreciated what a long and happy life he had enjoyed with Kara.

Then he stepped into Kara's wagon, starting the engine and backing out of the garage. Under the circumstances, it made more sense to leave the Porsche behind with his family. It was the last familiar sight he saw before the overhead light in the garage went out with the closing of the door, leaving his home in darkness.

The morphine was hidden in a place less than an hour and a half from his house in Plantation. Ironically, it was an area that had undergone a minimum of change since he had buried it there in the fall of 1945. There were now a variety of roads and highways providing access to what had once been an isolated finger of inland water along the coast, but the land itself had remained basically undeveloped, relegated during the early Fifties to a state park.

The actual spot where he had buried the suitcase was not ideal, but for a sight chosen with a minimum of planning, he could have done far worse. He would have to pull into a parking lot, but there were seldom cars there as late as midnight, and the cabin that housed the local ranger was over a half mile away, well shielded from the sight of his headlights by areas of intense vegetation.

In the opposite direction was the beach where Sam had gone on another night so many years earlier. It was white with natural sand, but it was hemmed in by overgrowth, and the water there was shallow and brackish enough to discourage most bathers. Sam had been there only once in the last ten years, noting that it continued to be deserted by most people for the open beaches and clear water nearer the parking lot.

He had a good ten-minute walk ahead of him after he parked the car in the empty lot, and he took a path through the undergrowth that added another five minutes to his trip in order to avoid going near any of the darkened outbuildings. He moved cautiously, knowing that although his presence violated no laws, he would be forced to return the following night if he should encounter anyone on the way to the water.

Twenty minutes later, he had settled into a position that overlooked the beach. A heavy cloud cover hid the stars, but the darkness only added to his sense of security. There would be more than enough light to orient himself at dawn, a full hour before anyone was likely to arrive at the park. And with that kind of an early start, he could be back at his office before noon, waiting for Vera's call.

The thought that he would be so close to home without returning to it took his mind from his surroundings for the next few minutes, and a slight rustling in the undergrowth behind him was the first warning he had that he might not be alone. By that time, it was too late, and a hand closed over his mouth before he could cry out or even turn around.

Kara could not be sure if the ringing of the phone had brought her out of her sleep too late to answer it, or if it had only sounded in some dream. In either case, she found herself awake near midnight, and the shadow of premonition caused her to bring a hand to her face.

For weeks, she had been bracing herself for the worst to happen, and the sixth sense which had helped her to survive very real dangers in the past told her that Sam had left for an appointment that had nothing to do with his business. They had been too close to each other from the start for any shift in the current of his feelings not to communicate itself to her by a variety of subtle signs on the surface. The lapses into periods of preoccupation which she had not seen since the years after the war; the prolonged and tender way he had made love to her before he had left that evening; his hope for Todd. Everything pointed to a preparation for a final parting.

He was gratified by the change in his son, but she saw something held in reserve when he discussed him. The elation that had marked their early victories together was missing, as though he would have to content himself with the mere promise of what he saw happening.

She sighed, angry over her own weakness, but rising from the bed in spite of it. She pulled on her robe as she made her way toward Todd's room, determined to indulge herself with the comfort of his presence. But there was no answer to her knocking, and when she pushed open the door to his room, the bed was smooth and undisturbed in the glow of the night-light.

The sight of the empty room communicated something that meant more to her than being alone, and she sank back against the door, remembering Todd's determination to protect his father and seeing other scenes from her memory. The janitor in the darkened hallway; the smoke streaming from the hood of the wagon; the unmade bed in the barracks, awaiting the return of her sister; her family, boarding the train in Vienna. Her faith had been driven deep inside her, but in the most elemental form, it still existed, and she pressed the backs of her hands to her eyes in unspoken prayer.

It would be so unfair to lose both of them.

No weapon appeared in the limited circle of Sam's vision, and he chose to surge against the grasp that held him from behind, straining for the first time in his life against a strength that seemed equal to his own. But the struggle came to an abrupt halt when a voice called out to him in a hoarse whisper. "Don't shout!"

The grip on him was relinquished, and Sam turned around, only to renew it in an embrace. "Todd!"

They held each other for a moment before Todd pushed away

to face him. "I didn't want you to make any noise," he whispered.

"My God, I thought you wanted to kill me!" Sam sank down into the hollow he had cleared for himself near the edge of the beach.

"If I had wanted to kill you, you'd have been dead before you had any time to think about it." After a quick survey of the area around him, Todd settled down beside his father.

Sam was rubbing at his neck, still dazed by surprise. "I can't believe you came up behind me without making any noise. You're a good—" He hesitated.

"—killer," Todd suggested evenly. "A former professional. Unfortunately, there haven't been any openings for me since I got back. Until now, that is." He confronted his father. "I've been watching since the night before last, ready to follow." He produced a pistol from inside his jacket. "I didn't exactly expect your consent if I offered to even up the odds."

Sam shook his head in the face of the suggestion. "There are no odds, and I don't need any help. I'm doing this to get even with myself. For something I set in motion before you were born."

"I'm not going back if that's what you're saying."

Sam gestured toward the darkness in front of them. "There's about two hundred yards of beach out there. When it's light enough to line up one of the palms along the edge of the sand, I'll take a rough bearing and start digging. The suitcase is less than four feet down, if it's still there. I guess it is. Judging by what's been going on down here with drugs lately, a find like that would have made the papers. Anyway, I think I can handle something that simple without hurting myself."

Todd continued to look at him with open suspicion. "Fine. If there's no danger, I guess you won't mind if I stay and watch."

Sam was about to protest, but he realized any objection on his part would be useless. There were a hundred ways he could free himself for his meeting with Vera the following noon. "Suit yourself," he said with a smile. He peered up at the starless sky before he leaned back into the brush he had tamped down behind him. "It's not the best night to spend in the great outdoors."

Todd stretched out beside him, placing the pistol on the ground between them. "I've slept there before. Standing up, and in the rain."

"I'm sorry. I'd forgotten."

"Don't ever be sorry for forgetting that," Todd said. "Good night," he added when he had rolled over on his side and was facing in the opposite direction.

"Good night," Sam said.

Todd had been keeping a tireless vigil since Sunday, and in minutes, his heavy breathing indicated that he had actually succeeded in getting to sleep. Sam smiled to himself, grateful for the opportunity to be with him again, and noting that for once, his son's rest seemed undisturbed.

But something came over Todd during the night, something that went beyond the restlessness that had marred his sleep since his return from the war. He woke up in a sweat, despite the coolness of the open air, drawing his breath in uneven gasps, as though he had been running instead of attempting to rest. He had been up for two nights in a row, but when he settled back down onto the soft ground, his eyes had barely closed again when everything came back to him and he remembered the dream. He sat up a second time, already shaking, and he realized that something more than his fatigue had made him especially vulnerable.

A slapping sound from the direction of the beach caused him to flail out at the pistol, rolling to one side of the hollow. He remained where he was, frozen with fear for close to a minute, until he identified the soft lap of the water. Even then, images that he had always succeeded in holding back flashed before his eyes, and it took a concentrated effort before he realized that his surroundings had merged with the landscape of his dream.

He had spent too many nights over there in similar places.

And this time, unlike his dream, the danger he felt was as real as the undergrowth around him, and the oil he smelled was from the workings of a gun he might use. This time, he could not leave the nightmare that was bringing it all back. Not unless he were willing to walk away from his father.

He shut his eyes against it, but what flashed before him there was even more vivid than the total suggestion of his surroundings, and everything that he had been avoiding for over five years began to play itself out in his memory, as if his mind were his eyes, and he had no way of shutting off his vision.

"She's coming!"

"Where?" Sam sprang up from the prone position of his sleep and took in the circumference of the cove with widened eyes before he turned to Todd. His son was doubled up beside him, rocking back and forth in a seated position with his arms wrapped tightly against his sides. "Todd, what's wrong?" He put his hands on his son's shoulders and leaned into him. "Where did you see her?"

It might have been twenty years earlier. Todd's face was streaked with tears and he spoke in the disjointed speech of a child. "She's everywhere! This is her place, here." He lost control of himself, and Sam waited, patting him lightly on the back. "I can't even shut my eyes!"

"Todd, it's a dream."

Todd released his breath and shook his head. When he spoke, his voice was still wavering, but Sam was aware that he was conscious of what he was saying. "Not this time. The whole fucking thing is coming down on me!"

"The war?" Sam brought his face closer to Todd's, peering at him and moving his arms around his shoulders.

"God, yes." Todd nodded and Sam wondered if he had ever seen an expression so vulnerable. "It's the end. I'm seeing the end again and I can't stop it!"

"Then don't," Sam said softly. "Just this once, let it come. For me."

They were two hours out from base before they reached the

village. Telling his father there in the undergrowth, he could smell the jungle they had emerged from, and feel the pull of his equipment against his shoulders. He had used a North Vietnamese pack the last few months he was over there. Most of the men found them more comfortable than the American issue, and Mai had managed to get him one from a farmer who said he had found it in his field. They had taken their time on the trails because things had been so hot for them lately, and later, he realized that anyone not worried about being ambushed could have left after his patrol did and been at the village before they arrived.

There were no burned hooches and dazed villagers waiting when Todd's group entered the large clearing. The V.C. had withdrawn without resistance days earlier, and the Americans found the area almost as they had left it before they were forced out. Todd's patrol was assigned the job of covering the fields that ran to the north of the settlement, and he had left the formation of a survey line to Ridings while he indulged himself in a cigarette, relieved that they had not seen any action.

When one of his men trotted up to him in the center of the village, he assumed that they were ready to make their sweep, but the marine was gesturing, and Todd saw a look of exasperation on his face as he approached him.

"Ridings don't want to start across."

Todd tamped out his cigarette and fell into step beside him, walking back toward the edge of the village. "I know," he said. "I told him to wait for me."

"Not even with you he ain't going," the marine said. "He's arguing about it with the old man from the village."

Todd could see the knot of his men at that point, surrounding the frail form of a villager who was tapping his chest and shaking his head in the direction of the field.

"I think Betty's out there," Ridings warned as Todd approached the group.

Todd paused and glanced in the direction of the field. Bouncing Bettys were mines that could be rigged in a variety of ways.

In a field, they would be tripped off by the weight of the man who stepped on them. When that happened, a sixty-millimeter mortar round popped up with a shortened fuse that usually set them off when they were waist high. The pattern of the explosion was a horizontal circle of metal that entered the body perpendicular to it, like a buzz saw. They were designed to cut people in half.

"What does he say?" Todd asked, pointing to the old man.

"He says there's nothing out there. But the V.C. are too comfortable around this place. I don't fuckin' trust him."

The old man waved his sticklike arms then, as though he had understood what Ridings was saying. Smiling, he raised his hand in the direction of the villagers who had gathered to watch from a distance. Then he turned to Ridings and spoke a few words of Vietnamese before he hobbled in the direction of the field, working his way slowly over the uneven ground with a stick he used as a cane. Ridings looked over at Todd and shrugged. "He's going out there himself. Just to show us."

Before Todd could react, a murmuring went up from the villagers behind them. A figure had detached itself from the crowd and was rushing toward the field, waving the old man back while the others called out to him. The old man had not yet reached the edge of the clearing, and he turned, making his way back to them with the same confident smile on his face.

"What's going on?" Todd asked.

"Same thing. They just want someone younger to do it, I guess. He could be dead of old age by the time he made it across."

"Betty ain't out there," one of the others concluded, pointing toward the field, and even Ridings hitched up his pack and moved toward the edge of the clearing ahead of the others, as if to compensate for his initial stubbornness. "That fucking kid's halfway across, and he ain't even looking down."

"That's no kid. Look at her ass. That's a slit."

The argument was settled when the figure turned around, waving them into the field. Even from that distance, the long dark hair and narrow waist of a woman were unmistakable. Ridings was well into the waving grass before Todd recognized her. It was Mai. At first, he felt a rush of warmth, and he waved, trying to get her attention with the thought that she had been unable to stay away when she knew where he would be going.

Then he realized that she had remained out of his sight, appearing only when the old man was being forced to precede them. Todd strode toward the edge of the field, and his pace quickened with each disturbing thought. She had made good time to arrive before they did, traveling the sort of straight line available only to someone who had nothing to fear from either side. "Hold back!" he shouted to the others about to enter the field, and he tore through the undergrowth toward the bobbing helmet that marked Ridings' position.

The recent past flashed through his mind with the acceleration of desperation, as though he were already dying instead of pounding through the grass waiting for the ground to erupt beneath him. Every time his company had been hit during the last month, his patrol had been a part of the action. And for the last month, he had been telling her where they would be going. Had she been present those other times, watching them draw fire from some enemy bunker?

"Don't move!" he screamed, coming up on Ridings.

Ridings turned as if to object, but the expression on his face went dead when he saw Todd bearing down on him.

"Daisy cutters!" Todd pulled him back by his pack strap and pointed at the tracks they'd made behind them in the grass. "Get out the way you came in!" he ordered, and then he ducked around him, running in the direction of Mai.

For the past twelve months, he had been developing the kind of instinct that meant his survival, but even as he gained on her, he held fast to the possibility that he was wrong. There were other reasons why she might have come, reasons that had to do with being young and frightened together in the same place, and touching in a special way that removed the threat of the war surrounding them.

But he never found out how much of what had passed between them had to do with her real feelings, and how much was a deception justified by her beliefs. In the end, he only knew that he had been right about her actions.

He could see that as he approached her, shouting her name. She waited, facing him until he was close enough to read the defiance in her expression. Then she turned calmly and trotted away from him toward the green of the distant jungle. He was less than ten yards behind her when either her luck ran out or she got what she wanted. In any case, some of the same fragments that cut through her body still had enough momentum to take out a good piece of his leg.

Fifteen minutes after he had finished speaking, Todd was still on all fours near the edge of the water. By that time, he was bringing up only phlegm, but Sam continued to stoop over him, patting him gently between the shoulder blades. When the shuddering motions finally stopped, Sam raised him effortlessly by an arm and half carried him back through the undergrowth to the hollow where they had been lying.

"Feel better?" he asked when Todd had settled down onto the mattress of the brush.

"Jesus." Todd let his eyes shut. "You ought to know."

"No, not yet," Sam said softly. "Telling you was only half of it. I still have to pay the price."

Todd's voice was distant with exhaustion. "I'll pay mine in the morning."

"You are the price." Sam reached over and squeezed his shoulder. "You didn't put yourself in that position over there. All you did was pay for it, like so many of the others. Now it's time to stop paying."

"Even though I killed her."

"That's not what it was, but call it that if you like." Sam settled down beside him. "What would have happened if you hadn't gone after her?"

"I don't know."

238 FINAL RECKONING

"Yes, you do. You would have lost one of your men. Would it be any easier to be Todd Clement now if that had happened instead?"

"I never saw it that way."

"You never looked at it. Sometimes that takes more courage than living through something the first time."

Todd nodded without opening his eyes. "Especially at night. I'll never sleep. Not the way most people think of sleeping."

"I think that might change." Sam's expression was hidden by the darkness. "You'll wish you hadn't lived with it so long, but I'm glad it came out while I was . . . here." He looked off in the direction of Plantation. "Maybe you should know now that things might happen tomorrow you won't understand. Not until you've had a little time. Just remember, I have to live with myself, too." He smiled then. "It's all going to be easier for me now, because the worst is over for you. Do you think you can accept that?" When there was no response, he bent down to find that Todd was already sleeping. "I guess you have," he said.

He listened to the even breathing of his son until he was satisfied that his rest would not be disturbed again. Then he leaned back himself, staring up at the sky with a feeling of exhilaration that he knew would keep him awake until the first light of morning. It seemed so much to him, the unexpected gift of that last night.

Todd was still sleeping when Sam pulled on his light jacket and rose quietly to his feet. He paused to look at the boy's placid expression as he stooped down to pick up the small folding shovel he had brought with him, deciding not to disturb him until he had uncovered the suitcase and was ready to leave. Then he turned and pushed through the trees, walking the periphery of the beach until he was about two hundred yards from Todd's position.

The sky had taken on a red glow where it met the narrow neck of the inlet, but the sun had not yet pushed above the horizon, and Sam held his glasses in the pinch of his fingers to prevent them from slipping off as he bent down to examine the trunk of each tree. He finally found his mark, a jagged rut in the smooth base of a palm, evener and narrower with time, but as indelible as the track of a scar. He took five measured steps in a straight line with the rock behind it and began to dig.

He had scattered sand in a wide circle around him, forming a depression in the beach that was close to three feet deep at the center, when he began to fear that he might not find what he was looking for. By that time, the sun was beginning to rise, and he turned toward the tree line in the growing light with the thought that he had oriented himself to the wrong mark. But a second glance convinced him there was no mistaking the jagged line he had cut so many years earlier, and he doubled his efforts, imagining that he already heard the sounds of early visitors approaching through the underbrush. Almost at once, the blade of the shovel slid off to the side of an object that was giving but resilient.

He fell to his knees then, scooping the sand away with the delicate hand movements of someone uncovering a relic from the past. Gradually, the rough covering of the canvas he had used to wrap the suitcase came into view, and when he had dug deeply enough to slide that away, he rose, brushing at the brown leather of the bag itself. He heard Todd coming up behind him, and he decided to wait before he opened it.

"You're too late," he said, swinging the suitcase out of the hole and turning with a smile.

"It's never too late, Sam."

He let the bag fall then, staring mutely at the gun in Vera's hands before his thoughts caught up with what was happening and his eyes settled on a face he hadn't seen in close to forty years.

Mai walked for Todd through the mine field yet another time, and he watched, fascinated not by what he was seeing, but his reaction to it. She was dead, he knew, and she had been his lover. There were other things he would never know, thoughts that might have remained in her head even if he could suddenly have been with her again. But he was at peace, and he could open his eyes during his sleep without turning them on himself for fear of what he might see.

He opened them as he was waking, stretching with the satisfaction of a rest he hadn't enjoyed for years. Then he sat up, squinting toward the beach, when he saw his father's place empty beside him.

For a moment, the scene before him was the field again, as if the morning light had formed some strange negative from the image of his dream. Mai approached him, the black of her pajamas turned a stark white, and her hair no longer ebony, but the pure blond that colored the opposite end of the spectrum. Everything young about her had withered, and she seemed the embodiment of age, sticklike beneath the folds of her clothing.

But there was still the same threatening aura communicating itself to him, and although he had never seen her, he knew at once that it was Vera.

Branagan crashed out of the undergrowth moments after Vera, lowering his eyes self-consciously when Sam shifted his gaze to him. "Hello, Sam. Long time."

The greeting was a mutter, and Sam squinted at the figure of an old man, trying to reconcile the person he was seeing with the familiar voice he had just heard. "Joe?" he said softly.

"Good to see you, Sam." Branagan worked his lips and looked sideways at Vera. "Sort of."

"We followed you all the way from Plantation," Vera announced with satisfaction. "We spent the night in the car, but we've been waiting here since four in the morning. We thought you'd make your move once it got light."

"I was going to bring it to you," Sam said calmly.

"In another twenty-five years?" Vera's anger cut through the words, and she actually pushed the pistol in his direction as she spoke. "I'll say the good-byes this time, Sam. And don't think anything you have up your sleeve is going to work. We heard voices this morning." She motioned to Branagan with her free hand. "Take a look near those trees where he came out," she ordered. "And keep your gun in front of you!" They both watched him shuffle across the crescent of the beach toward the place where Sam had spent the night. Then she turned on him again, smiling with an obvious satisfaction. "We'll be on our way as soon as we're sure you're alone. You can just keep your hands in your pockets until Joe gets back."

Sam might have made his move then, but he wanted to know that Todd was in a safe position before he acted on his own, so he waited, studying her while she alternated glances between the bag at his feet and the edge of the undergrowth where Branagan had disappeared. Now that the moment had come, he was as calm as he could have hoped to be before seeing any kind of action. The confrontation on the beach was almost identical to the one he had planned to play out later that day under similar circumstances, so he had already prepared himself for everything except the presence of Todd. And Vera's appearance.

Her looks might have held up better away from the glare of the sun, but light had become her enemy, and it seemed to him that time had stripped away the veneer of her appearance along with the good years, exposing what had always been beneath it. It was as though something had come into contact with the perfect porcelain beauty of that face and shattered it, leaving a thousand cracked pieces masked around the faded blue of the eyes. The network of wrinkles went far beyond the normal process of aging, with each fold of skin separated from the next by creases so deep they were bordered in black. The total effect was a devastation that differed so much from Sam's memory it appeared to him as a deformity, and he was visibly shaken when he thought back on the world that had been his past.

She caught him looking at her then, and she narrowed her eyes with suspicion, raising the gun to the level of his face. "He should be back by now. Are you sure you're here alone?"

Sam looked past the pistol and found her eyes. "I came with Eddie," he said calmly. He was protecting Todd, but it was only a half lie. The sun had pulled away from the water, lighting the beach, and he recognized the bright stretch of sand as the same one he had seen during the delirium of his fight with the Japanese. He smiled then, finding it strangely appropriate.

The expression infuriated Vera. "It's still Eddie, is that it, Sam? And Eddie's mother, and your mother. And me! Are there still a thousand reasons that make you better than everyone else when you take what you want? Is that why you ran off with the morphine? To save Joe?" She stabbed a finger at the suitcase lying near his feet. "Well, I've got news for you. You're no better than the rest of us! Hand that over now, and I'll keep it. At least I admit I want it, for the money! You can go back to that upstanding life you bought after the war and keep lying to yourself."

Sam's expression remained placid in the face of the outburst. "I'm done lying, Vera. And I'm not handing over anything."

Something was coming to life inside Joe Branagan. As soon as he caught sight of Sam Clement emerging from the undergrowth, the vague feeling of uneasiness that had come over him during the past few weeks quickened. It was not the first time he had seen Sam, but his other observations had been made from the considerable distance of the marina. With Clement in clear view on the beach, he was no longer the vague figure from his past who had wronged him, but the past itself.

Up until that time, Branagan had consoled himself with the thought that he had taken Sam's place, becoming Vera's lover and moving toward the affluence she had shared with Sam and now held out to him. But in the stark light of that dawn, he felt suddenly cheated, and all of the lore he had created for his own survival faded under the scrutiny of Sam's curious glance.

That look told Branagan a great deal. For the second time since the war, it was clear that Sam had chosen the right way, and the expression on his face reflected it. Had he been angry, or even derisive, Branagan would have lost little of his conviction.

But there was neither fear nor resentment in the look Sam turned on him. Only shock, and pity.

Their separate lives were written on their faces, Branagan realized, and if Clement was older, he was still unbent by the years that had ravaged Joe since they had met on the Newark waterfront over thirty-five years ago. In the revelation of that moment, Vera withered on the sand beside him, becoming what she had always been. She was no longer regal, and nothing but anger and bitterness remained to inherit in the world that Sam had abdicated so many years ago. It was Clement's new life that Joe envied, and he knew then that he and Vera were separated from it by more than money.

He had sensed this truth when he captured Kara, although he denied it at the time. She was everything he would have wanted for himself in a woman, and she had the same inner strength he had always envied in Sam. When she had actually responded to his touch that night in Miami, he was excited by more than her physical presence. For a moment, he believed even in this late stage of his life he could take something away from Sam. She had turned on him, of course, and facing her husband on the beach that morning, he realized a woman like Kara was so far beyond what he had become, he might just as well have attempted to couple with a different species.

Branagan continued to push dutifully through the brush, but he was haunted by the ghost of a former self he had seen in Sam's eyes, and he was filled with an unfocused anger because of it. Vera had kept him from his drinking during the vigil of the last three days, and the unusual clarity of his mind not only prompted some very basic realizations, it made them acutely painful.

He did not know who to blame for what he had become. He only knew he could no longer blame Sam, and the frustration of a wasted life grew inside him without any release. He was lost, and all the money that morphine might bring could not redeem him. For months, he had prepared for one final fight left deep inside him, and in a few brief moments on the beach, he had lost his cause.

But even if his anger had been directed outward, it would have made very little difference under the canopy of the jungle he was searching. Todd Clement was a match for trained men half Branagan's age, and he fell on him soundlessly from the thickness of the branches that overhung the path. Like Sam, Joe never even had the chance to cry out.

Vera squinted against the growing glare of the sun. Then she pulled back the hammer of the pistol with her thumb and locked it into place with an ominous sound. "Give it over, I said. Or you'll get what you deserve."

But Sam shook his head with the same neutral expression. "I want what I deserve, Vera. Unless you're willing to destroy this."

She continued to motion toward the suitcase. "Don't tell me what I should do. You don't have any choice."

"I think he does." The voice came from a break in the tree line about twenty yards behind her, and they both turned to see Todd emerge from the woods. He was holding Branagan against his chest with enough force to raise his feet from the ground, while his right hand pressed the barrel of the pistol firmly against the old man's temple. "My father for your friend here," Todd called out, half dragging Branagan to within a few yards of Sam. "And I'm not only good in the jungle. I can actually shoot." He bobbed his head toward Vera. "Your choice."

"My choice!" Something like a laugh escaped Vera's lips, and she glared at Todd without turning the pistol from Sam's direction. "A million dollars for what you have? For that thing under your arm?" Her eyes narrowed as she shouted at Branagan. "And you, you fool! You let him take your gun and he can't even walk straight!" She looked back at Todd. "I hope you blow his brains out."

Branagan's mouth fell open and he let out a sound that might have been forced from his lips by a blow to the body.

But Sam had fallen to his knees over the suitcase, and both Vera and Todd turned to look at him. "I'm opening it for you," he said, looking calmly past the leveled gun, and he pulled back the rusted clips that fastened it. The straps fell away while he was unbuckling them, and he lifted the lid without any difficulty, coming slowly to his feet with the neck of a large cellophane wrapping bunched up in one hand. It was heavy enough to make his arm shake with the effort. "We didn't have any plastic back then, did we Vera?"

"Now," she ordered, focusing on the motion of his hand. "I want it now!"

Sam let his fingers fall away from the neck of the wrapping until a fold of the cellophane came loose, and the morphine began spilling out onto the sand under its own weight. "Think of it, Vera! This could be the end of it once and for all if we let it!"

"You bastard!" She would have shot him in that moment, but she was distracted for an instant by Branagan, whose quiet moaning had suddenly erupted in screams.

"You!" he shouted at her. "I'm not your thing! You're the thing!"

The time she took to look at him was all Sam needed, and he went for her, closing the distance between them in a few short bounds.

Todd saw what was happening, and he raised his pistol in the grip of both hands just as she turned back toward his father. But Branagan had used his release to join Sam in his rush, and in the time it took him to reach Vera, his body shielded her from Todd's line of fire.

In the end, Branagan shot her himself, tearing the gun from her hand in a frenzy of screaming and turning it on her long enough to send her sprawling back onto the sand with three shots staining the center of her uniform. But it was Sam who bought him the time, taking the only bullet she fired in the side of the chest before Joe collided with her and captured the gun.

Todd was at his side seconds after he hit the ground. "Jesus, not now!" he pleaded, pulling off his shirt and folding it into the tightness of a pad. "In the name of Christ, not now!"

There was still life in Sam's expression, and he found Todd's eyes without moving his head. "Now is fine," he said softly. "Now I'm even." He shut his eyes briefly while Todd clamped the shirt over a growing red area on the side of his chest. Then he blinked up at his son with a smile. "All during the war, people kept telling me that anyone could die. It's not so easy."

"That's because you're not dying, goddamn it!" Todd looked up out of habit, listening for the chopping of helicopter blades before he remembered there was no help he could summon from the sky. Then a sound from the tree line caught his attention, and the smiling head of a seahorse came bobbing through the undergrowth, wrapped in the form of a life preserver around the waist of a small child.

Branagan was still sobbing over the lifeless form of Vera when Todd called out to him. "Get over here!" he ordered. "There's help back at the park if we can get him there in time!"

Jon Chaiten was still in his uniform when he gunned his car up to the emergency entrance of the hospital and ushered Kara out of the front seat. As well as working with veterans' groups, one of his major duties during peacetime involved recruiting, and he had been holding a meeting in his office when Todd's call reached him. By then it was late morning, and he had arrived at the Clements' home just before noon. Todd told him to say that Sam had been in an accident, but Kara seemed to have been waiting for him when he knocked on the front door, and from the look she gave him as she opened it, he might have been wearing the uniform of a policeman instead of a marine.

"Is my husband dead?" she had asked before he had even introduced himself.

She was calm during the ten-minute drive to the hospital, asking politely about the time he had spent with her son in the service, and when Todd greeted them at the door to the emergency room, she embraced him quietly before he guided her in the direction of the elevator. Chaiten waited downstairs in the crowded reception area after he had parked the car.

Todd found him there an hour later when he returned from his father's room. "It's not good, but he's still alive," he said, sitting down next to him and staring into the fold of his hands. "The bullet's out, and they've replaced the blood he's lost. Now there's nothing to do but wait." He raised his eyes to Chaiten. "Thanks for the help."

"Thanks for calling."

Todd flashed him a tight smile. "Who else would I call once the shooting started?" He looked off through the window they were facing. "I actually reached for a radio after it happened. I wanted him dusted off. Then I realized there weren't any choppers. But you should have seen it once we got him out to the parking lot. Three police cars and an ambulance. We raced off to the hospital in a goddamned caravan. All for one chest wound."

Chaiten nodded knowingly. "Of course. Back in the U.S.A."

Todd found his eyes again. "You know, it was all I ever wanted in the middle of that nightmare we lived through back then. I really would have settled for that. Not to live. Just to have every death mean something, instead of being in a place where there wasn't any room for those kinds of feelings." He worked a hand against his mouth and shook his head. "My God, that doesn't even help a little now. He has to live."

Chaiten put a hand on his arm. "It can happen. We both know that."

As if in response to what they had been saying, one of the nurses who had just emerged from the elevator scanned the room and hurried over to Todd. "Mr. Clement?"

Todd and Chaiten came to their feet together.

"I'm afraid your father's had an arrest. The doctor's with him now. You can go right to the room with your mother."

Joe Branagan came up to fire his gun beside Sam. It was the Tom Mix Peacemaker his father had bought him for his eighth Christmas, and as he rested its barrel on the cinderblock ledge of the cellar window, Eddie looked over from his position by the opposite wall and gave them the high sign. Then all hell broke loose as the forces of the Kaiser surged across Clay Street, and the three of them fired at a pace unrelenting enough to make their throats sore.

There was still danger out there when they turned away from the windows, but it waited for their attention while Greg Harms banged down the stairway, balancing a tray with four glasses of root beer that Mrs. Branagan had sent from upstairs. They drank without pausing for breath, sucking noisily on the ice cubes afterwards while they sat in a tight circle and discussed the various combinations possible in trading weapons.

It was warm in the bunker of Branagan's basement, and the sweat ran down the flaps of the aviator's cap Sam was wearing, cooling the nape of his neck and bringing back the hot, wet leather smell of baseball season. At the window again, he fired louder and longer than any of the others, until his father, coming home from the plant with his lunch pail under his arm, smiled at the sound of his voice before taking the steps to their apartment on the opposite side of the street.

Sam surrendered the comfort of that bunker only twice. The first time, a vague feeling of apprehension that had nothing to do with the weight on his chest caused him to force open his eyes. But there was nothing to fear. Kara was there, waiting, and she must have seen the feeling in his eyes, because she smiled, reaching out and squeezing his hand. There was a hand on hers, and Sam pushed his vision just far enough to find Todd's face peering at him anxiously from over his mother's shoulder. He knew then that he wasn't in the same room that had been haunted by Vera, and that time had replaced her with the return of his son.

He let them go after that, drifting back to the comfort of the basement. Shells were falling onto the pavement outside, lighting up Clay Street in vivid Fourth of July colors. One or two sparklers drifted through the window, and the four of them scrambled over each other in a rush to throw them back in the direction of the enemy. Finally, a rocket settled onto the faded linoleum of the floor, and Sam distinguished himself by being the first in the game to reach it. He held it out for all of them as he carried it to the window, but it was Eddie who took it, and the others faded from Sam's vision as his best friend raised it in anticipation. It flashed in his hand soundlessly, and in a burst of color that seemed to please Eddie, it lit the smile on his face. Then all the light turned to darkness, and Sam knew that Eddie was gone from his dreams, to live as he had once been within the confines of his memory.

The nurse at the monitor hesitated only long enough to confirm the reading before she called out to the doctor without turning away from the screen. "I've got a heartbeat again," she said.

Sam might have been the veteran, rising from his wheelchair with the support of Todd and Chaiten, who flanked him during his halting walk to the open door of the car. When he was resting comfortably in the back seat, Todd and his friend remained there with him, while Kara shared the front seat with the driver. She felt more protective in the forward position. It was the same reason she had chosen the anonymity of a hired car for the homecoming, and she thought about her misgivings during the twenty-minute ride from the hospital.

For Kara, life under any conditions was a gift, and Sam's complete recovery was all that she could have asked for herself. But as she watched the familiar landscape of her town roll by the windows of the limousine, she thought of the city she had known as a child, and how it had turned on her without pity or warning, becoming a different place. The people they had known might do that to her husband, and it would matter to him, just as clearing his own conscience had mattered after the passing of so many years.

The conversation that came to her from the back seat was warm and animated. Todd's voice had come to life during the past week, and when he spoke to his father or his friend, something in it echoed a younger son she thought she had lost almost a decade ago. And in everything Sam said, in the very position he took against the back of his seat, there was a sense of relief apparent to Kara, making her realize that for the moment, the only respect he needed was his own. As the car turned from the wide avenue into the side street that held their home, she hoped that would continue to be enough for him.

Branagan had helped, she reminded herself. The story he had told the police was more a confession of his own sins than an account of what Sam had done in the past. There would be no charges against her husband, who had destroyed the last vestige of his former life on that beach, and had come close to destroying himself because of it. If she remembered Branagan's hands on her body, she would also remember the weeping voice on the phone when they had allowed him to call Sam, and she was grateful in spite of her pity that in the end, he had turned on himself rather than continuing to strike out at others.

Kara was the first to notice the strange car in the driveway as they approached the house. She had been home only twice during the last two weeks, and that had been late at night. She told Todd she was taking a room close to the hospital to be near Sam, but even when he was out of danger, she continued to stay at the motel. Todd had heard nothing but expressions of concern when he returned to run the business, but Kara reminded herself that those people were employees as well as friends, and she continued to read the accounts of the shooting in the papers, bracing herself for a judgment that haunted only her.

"I hope that's not another new car in our driveway," Sam observed quietly from the back seat, and the others laughed appreciatively.

"I don't know about it at all," Kara said, forcing herself to smile. "The boys must help you in from the street, then. I will go ahead to unlock."

She pushed open her door before the driver could come around to her side, walking rapidly across the lawn with her eyes straight ahead. Before she moved out of earshot, she heard the men emerging from the back seat behind her, speaking of lunch.

She was nearly to the door when the voice caught her, and her fear must have been betrayed by her face, because Rowena Bloom took a step back in the direction of her own home and immediately apologized.

"I'm sorry, I must have surprised you!" The penciled eyebrows rose before she waved her hands in her normal pattern of speaking. "Well, I've been waiting for you to get home, and I almost missed you as it was. The car was Bess's idea, but it was my job to move it." She pointed across the street to the Fowlers' house with the keys she was holding in her hand. "They're out for the afternoon, so I'm keeping watch." Rowena spread her arms in the face of Kara's expression. "The media people, I mean. They were driving right up to the house to take pictures. I've cleaned up your front beds more than a few times what with everyone tramping down the landscape." She paused long enough to raise her eyes in Sam's direction as he stepped out onto the softness of the lawn. "Thank God, he looks fine," she sighed. And then she rushed on. "Well, at least the car forced them to walk in from the street, and by then we could head them off." For a moment, a look Kara had never seen before came over Rowena's face, and her neighbor stepped closer, reaching out briefly to clasp her hand. "I can't tell you how happy we are it's all right, but there's time for that later. Right now I'm sure you want to be alone."

She turned in the direction of her house, and she had reached the border of their yards before Kara could respond. "Thank you," she managed.

Rowena waved a hand behind her back without turning around.

Kara looked at the Fowlers' house then, before taking in all of the homes lining their street. She knew in that moment a question had been answered, that her husband's reckoning had also exorcised a secret fear buried deep inside her since childhood. The thought drew her glance to Sam, who was making his way across the lawn with Todd while Chaiten trailed behind, helping the driver with their suitcases. She could not fully understand what had happened during the past few weeks. It had come on them as unexpectedly as the bad times that had changed her life forever so many years ago. But taking in the two men approaching her across the lawn, she was suddenly glad for it all.

Todd looked up then, reflecting her expression with a smile of his own as he approached the porch, straightened under the weight of his father.